FOR THE 1000TH TIME

Love In Vancouver
Book One

JEN-LEA MERCY

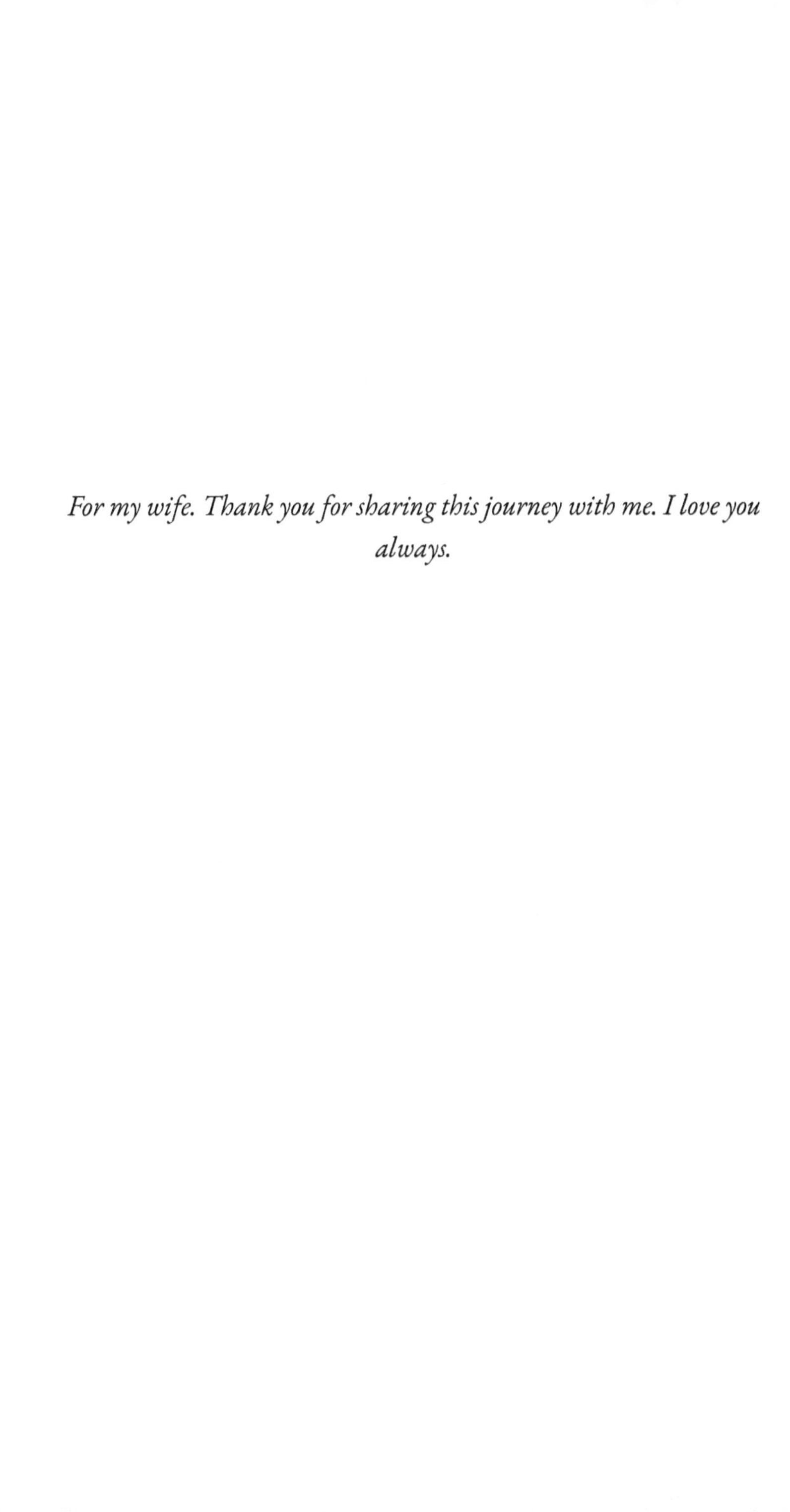

For my wife. Thank you for sharing this journey with me. I love you always.

A Thank-You from Jen-Lea

It's taken a long time for Abi and Tess's story to come to fruition! Seriously, there were days when I doubted just about everything but Abi's infinite affections for Tess LOL, but I'm so happy I didn't give up.

I'm *thrilled* to share my debut sapphic romance with such an incredible community! Thank you for taking a chance on me, and I hope you all love Tess and Abi as much as I do.

Thank you to everyone who has helped shape this novel into what it is today! I'm so lucky to have a supportive team who offers endless encouragement. A special shout-out to my editors and proofreader: Colleen, Allister, and Amber, and also my beta readers: Amber, Sarah, Meghan, Ami, Vanessa, Debbie, and Melissa. You guys rock!

I would be remiss if I didn't also show my appreciation to the West Prince Arts Council. Thank you for helping writers like myself pursue their dreams.

Chapter One

Abi

I shouldn't have taken my clothes off that night.

She'd done a lot of foolish things in her twenties, but getting naked four years ago with her best friend Taunya's sister took gold for the Olympics of bad ideas. No, getting *caught* took gold, if winning at a losing game was something to be proud of. Abi scoffed, lost in humiliating memories of her last few moments with Tessa Moore. It had taken a long time to admit she shouldn't have been anywhere near Tess's bedroom the night of her going-away party.

And going home for Tauni's wedding is already dredging everything up again. Lucky me.

Abi sat at her desk, her brow furrowed as she thought of years past. In some ways, she could hardly recognize the girl she'd been at twenty. She'd grown up, but that didn't necessarily mean she had what it took to see Tess again. With a whole week of bridal party events happening before the wedding, there would be no choice but to face Tess — *or* what had happened between them.

"Young! Marianne's running errands, so I need you to grab me lunch."

She inwardly winced at her boss hollering through the open office door, as well as Margo's tasteless penchant for using Abi's surname whenever she barked an order. And why couldn't another intern go grab lunch? Abi had really thought that when she landed the marketing coordinator job, being Margo's errand girl was done with.

Standing up, she gave the stack of reports on her desk the stink-eye. Abi had enough of her own work to do to worry about making lunch orders too. Here she was, scurrying around the office like a frantic chicken as she prepared for her first summer vacation since graduate school.

There was still tons to do before she could enjoy that vacation. Marketing reports needed filing, social media posts waited on standby, either for scheduling or closer edits for the upcoming weeks, and she still hadn't confirmed her arrival into Vancouver International with Taunya. During this last week, Abi had doubled her work tasks and even delegated a few of them to her boss's newest intern. However, there was still a significant amount to get done before heading home to pack. She let out a tired sigh, knowing packing for the trip was yet another task she had put off until the last second.

"Of course, Ms. Tremblay, right away." Abi plastered on a smile. She grabbed her purse to sling the strap over one shoulder, walking the few steps to Margo's office. "Anything in particular?"

Silently, she ran Margo's past lunch options through her head, grateful that her boss was predictable. No matter how sweltering the August heat of Toronto got, Margo Tremblay had always ordered the soup of the day and a sandwich. According to Marianne, things hadn't changed.

"Surely you still remember what I like, Young," Margo snapped, her eyes blazing with fury as she snatched her cell phone from her desk. She leveled her cold gaze on Abi. "If you can't remember lunch details, how are you supposed to remember design details for a client?"

Abi tilted her chin and stood her ground. Since the older woman was her boss — and ex, unfortunately — she bit back a retort. Things hadn't always been so ... *tense* between them, and Abi hated her part in why Margo was such an insufferable bitch these days. She'd tried to make it work, she really had, but love, as it turned out, wasn't something she could just give to anyone. In fact, Abi was fairly certain she had zero control when it came to matters of the heart.

Margo was the first to break eye contact, and Abi watched as she folded her arms across her chest and looked away. It was no secret how important this job was to Abi, and ever since she ended things between them six months ago, Margo had lived to make her sweat. She'd have quit already, except she didn't want to be back at square one, begging for handouts at a lesser company. MT Marketing was the most sought-after company for any newbie trying to make it in the design world. Founded by Margo and two of her friends, it was world-renowned for its ability to take smaller companies and give them the makeover and exposure needed to succeed on an international level.

"Not at all," Abi replied, smoothing down the few wrinkles in her skirt. "Since it's the end of the week, I'm guessing a sliced turkey on rye bread is a safe bet. No lettuce, extra pickles. And the soup of the day, of course."

Abi bit the inside of her cheek as those searing blue eyes momentarily scrutinized her. Margo's gaze landed on Abi's open-toe pumps first, and as they made their way up the length of her body, lingering on her breasts stuffed into her royal blue blouse, a pinch of unease settled in the pit of Abi's stomach. Only one other person had ever looked at her with such blatant appreciation and desire. How could Margo and Tess look at her the same way, and yet the shivers skittering down Abi's spine were for wholly different reasons?

"Young, what are you waiting for? Validation? Get going already!"

"I'd be waiting an awfully long time if that were the case," Abi muttered and hurried out of her office. It always made for a hellish workday when Margo got in one of her ogre moods, and the elevated tension in the office rattled Abi every time. Her fingers trembled as she punched the button for the elevators, and she breathed a deep sigh of relief when the doors opened. She stepped inside, grateful when no one else accompanied her down to the main floor. For a moment she stood with her eyes closed, enjoying the silence. Her mind was blank for all of ten seconds before she heard her cell phone vibrating inside her purse. When she pulled out the device, an instant smile appeared as she noted the new picture message. Abi's good friends, twin sisters McCoy and Sloane Miller, sat straddling their mountain bikes as they posed for the selfie. The B.C. cliffs acted as a backdrop in the photo, and the caption underneath read, *Getting our last ride in until Tauni's wedding! Can't wait to see you tomorrow, Abs. Love you lots.*

"Love you more," Abi murmured, eager to see them, as well as Taunya and their friend Krystal. It had been the five of them against the world since she and Taunya met the other girls years ago at Simon Fraser University. Video chats were amazing, don't get her wrong, but they weren't the same as visiting with friends. It would be good to catch up and spend quality time together over the next two weeks.

Abi bit her lip, conflicting feelings of seeing Tess consuming her once again. There was still so much left unsaid regarding their night together four years ago. Abi and Taunya had managed to mend their friendship, both choosing instead to dodge the hard, unfinished topic of Taunya catching her sister and Abi in bed together rather than hash it all out. Their verbal exchange the morning following her going-away party had been heated, and it had taken a long time to understand Taunya's point of view about possibly being caught in the middle. After that, Abi never had the courage to broach the subject again.

She rolled her shoulders, hoping to loosen the stiffness and shake off the nagging voice in her head. Abi was over whatever had — or hadn't — happened emotionally between her and Tess. Her years of pining for her best friend's sister, who was six years older, had come and gone. She wasn't twenty years old anymore, sneaking away from her party to take her shot with her long-time crush. She was headed home to be a bridesmaid in Taunya's wedding, something they'd talked about thousands of times when they were kids.

The café bustled with activity by the time Abi arrived. Every table was filled, and seven people waited in line to order. Abi cursed under her breath, recognizing the faint pinch of anxiety brewing below her sternum. She glanced at the clock behind the counter attendant and checked the time. Of all the days for Marianne to be out, it had to be this one. Honestly, Abi's life wasn't turning out at all like she'd envisioned when she moved. She was stuck in a city with no view and slowly working herself to death for a woman who'd become as cold as Toronto's February chill. Though she worked in a field she loved, and had friends she lived with, something was missing. The way she was with her roommates wasn't the same as the closeness she'd felt with Taunya and McCoy or the tenderness she'd felt for Tess.

Abi heaved an annoyed sigh, hating that even after all this time, Tess still regularly consumed her thoughts. Her ash-blonde hair, the warmest brown eyes Abi had ever seen, or the way Tess's lips had tasted or how magical their bodies felt moving together. As often as she tried not to, she wondered about Tess. How had the last four years changed for the other woman? Where did she live now? Was she happy? Or, the biggest, most humiliating question of all — did Tess think of her?

In the few times she'd been back to Vancouver to visit, she'd only seen Tess once, completely by accident. They'd walked by one another at a pub one night when she'd been out with the twins. If Tess had recognized Abi, she'd hid it well. It seemed like Abi wasn't the only one trying to forget that night or what was said.

I was so obsessed with her.

Taunya might have barged in on them and by proxy acted as a wedge between her and Tess, but it was Abi's big mouth that, despite her best intentions, had driven Tess away. That night ended with Abi crying herself to sleep in McCoy's protective arms. And by this time tomorrow, Abi would be well on her way to seeing the one and only woman who truly broke her heart.

By the time Abi got to the front counter and placed Margo's order, ten minutes had passed. The pressure of being late brimmed to the surface, and she found herself drumming her fingertips impatiently against her thigh. Margo was going to kill her. *Why* hadn't she anticipated she'd be left with ordering lunch? She should have known better than to let thoughts of her vacation take priority. She'd been working at MT Marketing long enough to know Margo's habits inside out.

"Here's your order, Abi." The café manager was behind the register now, his sympathetic smile just making things worse. "Boss rushing you again?"

"No," Abi expelled, exasperated with herself. She took the paper bag from him a little too fast in her panic. "This mess is on me. Thanks, Adam!"

Margo was on the phone when Abi came rushing back into the office. She set the takeout bag silently on her desk, hoping to make a quick escape, but Margo held up her hand to wait.

"Yes, I understand. I apologize for — yes, okay. I'll make sure of it."

From what Abi could gather from the bits of conversation, Margo was getting a tongue-lashing from whoever she was dealing with. Abi hid her smile, peering down at the decorative rug in her boss's office. Margo wasn't known for her patience, and Abi could hear her voice escalating.

"Fucking insipid *morons*!" Margo finally snapped as she slammed the receiver down in its cradle.

"Who this time?"

Margo glared across the room at Abi, her words pushing out in a low growl. "That was the head of Beauty Is Blush on the phone, demanding we make immediate design changes to their website by Monday's end."

"Oh, wow, that isn't very much time." Abi winced as Margo shot her *that* look, the one where she knew she wouldn't like whatever was about to come out of her boss's mouth.

"I need you this weekend, Abi. Postpone or cancel the flight, whatever you need to do."

Abi's lips parted in disbelief. "What? No way! I've had this trip booked for —"

Margo raised her hand again, stopping Abi mid-rant. "I can't do this with you anymore, Abi. *You* ended things and then *begged* me to keep this job, remember? You made a convincing argument about how important it was to *you*, yet now you're flying out to B.C. for two weeks and deserting me again!"

Abi ground down on her molars, breathing in deeply to remain calm. If she dug deep enough, she might find the inner peace she sought. She could feel her pulse thumping against the column of her throat, *tick-ticking* in time to each one of Margo's jabs.

Uncomfortable silence settled over the room as they stared one another down. Abi reminded herself she wasn't in the wrong here. She'd worked her ass off for months to ensure they granted her this vacation. It didn't sit right that Margo would take things so personally and so out of context. Abi was leaving for vacation, yet Margo made it sound like she was breaking things off again. "I'm sorry the wedding isn't at a better time," she offered, trying to understand the situation from Margo's point of view.

A heavy sigh escaped Margo, and she looked away, regret clear in her eyes. Abi remembered that look well. It was the same one Margo had shown for the first three weeks after their break-up, any time they would make eye contact. Regret, hurt, Abi had put it there. She watched Margo take a moment to peer inside the takeout bag before their eyes met again.

"I'm sorry," Margo began, and Abi's jaw slackened at the apology. "That was uncalled for. I just … I need you here Abi. I hate that I do, but the main team is working on another deadline. You're the only one familiar enough with Beauty Is Blush's brand to pull this off."

"And I'm sorry, but I can't cancel my flight. I have a couple of the interns scheduled to help, and Marianne is a good assistant. She can do more than answer phone calls and run errands."

That brought on another scowl. "She doesn't have the design experience required for a website change. How about working remotely?"

Abi shook her head, frustration causing her cheeks to flush. "No, again, I'm sorry, but this vacation is mine. Don't take it from me, Margo."

Margo came around the desk, standing mere feet away from Abi and entirely too close for her growing anxiety. "Don't make me, Abi, please? I can make it up to you in the fall. I'll fly you anywhere you want to go."

Abi's quick inhale was lost on Margo, and she watched in shock as the desperate woman reached for a strand of Abi's hair. "What do you say?"

Angry tears stung the backs of Abi's eyelids, and her fists clenched at her sides. *This* was why companies discouraged interoffice relationships. Yes, Abi had been the one to break things off, but Margo was being unfair and manipulative. If she wasn't going home for her best friend's wedding — a wedding she was a *part* of — Abi would likely consider rescheduling. It would be an ideal opportunity to get back on Margo's good side, but it just wasn't possible. Taunya meant too much to Abi, and Margo hitting on her had crossed the line. Abi had made their non-relationship abundantly clear months ago.

Enough was enough.

She ripped her access card off her belt, images of her old life in Vancouver flashing through her mind as she placed the plastic on Margo's desk.

"You know what? I can't do this anymore, Margo; I quit."

Chapter Two

Tess

Tessa Moore eased seamlessly in and out of traffic, her thighs hugging the sides of her black Ducati as she merged the motorcycle into Vancouver's midmorning traffic. She was already late opening her barbershop, having no choice but to reschedule her first client so she could fit in yet another errand her sister had so *helpfully* sprung on her that morning. Taunya had been driving her nuts for months over every nitty-gritty detail of her upcoming wedding. She was usually the more decisive one in the family, helping make life-and-death decisions every day as an intensive care nurse. After sending Tess to evaluate possible bouquets, she and her fiancé couldn't agree on, *for the fourth time*, it was clear her younger sister was on a fast track to becoming ... Bridezilla.

Tess shuddered at the thought.

She arrived at her barbershop minutes later, preoccupied and flustered, parking the Ducati in a well-kept alleyway between her building and her favorite café. She sighed, not moving for a moment as she got her bearings. There was no easy way to put it: the sooner Taunya married Derek, the sooner Tess's life could go back to normal. Some days, it seemed like she was losing her mind; Tess, not Taunya, although considering her sister had sent Tess to give an opinion on whether daisies or carnations better suited the wedding theme, the jury was still out.

Climbing off her bike, she carried her helmet in one hand and headed for the street entrance of the café. The bell above the door jingled as she entered, and the husband and wife duo behind the counter turned toward the sound.

"Tessa, you made it!" Ezel fondly called out, and with his thick accent, even the simplest greeting sounded distinguished.

"Good morning, Ezel, morning, Aiyla," Tess replied as she approached the counter. She'd been hooked on their Turkish coffee since the day she'd stepped foot in the quaint café, so much so that they had her usual routine memorized by now. "I'm getting to the shop a little later today, but," she took notice of the several occupied tables and smiled, "doesn't look like you missed me."

"Ah, nonsense! That smile is always missed," Ailya corrected, lifting a decadent Turkish cookie out of the display case and placing it in a takeout bag. She handed it to Tess. "For a trade, as always."

Tess bit back another smile, accepting the hot coffee Ezel passed her as well. "Doesn't seem a fair trade, Ailya. You come for a trim and wax once a month, while I'm here daily, getting served coffee and Şekerpare cookies."

"Sometimes twice a day," Ezel surmised, grabbing a damp rag by the register to wipe down the counter. "You cut hair for a family of five. Seems a good trade to me, no?"

"Don't forget occasional weekend babysitting."

"Okay, okay." Tess chuckled. "Well, I thank you. Have a good day, guys."

"You as well, Tess!"

Tess was still grinning as she made her way next door to her shop, which was conveniently located on the first floor of a dance studio. Half her clients carried over from the dance studio. Tess had struck gold coming across this prime real estate two years before. With the help of her parents and a government-aided business start-up, she was able to convert the old convenience store into the barbershop of her dreams. After being under her ex's thumb for so long, the no-strings-attached aspect of owning something became more important to Tess than anything else. Not to mention, having Tess as competition rather than working under Chantelle had likely been a proverbial kick to her ex's ego.

As always, the weight of the world fell away as Tess stepped over the threshold of her shop and closed the door. It might not be a big deal to some, but having her own business had been a lifelong dream. She loved the feeling when she walked through the front doors, the smell of cleaner and yesterday's hair products still lingering in the air.

Tess stripped off her leather jacket, carrying it with her to the back room near the washroom to hang on a hook. She then swapped her black riding boots for a pair of blue Nikes before turning on the lights. Her first appointment wasn't due for another ten minutes, so she took a seat at her crowded desk. As her laptop was booting up, she dug into her desk for her bottle of anxiety meds, slipping one under her tongue. Like the rest of her day so far, she was a little late in taking her dose and hoped it wouldn't make much difference. The last thing she needed was to be on edge at dinner that evening.

As soon as she was connected to her shop's Wi-Fi, she clicked into her email. She had all the accounts on her laptop set to recognize her because she never remembered her passwords. It was embarrassing how clumsily she navigated the Internet. When she wrote the passwords down in one of her notebooks, she misplaced their location. Her sister teased her mercilessly about how Tess was born in the wrong generation, and at times she agreed.

After confirming her upcoming supply order, she opened her Instagram account. If it wasn't for her best friend Stacey helping set up her account, Tess doubted she'd even be able to do this much. It was the same with TikTok. She hadn't attempted to post anything on there, but she had pictures of clients' haircuts and a few of her Ducati on Insta. With a mere two hundred followers, it wasn't a great marketing strategy so far. If Tess were savvier with social media, she was certain her business would flourish, rather than the word of mouth she currently relied on. She got by, but her financial success was nowhere *near* where she'd imagined it two years ago. She was almost thirty-one and still living on her parents' property — in a detached living space, but still.

So Vicki keeps reminding me, Tess thought, sitting a little straighter in her seat as she considered her current girlfriend. Their six-month anniversary had come and gone, and, honestly, Tess felt like they had nothing to show for it. What had started out as a promising relationship changed into something else the moment Vicki informed her she didn't want kids. The dream of one day creating a family with a partner had been all but extinguished the moment she walked in on her ex with another woman, and yet four years later, a part of Tess still held on. It wasn't until her brief discussion with Vicki that the last of that hope sank like a lead balloon. She discerned that one day she would need to choose — settle down with someone like Vicki or face motherhood alone. With her terrible track record in relationships, maybe having both was too far-fetched for someone like Tess.

She sighed as her mouse cursor hovered over her sister's latest Instagram post. There was an old photo of her and her friends together with a caption stating, *The fab five reunite tomorrow night!* and Tess was positive Taunya had rhymed on purpose. She was the flashy one in the family, forever doing what she could to make a statement.

Abi Young posed in the center of the group shot, making the peace sign and sporting a goofy smile spread wide over her pretty face. Tess swallowed past the rush of emotion bubbling to the surface at the sight of her. Guilt and shame from years ago still gnawed at Tess, and the heaviness she felt after all this time draped across her insides like plate armor. What would it be like seeing Abi again? Knowing they were both in Taunya's bridal party had Tess on edge. Could they last two weeks without bringing up what happened, or would Abi demand they talk about it? Did she hate Tess for how she'd handled things? Tess fingered the rubber band she always kept around her wrist. Her part in the night of Abi's going-away party should never have happened. She wouldn't have even been there had she not recently packed a bag and walked away from her life with Chantelle. Abi had caught her in a vulnerable place, but that was no excuse for how Tess had treated her.

I just need to get through the next two weeks. That's it, that's the goal.

Tess could not, under *any* circumstance, cause drama for her sister before the wedding. Besides, she'd had at least one definitive moment in the last four years where she could have apologized to Abi but chickened out at the last minute. She'd been at O'Rourkes with Stacey on the same night as Abi. Tess could have said hello, apologized, and bought Abi a drink but did none of those things. Instead, she'd held her breath and walked past Abi without even looking at her. *Pathetic* — that was Tess in a nutshell.

The bells above her shop's door jingled, startling Tess, and she peeked around the corner to see a familiar face.

"'Morning, Tess! Thanks for squeezing me in on such short notice." The older woman chuckled, talking over her shoulder as she shut the door. "My daughter thinks I'm ridiculous, but I refuse to let anyone else touch my hair."

A bright smile lit Tess's face at the compliment, and she quickly forgot about her own life drama. Hopping from her chair, she closed the distance between them. "Hi, Liz. Please, have a seat." She gestured to her hairdressing chair, holding it steady as Liz sat down. "You've been saying that for a year and a half," Tess added, draping the cape around Liz's front. She clipped the fabric around her neck. "Hard to believe we've known each other that long."

The skin around Liz's blueish gray eyes crinkled as she smiled at Tess in the mirror. "And I've meant it, too. Not only do I get a great cut, I get to see you, who I'm pretty darn fond of."

Tess laughed, shaking her head at her friend's teasing. She pumped a bit of her water from her spray bottle to dampen Liz's thick gray locks before she reached for the hairbrush.

"How is your grandson doing lately? Last time we spoke, you mentioned he was still struggling."

"Kristopher is … okay. He likes to keep busy, you know? Says it keeps his thoughts productive."

"I understand that, believe me." Tess gave a solemn nod, her expression downcast as she finished the comb-out. "Depression is hard to overcome. Sometimes I worry I'll lose myself again, and it's been four years for me. Has he … does he talk to anyone?"

"He has a therapist, but I never know if the sessions are helping," Liz admitted, watching Tess in the mirror as she selected her swivel scissors.

Tess considered Liz's words, understanding a bit about Kris's struggles. She'd given therapy a try post-Chantelle but quickly found it wasn't for her. Music was what helped her, playing her guitar and singing by herself or with her mom. It had been an effective way to forget Chantelle's betrayal.

"I know our stories are drastically different, and I'm no professional, but I'd be willing to lend an ear if he ever wants to talk."

"I'll let him know, thank you, Tess. Now, how is that girlfriend of yours?" Liz shot Tess a wistful smile in the mirror, as though mentioning Kris had brought on a wave of sadness.

Tess returned her smile with one full of kindness. "Vicki's good. It's her birthday, so I'm treating her to dinner at this fusion place on the Westside."

Liz arched her thinning brows, her expression a cross between humor and speculation. "Not on that bike, you're not."

Tess laughed at that, but her stomach was twisting from the nerves. Her lack of a car was yet another thing she and Vicki clashed over. Perhaps it was Tess's fault her future wasn't going in the direction she wanted. Would she have to trade in her motorcycle before she found a woman who also wanted kids?

Tess – 5:47PM

I'm here already, just outside waiting

Tess had just pressed *send* when Vicki's newer-model Acura pulled into the crowded parking lot. She tucked her phone into her leather jacket, adjusting the collar on her blouse and watching as her girlfriend found a place to park. When Tess made the reservation for Desmarais, a French/French Canadian Fusion restaurant Vicki had been wanting to try, they'd confirmed it was semi-formal dining. It was a higher-end restaurant, one that Tess couldn't exactly afford, but Vicki had dropped the name enough over the last month that Tess could safely say she'd gotten the hint.

"Wow," Tess said as Vicki sidled up beside her.

She wore the ruby-red sequin dress Tess had bought her while they were visiting her family in Calgary the month before. It was gorgeous, hugging Vicki in all the right places, and Tess could almost forgive the number on the price tag. Desperation to win people over was one of Tess's less appealing qualities, according to her best friend. Stacey had almost hit the roof when Tess told her she'd impulsively bought a three-hundred-dollar dress for someone else. Shaking off the memory, Tess cleared her throat, rising on her tiptoes to give Vicki a light kiss on her cheek.

"You look beautiful, V."

"Thank you," Vicki replied, shifting her head slightly so her lips could claim Tess's. When she pulled away, her brows scrunched together as she took Tess in. A light laugh escaped. "What are *you* wearing? I knew I should have met you at the love shack after work."

Tess huffed a laugh as well, but Vicki's words rubbed her raw, and the evening was just getting started.

"My home is not a 'love shack,' V, seriously." Glancing down at her clothes, Tess couldn't see the issue. She'd gone home to shower and change first, and her outfit was tidy. She'd even worn her flats, which wasn't something she usually did because it was dangerous on her bike.

"I guess not, since it's too cringy for sex with your parents right next door." Vicki laughed again, looping her arm through Tess's as they headed inside the restaurant. She swept her free hand over her dirty blonde curls, acknowledging the host waiting to greet them before glancing at Tess again. "You're coming back to mine after, right? Figured we could skip Netflix and go straight to the chill."

"Oh," Tess said, always a little shocked at how little romance and friendship their relationship offered.

Vicki had been blunt from the moment they met six months ago during one of Tess's jam sessions at the seniors' home where Vicki's father lived. He suffered from dementia, and while she was visiting him one afternoon, she'd caught sight of Tess playing guitar. She'd asked her out that day. Dating had never come easily to Tess. She was awkward and shy and never had the best self-esteem, even pre-Chantelle. So, when Vicki showed an interest in her, Tess had been ecstatic in the beginning. The sex had been amazing — it still was, if she was honest — but it felt like something was missing. Even taking Tess's desire for children out of the equation, something important in their relationship repeatedly fell short. The thought of moving on again, admitting she'd failed at yet another relation-ship, kept Tess rooted in place. She held on, hoping that whatever magic she'd felt in Abi's arms would spark in Vicki's. There were times when it seemed impossible. Four years later, and Tess couldn't remember another woman looking at her the way Abi had.

Vicki *never* looked at her like that.

"Good evening, *bonsoir*," the host greeted them warmly, glancing at first Vicki before landing on Tess. "Welcome to Desmarais. Do you ladies have a reservation?"

Tess cleared her throat, wanting to shake off the unease that she was supposed to be somewhere else. "Yes, under Moore, please."

"How long do I have before your sister steals you away?"

Tess thinned her lips at Vicki's question. "I invited you along for some of it, you know."

Vicki scoffed. "I have no interest in being the odd girl out. Besides, the bucket list sounds lame. I just want a time frame so I can schedule my week."

Tess looked away so Vicki couldn't see the roll of her eyes. Everything was about her, all the time. Tess had met her family, had spent time with her friends, and yet Vicki always made one excuse or another not to meet Tess's.

"Ah, here you are. Right this way," the host announced, breaking the stifling silence.

Tess breathed a sigh as Vicki sauntered ahead of her, swaying her hips in the process and looking every bit like she was modeling her dress on the catwalk. The handful of heads turning her way was precisely the attention Vicki craved, and trailing slowly after her, Tess's own insecurities were at an all-time high.

When they reached their table, Vicki turned to catch Tess's reddening face with a smirk. "In the future, I'm choosing your outfit, okay? You'll look hot, I promise." She waited for Tess to pull her chair out before taking a seat and adding, "Thank you."

"You're welcome," Tess murmured, choosing not to respond to the clothing remark as she pressed a soft kiss to Vicki's expectant lips. She finally felt herself relax slightly as she took her own seat. She unzipped her leather jacket, shrugging out of it in time to see Vicki's disconcerting gaze. "I wore a blouse?" she said, but it came out more as a question.

"I can see that. It's your go-to," Vicki snickered as she used air quotes, "'going out' top."

"Eh, okay," Tess replied, unsure of where this conversation was going.

What was Vicki expecting, for Tess to miraculously transform into some kind of alpha lesbian raging with overconfidence and good looks? That would never happen. She knew someone who fit that description, and Tess was nothing like Taunya's friend, McCoy Miller. The first time she'd met the mechanic during her sister's first year at Simon Fraser University, McCoy was seated in a booth at the pub with a beer in her hands and a woman hanging off each arm — Abi being one of them. Tess never had confidence like McCoy — when it came to style or with dating — and never would. Vicki and Abi would both find someone like McCoy ten times more appealing than Tess.

A server arrived with ice water and menus, but Tess no longer felt like being there. She'd grown up around parents who loved each other. To this day, their relationship was balanced and healthy, so Tess had a pretty good idea of how her partner should treat her. What was it about her that made her so unlovable? Tess gave it her all when she dated someone, but no matter what she did or said, Vicki had to psychoanalyze it from the ground up. There was a world of difference between them, one Tess wasn't certain she wanted to break through. They were too different, heading down opposing paths in life. She never knew what mood Vicki would be in, and she hated feeling like their entire relationship consisted of Tess walking on eggshells. How much more of this could she take?

Chapter Three

Abi

EACH TIME ABI WALKED through the arrival gates at Vancouver International, she swore she felt a little more homesick. Bittersweet emotion choked at her, causing her heart to ache in ways only her first love could accomplish. It didn't matter where her career took her around the world, Vancouver would always be her favorite place. Everyone she loved was in the city and surrounding areas. She'd fully planned on returning after graduation, but after what happened with Tess, she knew it would be best for everyone involved if she stayed away.

In the end, time hadn't healed her heartbreak, but space had — and a *lot* of college hookups. If it weren't for the constant state of slight nausea at the thought of seeing Tess again, Abi could almost believe she was immune to the barber. And *that's* why even though now she was jobless and could move anywhere, it would never be Vancouver.

Abi spotted Taunya in the waiting area, her silky black hair pulled back in a ponytail and wearing a white halter top and navy capris. She held a cardboard sign almost as big as her that said, *T's number one bridesmaid.* Those blasted tears Abi had been holding on to sprang like a leak as she threw her arms around her best friend. "Tauni!"

In that moment, precious memories of growing up together rushed through Abi's mind. Gone was their fight over Tess so long ago, or the semi-awkward visits since. This was the best friend who'd sat beside her in first grade, the one who had swapped lunches with her and played hopscotch during recess. They'd played Barbies, and house, and made future wedding plans. Abi had lost count how many times they'd comforted each other in their teen years. Growing up, they'd talked about everything and anything, *except* for Tess. Abi had always known her crush on Taunya's big sister was off limits, but that hadn't stopped her from etching their names into notebooks or her favorite backyard tree. When she was fifteen, Abi thought Tess was every teenage lesbian's crush. It had taken five more years and a broken heart later, but as a grown-up she'd finally seen Tess without those rose-colored lenses.

You know that's not fair. She was hurting, and you took advantage of that.

Taunya buried her face in the crook of Abi's neck, squeezing her so hard, she thought a rib would crack. "It's so good to see you!"

They laughed once they realized they were blocking foot traffic. Abi wiped away her tears, and they moved with the crowd toward the luggage pickup. Taunya practically beamed as she peered at Abi, her pretty, earthy brown eyes full of warmth and affection.

"You've got that pre-wedding glow about you, friend."

"No way. I've got a bridal party glow." Taunya's grin was contagious, and she reached over to squeeze Abi's hand. "Do you know it'll be the first time in four years all my friends are together? I didn't think I'd be this excited to road trip around the province for a week of activities, but I'm stoked!"

Abi spied her suitcases making the way around the conveyor belt. "Is ah … is everyone participating? The fab five?"

"Yeah. They're over the moon that you're here, Abi. Coy wanted to come with me to pick you up but was elbows-deep inside someone's engine when I called." Unable to help herself, Abi cracked up, and as usual, it took way too long for Taunya to grasp her unintentional pun. Then she was laughing too.

"Oh! And my parents insisted on a welcome-home dinner tonight. Mom's making your favorite, spaghetti and homemade rolls." Taunya reached to help Abi with her luggage, adding in a much more subdued voice, "Tess'll likely be there too."

"Tess?" Abi squeaked. A lightning-hot image of the small blonde gyrating against her flashed through Abi's mind, and for the briefest second, her legs wobbled.

"Yeah, will that be, like, okay? If not, I can call her and —"

"No, no of course it is," Abi interrupted, but her voice sounded off, even to her own ears. "You just caught me off guard. Tess is…" she gave a helpless shrug, and finished lamely, "you know, old news."

Taunya's eyebrows knitted with blatant uncertainty, but she just nodded. "Okay."

Abi gave an uncomfortable swallow, silently questioning her life choices as she sensed the familiar pressure building in her sinuses. She didn't know why she was getting so upset. Tess was Taunya's maid of honor and would no doubt be participating in the bridal events this week, but Abi foolishly thought she'd get away without seeing her this weekend. It would have been nice not to be thrown right in Tess's line of sight the moment she landed. After all, Tess was six years older, and save for having a pretty good relationship with Taunya, what desire would she have to welcome Abi home? Especially after the way things were left between them.

"I appreciate Bobby and Audrey going through the trouble," she murmured when it was safe enough to speak. She darted a glance to her friend, giving her a tight smile. "But I guess I assumed you wouldn't want to immediately put Tess and I together. Not that it matters anymore, it's just that a heads-up would have been nice." She was blabbering, but it couldn't be helped. Knowing she'd be seeing Tess sooner than later had Abi feeling *some* kind of way.

Taunya looked stricken, like perhaps she was genuinely aware and apologetic for her part in keeping Abi and Tess apart in the past. Her lips parted, but when she didn't speak, Abi looked away. If she was going to get through the next couple of weeks, she needed to make sure she didn't end up down the same lovesick rabbit hole she'd been in for a good chunk of her life.

When Taunya pulled her blue Toyota Corolla hatchback into her childhood home forty minutes later, Abi automatically went on a lookout for Tess. Dinner was still hours away, so she was genuinely surprised when she came across the familiar motorcycle parked in front of the two-door garage of the main house.

"Isn't that Tess's bike? I thought you said she had her own place again." Surely Tess hadn't shown up *this* earlier to dinner? Not when it meant spending longer than necessary with Abi.

"Yep," Taunya deadpanned, pointing to the rustic outbuilding separated from the main house by a row of cedar trees. "You're looking at it. I guess when it came down to it, getting her business off the ground was more important than impressing women with her independence. Her girlfriend stopped by once when it was time to meet the parents, and then no one saw her again."

"Tess has a girlfriend?" Abi blurted before she could stop herself. She clamped her mouth shut, ignoring the instant flicker of pain she felt at the news. She would not get upset. She did not care. Tessa Moore would never be hers.

Then why can't I fucking breathe?

"It's been four years, Abi." Taunya made it sound so reasonable, as if there was a time limit to heartbreak, but then it dawned on Abi. Tess getting over her cheating bitch of an ex was a little different from Abi pining for Tess since the age of fifteen. Taunya's awkward laugh filled the car's silence.

"I mean, their relationship seems fairly new, if that's any consolation. And Mom and Dad hate her. I haven't met her, but she sounds snobbish."

Abi nodded, not really listening anymore. Hot, angry tears brimmed from her eyes, and she reached for the door handle. She was angry with herself, humiliated that she couldn't get her shit together. She'd been back less than two hours and was already making a fool of herself.

Taunya's hand landed on her arm, "Abi, I ... we've never talked about ... *that*, and I–I need to apologize."

"It's fine," Abi answered in a tone less than convincing that everything was, in fact, *fine*.

"It's not, though, is it?" Taunya asked, her voice small as she gave Abi's arm a gentle squeeze. "I was young and immature, and ... fucking *awful* to you. And Tess. I–I wish I'd never gone to check on her that night. If I hadn't, maybe ... maybe you and her—"

"Stop," Abi whispered, reaching up to wipe away the last fleeting tears from her eyes. She accepted the tissue Taunya handed her, swallowing hard before adding, "It wasn't just your fault. I–I was scared that Tess would believe all those things you were saying, that you'd get caught in the middle and have to choose sides if we dated, so when you left, I panicked."

A choked laugh escaped Abi, and she glanced over to see the sympathy in Taunya's eyes. She grimaced and with a helpless shrug admitted something she'd revealed only McCoy. "I told Tess I loved her. I–I would have given up Toronto for her, Tauni." It was a harsh reality she grappled with much later, but Abi would have given up just about anything to be with Tess. "She said she'd made a mistake, and that ... that I was too young to know about love."

"Oh, Abi," Taunya said, pulling Abi into her warm embrace.

It felt good to finally breach the off-limit topic they had actively avoided for years. *Better late than never,* she supposed.

"I'm so, so sorry, babe."

Abi's chest was tight from the pain of old wounds that refused to heal. "Yeah. Me too."

They sat in silence for a while, both lost in thought. Abi's face felt flushed, her eyelids swollen, and she wondered how she would get inside the house to the bathroom undetected. The last thing she needed was to run into Taunya's parents and have to explain her immediate meltdown on arrival. She glanced out the windshield, taking in the Moore property like she'd done thousands of times growing up, her chest aching with the familiarity. She felt like she was finally home. She had borne witness to so many events in the Moore household, from the summer Bobby, Taunya's father, built a spacious backyard deck to the day they'd installed the pool. Every school dance and graduation, Abi had shared with Taunya, either at the Moore house or down the street at her childhood home.

Abi sighed wistfully, taking another look at the annex that was Tess's home. It was barely more than a man cave or an extra large shed with vinyl siding that matched the main house. Two weeks living so close to Tess would be agonizing. She'd rather have taken two weeks of shit from Margo than feel the heartbreak from Tess all over again.

"For the record, I think Tess was wrong," Taunya finally said, rubbing Abi's shoulder in slow circles. She kissed the top of her hair. "I always knew you were crazy about her, but I ... I guess I never thought *she'd* see you ... in that way."

"I don't think she ever did. See me, I mean. Until that night." Abi's smile was sad as she remembered the initial shock, followed by desire, on Tess's face. "I'd never felt more beautiful than when she looked at me."

Silence again, before Taunya murmured, "Are you going to be okay being around her? I'm sorry I didn't mention she lived here. I sort of feared you wouldn't come if I did. We can stay at my apartment if you'd rather, but it would be a tight fit with my roommates and Derek. Maybe Coy and Sloane could put you up?"

Abi shook her head. Although she loved McCoy, there was no way she could live under the same roof as her for two weeks. Just the thought of her many hookups coming in and out at all hours made Abi ill. She would have stayed with her parents, but they'd moved to Vancouver Island a few years ago and the distance wasn't practical.

"I'll be fine crashing in Tess's old room. It's not like she lives in the house anymore."

Taunya let out a huff, pointing out the windshield, where Tess was indeed leaving the main house, keys and phone in hand. *Sweet baby Jesus,* Abi thought, her cheeks flaming as she locked in on the shorter woman straddling her bike a few feet away. Her breath caught as she soaked up those lean yet powerful thighs inside a faded pair of denims. Just like that, Abi's wayward thoughts took her back to Tess's bedroom for the umpteenth time that morning. Tess noticed them watching her and gave a little wave.

Taunya snorted, releasing Abi and joking, "You sure? Tell that to your lovely lady parts, babe. You're biting your lip and everything."

"Shit, I am?" Abi flew up in her seat, adjusting her crop top and praying her makeup wasn't smeared all over her face. She needed to get it together.

"What happened to the self-aware girl I grew up with?" Taunya continued, giving Abi a toothy grin as she pocketed her car keys. She took out a small sleeve of wet wipes, using one to help tidy Abi's makeup. "Own that shit. I've had four years to get over any hang-ups I have of you two together. If you still want Tess, let her know what she's been missing. And for fuck's sakes, remind her of her worth. Chantelle obliterated her self-esteem, and from what I hear, Dicky Vicki isn't much better."

"She's had tons of opportunities to reach out," Abi reasoned, watching Taunya push her door open, and scrambled to get out of the car as well. They met in the middle, where she finished in a hushed whisper, "I *am* self-aware, but it's meaningless if what I feel is one-sided. I still have *some* semblance of self-respect."

Taunya clasped Abi's hand in her own, tugging her toward Tess. Abi's legs shook as the distance separating them shortened, and she briefly worried if she'd break an ankle from something as simple as walking. She should have worn sneakers and packed the high heels, not the other way around.

"Have you been here long?" Taunya asked once they were standing beside the bike.

"T–Tess, hey." Abi's voice trembled.

Just perfect — her time home was starting off with a hearty dose of humiliation. Being within touching distance of Tess, she was acutely aware of her body's carnal reaction. How her heart quickened or how her thighs quivered at the sheer possibility of Tess desiring her again. Abi's gaze darted briefly to Tess's thin lips before meeting her eyes once more. She plastered on what she hoped was a smile and gave an awkward little wave.

"Not very long. I'm about to do a grocery run for Mom," Tess explained before giving Abi a faint smile. "Great to see you, Abi."

And just like that, Abi was sucking in a sharp breath, wholly unprepared for the emotional rollercoaster rushing to the surface. Her heart swelled as the last four years melted away with just a smile, and for a moment all she could do was stare dumbly back at Tess. Words became lost on her. Without another word, they watched as Tess put her helmet on and left, Abi still grappling with all the new and old sensations coursing through her. If it was possible, Tess looked even better than when Abi had last seen her. Her face was a little fuller, her hair a little longer, and there was a quiet maturity about her that Abi gravitated toward.

She startled when Taunya patted her back, laughing. "What'd you say before about being over Tess? 'Cause I'd say it's not quite over, babe."

CHAPTER FOUR

Tess

"You're the one who chose dresses for your wedding."

Tess looked from where she lathered butter over a slice of home-made rolls, taking in the conversation between the three other women at the table. Taunya sat beside her, with her mother, Audrey, on the far end and Abi across from her. They'd been discussing the wedding in detail, from the upcoming bridal shower all the way to the fabric of the dresses chosen. Wearing a dress wasn't Tess's first choice, but she didn't *not* like them. They just made her stand out, whereas she had always preferred to fade into the background as much as possible.

"Only because Derek's mom was pressuring me. You've seen the dresses she picked out! The color would look better as a curtain," Taunya complained, lifting her glass of red to her lips. "I get that it's too late, but I worry McCoy will feel like she's sticking out in the pictures, being the only one with a tux."

"Coy'll be fine. Honestly, she'd be more uncomfortable if you'd made her wear a dress," Abi threw in, her voice as sweet as Tess remembered. She couldn't get enough of it, truthfully, and eavesdropping on their conversation was affecting the one she meant to be participating in with her father.

Bobby reached in front of Tess for the plate of dinner rolls, and she pulled her gaze away from Abi. It didn't matter how they had parted; Abi still smiled at Tess in the exact same way, like Tess being in the same room with her was making Abi's day better. It was pathetic, Tess knew, but being around her was almost enough to forget Abi was the same woman who'd left Tess's bedroom in tears years ago.

"I plan to be at the river by six tomorrow morning, if you want to come," Bobby quietly mentioned, his voice as gentle as his personality. Tess couldn't recall a time when her father had ever raised his voice higher than what could be considered a half-muted decibel. He was the strong and silent type, only bringing to the conversation what was necessary. Even though Tess was closing in on thirty-one, he was still trying to make a fisherwoman out of her. She was too soft to tell him that killing the fish upset her, though a part of her remained secretly grateful he'd always tried to include her in things. Taunya had been the diva child, one hundred and ten percent femme, so when she'd turned her nose up at any activity that could potentially get her dirty, Tess had just known the expectation would fall to her.

"Maybe, thanks." Tess flashed him a small smile, wishing she could be more eager about the idea. They'd tried bonding over other things in the past, but it was tricky when they were so different. Her father could be as introverted as Tess but also had mad skills inside a courtroom. He even went for drinks voluntarily with his coworkers and watched football and hockey games with his old college buddies. Tess was content to live a simple, *much* quieter life. "It'll depend on how much sleep I get tonight."

"I just wish I hadn't listened to Derek's mom. She's so bossy, and bridesmaids wearing tuxes is a legit thing right now. Couples are moving away from traditional weddings, you know?" Taunya's hands were gliding through the air as she spoke, and once again Tess found herself watching Abi instead. Taunya hadn't stopped talking about the wedding since the day Derek proposed, and it was to the point, unfortunately, where it went in one ear and out the other for Tess. She'd much rather turn her attention to their guest.

Has Abi always been so beautiful?

She'd always been a pretty girl, but when had Tess begun to notice? She was dying to speak to her about that night. Apologize for her behavior and what came after once and for all. Tess had been vulnerable, heartbroken over Chantelle, and when Abi had slipped into her bedroom — looking very much a sexy temptress with her sights set on seducing Tess, it was all over. Her willpower had melted the moment Abi's lips landed on hers.

"Honey, I know you're stressing over last-minute details, but it's way too late to make drastic changes. I promise your wedding day will be perfect exactly as you've planned it." Audrey's tone was rarely quiet, but she often had a soothing effect on her daughters' moods. She was well versed in talking Taunya down pre-meltdown and did a bang-up job acting as mediator and cheerleader when it came to Taunya's moods. They were lucky to have such an amazing mom. Besides Stacey, Tess could unabashedly admit that Audrey was her closest friend.

"I agree with your mother. I don't see the point in hashing it out if it's not going to happen. You'll give yourself an ulcer before your honeymoon," Bobby said, taking a bite out of his pasta. Audrey had insisted on making one of Abi's favorite meals to welcome her home, so Tess had walked into the kitchen hours earlier to a pot of spaghetti sauce simmering on the stovetop. Audrey had made it her mission to cook as many things from scratch as she could while Tess and Taunya were kids. Once Taunya started school, Audrey went back to work as an admin assistant, and the task of breadmaking was pushed to Sunday afternoons.

Tess's cell phone went off for the third time, vibrating in the back pocket of her jeans. She grimaced, silencing the call and hoping no one else heard it. Vicki had been lighting up her phone nonstop over their supposed plans that evening. Taunya wasn't the only one stressing. Tess felt queasy, not understanding how their communication could be so off.

"Tess? What do you think?" Taunya asked.

"Hmm?" Tess focused on Taunya, aware of her slumped shoulders and panicked gaze. The upcoming wedding was certainly taking a toll on her sister.

"I think..." Tess began, careful to keep her voice as sympathetic as possible. The last thing this conversation needed was a hint of sarcasm. She stiffened when her phone vibrated again, but she resisted the urge to reach for it with everyone watching. Abi especially. Her gaze was on Tess, making her squirm in her seat. She swallowed the bite of spaghetti still in her mouth. "You did a wonderful job, Tauni. You're checking off boxes you've wanted your entire life. It doesn't matter what anyone else thinks, so long as *you're* happy. You and Derek."

"Well said," Abi added from her seat across from Tess. Her bright smile was intoxicating, sucking Tess into her vortex until she was blushing under her scrutiny.

"Can't you silence that or something?" Taunya demanded as Tess's phone vibrated once more. It wasn't like Tess worked on-call, although sometimes it felt that way with Vicki. She hated when Tess missed her call, which probably explained the rapid messages.

"Sorry," Tess muttered. Her blush deepened as she pulled out her phone, peering at the latest text.

Vicki – 5:59PM

> WE had plans first. I canceled with work friends to spend time with you.

"Is the shop on fire?" joked her mother.

Tess glanced up to the four pairs of eyes on her, waiting for a response. It was deathly silent in the kitchen as she quickly responded to Vicki's last text before returning her phone to her pants pocket. Sweat broke out along her back, and she had the biggest urge to flee the room and call Vicki in case her message was misconstrued in some way. She hated that about herself, how her desire to people-please rose above rationality. Knowing Vicki was pissed had her hands shaking, but she refrained. At least with a text message she could still hold her ground somewhat. Tess knew if she got on the phone, she'd be sacrificing plans she'd made with Stacey in no time. Not to mention it felt rude to take off while her family welcomed Abi home.

I'm always letting someone down.

"Tess," Bobby murmured, and her eyes flew up to meet his. He reached for her hands, squeezing Tess's fingers, his silent, all-knowing gaze observing their slight tremble. "Do you need to go?"

"No, um..." Tess shrugged, offering him a tremulous smile. She didn't dare look at the others; interrupting their meal and wedding talk was humiliating enough. Tess knew she would spiral in seconds if she caught even a hint of sympathy in Abi's eyes. She was always so sweet like that. Tess's throat was raw. "It's V ... Vicki. Miscommunication for our plans tonight."

"Isn't Stacey on her way over with the kids?" her father asked, helping himself to more salad.

"Yep. I–I must have forgotten to mention it to V."

She could have *sworn* she'd informed Vicki of the plans tonight. In fact, if memory served, she'd practically begged Vicki to join them. The one time she'd met Tess's parents hadn't gone as well as she'd hoped, and she was looking forward to another chance for them to get to know her girlfriend.

"Vicki's too pretentious to spend her evening here," Taunya interjected with another sip of wine.

"She isn't, she's just ... shy," Tess reasoned, although even she could hear how utterly lackluster her excuse was. Vicki was anything but shy, but what should she tell them instead? Vicki didn't have any interest in getting to know Tess's loved ones? That they'd only been an item for six months, and to Vicki meeting the parents was more of a year-end goal? Except that her opinion was flawed. She'd had no problem dragging Tess home for *her* family reunion the month before just so she wouldn't show up there alone.

"With a hundred thousand followers on TikTok, I doubt very much that she's shy, Tess. She posts thirst traps several times a day." Taunya laughed. "Vicki's an attention whore, and that's saying a lot coming from me."

Tess's fight-or-flight response kicked in, her chest squeezing at Taunya's words. It didn't matter to her that Vicki was popular on social media. She worked in fashion, so of course she would want to get on there and show off her outfits.

"She has a couple of videos with *you* on there too, but I bet you didn't know that."

Tess *didn't* know that. Trepidation latched on to the crushing feeling in her chest, and her fingers found the rubber band around her wrist. She toyed with it under the cuff of her long-sleeve, itching to snap it into her skin. The stinging feel it left behind often helped to slow her racing thoughts. Why had Vicki posted videos of Tess without her permission? Was that a typical thing to do in relationships? Tess didn't have a TikTok account, so she couldn't be tagged, but a heads-up would have been appreciated.

No, she was overreacting, like she always did. Taunya was just trying to get a rise out of her, and it was working. It didn't take much for Tess to overthink or allow her paranoia to consume her. Chantelle had often complained how she couldn't let things go. It was no doubt what led Chantelle to cheat on her. Tess wasn't sexy or confident, like other girls. Both Chantelle and Vicki had taken an interest in how soft-spoken and bashful she was, but in Chantelle's case, those parts of Tess eventually became annoying. She was worried constantly Vicki would feel the same.

"Thanks for supper," Tess said, acknowledging her mom with a small smile before getting to her feet. She carried her dishes to the sink, acutely aware of her family's whispers in the background. Her sister would never understand. She'd met Derek in college and had been fortunate enough to experience that rare, instant love. He'd caught her throwing up in the bushes at a party, offered to hold her hair back, and that was that. People like Tess had to hold on to what came to them, regardless of whether it was romance-novel-worthy or not. It was the only way to ensure they didn't end up growing old alone. "I'll be back over in a bit," she added, bending to give her mom a quick kiss on the cheek.

"Sure, honey."

She all but launched herself out of the side entrance of the house, eager to steal away from the judgment in the room. Hell, having Abi there as a witness made everything so much worse.

Reaching for the rubber band again, Tess pulled it back as far as it would go before releasing it. *Snap!*

It pained Tess how much power she gave to others. She knew she did, but for the life of her, she couldn't stop. She should be able to shrug off unwanted opinions instead of allowing them to fester until she doubted everything she'd originally thought or the actions she'd taken as a result. A confusing conversation could quite literally keep her up at night. Was that normal? Was it standard to toss and turn and rehash an entire conversation until she was no longer certain what was or wasn't said in the first place? The sinking feeling of someone being angry with her hit her the worst.

Snap! Snap!

Thoughts of Taunya and Vicki still weighed heavily as Tess traveled the short distance to her home away from home. Stacey was due to arrive any minute, a plan they'd made a week ago or more. Long before Vicki would have arranged anything. Like a Jack-in-the-box, Tess's nerves were tightly wound as she changed into her bikini top and swim shorts, and for once, the rubber band wasn't helping. When she got like this, it was usually best to find some alone time and decompress, but tonight it would be almost impossible. She sat on her bed, replying to Vicki one last time and inviting her to come to the house for the evening, but Tess knew she wouldn't.

"Ugh," she grumbled, catching her reflection in the mirror. Dull brown eyes stared back at her, and for the life of her she couldn't figure a way to get life back into them. She should be happy, not feeling whatever *this* was.

"Please be chill tonight," Tess muttered, grabbing a tank top from her dresser and pulling it on over her head as she slipped into her flip-flops. Then she took her regular dose of anti-anxiety meds before expelling a deep breath, silently counting to five before swinging open the door to the annex. She slammed right into Abi, who must have been about to knock, sending the younger woman teetering backward off the unlevel patio stones in front of the entrance.

"Shit, sorry!" Instinct had Tess grabbing Abi's slender arms to yank her forward again. She must have been stronger than she realized, or Abi frailer than she looked, because seconds later she crashed into Tess.

Abi yelped in surprise, but once the initial shock wore off and her body was pressing into Tess's against the closed door, her hands fell loosely to Tess's hips. Those haunting blue eyes peering down at her made Tess gulp. "You have insane reflexes," Abi remarked, and her low, throaty voice caused Tess's breath to quicken and her stomach to flutter.

"And you have..." She struggled for a reply, but nothing witty came to Tess as her attention fizzled into nothing but a jumble of nerves, sexual tension, and chest palpitations. Hell, she hadn't felt this giddy this close to a woman in four years. The feeling was more than mere attraction for Tess; it was as if her soul recognized Abi's, like Tess's body intimately remembered the way Abi's had yielded underneath her all those years ago. The fire in those icy blue eyes consumed Tess, possessing her, and for a moment all Tess heard beyond their ragged breathing was the rapid pulse rushing to her ears.

"I came to see if you were okay." Abi's hooded gaze was still locked on hers, and when she gently lifted her hands off Tess, it was all Tess could do not to pull her back. She watched her swallow, her eyes tracking the subtle movement. Was Abi nervous too? "You left the house pretty quickly."

"Oh, yeah." Tess shrugged it off, her gaze slipping from Abi's. She stared at her feet instead, appreciating Abi's painted toenails in a sexy pair of strappy white stilettos. A silver ring rested on the middle toe of both feet. "Tauni thinks everyone should act like Derek or there must be something wrong with them. I'm fine, though, really."

"Okay, if you're sure."

Tess darted a quick glance up at the obvious doubt in Abi's voice, about to respond when car doors slammed several feet away. She canted her head in the driveway's direction, watching as Stacey pulled a bag from the trunk.

"I'm heading inside, but…" Abi began, gaining Tess's attention once more. Her bottom lip was pulled between her teeth like she was deep in thought. "Your sister's not wrong, you know. You deserve someone who worships you like Derek does Tauni." Their eyes met, the flickering emotions cycling through Abi's on a front-row display. She'd always worn her heart on her sleeve, Tess remembered, but they couldn't go down that road again. *No way.* Taunya was right in saying it would never work between them. Tess was merely a curiosity, an experience that was interrupted, like a film shut off halfway through. Once the forbidden fantasy Abi had of them was fulfilled, she'd quickly grow tired. Tess was introverted, plain, and boring and in no way good enough for a girl like Abi.

"Tessi!"

Tess turned just as a miniature person barreled into her, wrapping tiny arms around her legs. "Hey, kiddo! Wow, you sure are getting big!" Tess exclaimed, stepping away from Abi to scoop the precious little blonde-haired girl up in her arms. She buried her face in Sierra's hair, praying her heartbeat returned to normal sooner than later.

Between the stress of dinner and Abi landing in her arms, she didn't think she could be more rattled.

Tess smothered Sierra in kisses, laughing as the little girl shrieked and wriggled to break free. When she glanced up again, Abi was disappearing into the house. Tess cleared her throat, aware their conversation was nowhere near finished.

Sierra's older brother stood a few feet away, a pleased yet reserved smile on his young face. Tess breathed his name out on a sigh. "Zeke, buddy. What, I don't see you for a few weeks and now you're too cool for hugs?"

"You're a quick study, Aunt T." Zeke flashed his dimples, dodging Tess when she made a grab for him with Sierra still in her arms.

"What about me? Do I get a hug?" Her best friend arched a questioning brow, trying and failing to hide her smirk. At five foot nine, Stacey Adams was considerably taller than Tess, with gorgeous hazel eyes, and she always kept her dirty blonde hair styled in a short pixie cut. Tess had met Stacey in the lineup for the water fountain in elementary school. Charlotte McGinnis had rudely butted in front of Tess, knocking her out of the way in the process with her backpack. Stacey had jumped in to intervene, shoving Charlotte out of the line and getting them both sent to the principal's office. She'd been Tess's protector ever since.

Tess set Sierra down, chuckling as she gave Stacey a quick hug. Her forehead reached Stacey's chest, and as always, it reminded Tess how awkward being short sometimes was. "I just saw you the other day when you came in for a cut, you goof."

"Yeah, and? I could be gone tomorrow, and then you'd be kicking yourself, wishing you had hugged me." She was joking because she was dark like that, but Tess grimaced at the thought.

"On that note," she said, clapping her hands with way too much enthusiasm. "How about we have some fun in the pool?" Tess smiled at Zeke and Sierra's excited cheers, her heart brimming with affection.

CHAPTER FIVE

Abi

THE INSTANT ABI MADE it into the Moores' house, she fled to the bathroom and locked it behind her. To say she was a hot mess was an understatement. Her heart and mind were at odds, warring with each other. Her *heart* grappled with the latest development on the Tess front, trying to reason with past rejection and the conflicting vibe Tess had projected. Her lady bits were throwing the tantrum of the year, horny and perplexed at the position she'd found herself in outside. Things were complicated, but for a moment Abi swore she'd felt a mutual attraction between them again. It didn't take a rocket scientist to see how unhappy Tess was in her current relationship. She deserved a woman who would worship the ground she walked on. By the way Taunya spoke, Vicki was toxic as hell. The question was, why couldn't Tess see that? What would it take for her to entertain the idea of a relationship with Abi, once and for all? She could ditch Vicki and finally be happy! But with the history she had with Tess, was Abi even strong enough to test those treacherous waters a second time?

She rolled her eyes, checking her makeup in the mirror and reapplying her lip gloss.

She'd been testing those waters since she was fifteen. Few people could say they fell in love with their first crush or that the frustrating six-year age gap had left much of Abi's love life in the hands of fate. She'd waited five years for her chance, only to blow it. Remembering Tess's vulnerable emotional state that night, it was possible Abi had made the wrong decision. She'd acted out of young love, desperate, eager to make Tess finally see her as a woman and not solely as her kid sister's best friend.

Unfortunately, the outcome had been nothing like Abi dreamed. She'd left with her tail tucked between her legs, her heart and ego bashed and bruised. If she could go back in time, she would have kept her clothes on that night. It had taken Abi a long time to understand, but Tess hadn't needed the distraction of her body. She'd needed a friend.

Now here was Abi, with no job, standing in front of the same bathroom mirror she'd given herself a pep talk in front of four years ago. Right before knocking on her crush's bedroom door. Not a damn thing had changed on her end, except that Abi was older. Not her love or hope.

When it came to Tess, Abi had learned long ago that tenacity was key. And whatever happened during her trip home, she vowed not to repeat the mistakes she'd made four years ago.

Abi weaved in and out of the crowded dance floor hours later, bobbing her head to the heavy bass. The DJ spinning tonight was new to the music scene and enjoyed mixing electro with hip-hop and R&B tracks. The beat was incredible, intense and sultry at the same time. The vibe in the place was killer, honestly, jam-packed with Vancouver's queer community inside a warehouse on the Eastside. It was an event one needed tickets for in advance just to get through the doors, and Abi was surprised to learn that McCoy had been planning this for weeks. Coy and the rest of Abi's friends, Sloane and Krystal, had arrived at the Moore residence dressed to the nines, not at all like they were staying for a bonfire. Tess was missing out, though she'd looked more than happy to keep visiting with Stacey and the kids.

Abi reached the bar, squeezing in beside two gorgeous drag queens sipping cocktails. The three bartenders behind the counter raced around, grabbing beers from the fridge or mixing drinks for patrons. Abi raised her hand, jingling her fingers in a small wave as she tried to get the attention of the bartender closest to her. The heavily tattooed androgynous woman noticed Abi and scowled before going out of her way to serve someone else. Abi sighed but refused to be put off. Sadly, wary — often belligerent — glances her way from queer women weren't uncommon. She got mistaken for heterosexual way more than she liked to admit. In fact, there hadn't been a time where she didn't make the first move in getting a woman's number. McCoy and Margo had been the only ones confident enough to approach Abi and risk getting shot down — or led on — by a "straight" woman.

A hand skimmed Abi's waist, teasing her, but before she could wheel around, McCoy's handsome face was there. She grinned cockily, those sexy dimples popping, and Abi watched as she easily got the bartender's attention and ordered a round of shots. "Who leaves their wing-woman on the dance floor?"

"A thirsty one. Think you can score some water with those skills?" Abi called out, noticing the rest of her friends were dancing off to the side behind Coy, sweaty and clearly drunk. Catching up tonight with the old gang was the most fun Abi had had in a ridiculously long time.

"You need swag, Abs. Gets 'em every time."

Abi rolled her eyes at the toothy, devilish grin McCoy gave her. Fisting the collar of Coy's shirt, she pulled her in to reply. "What I need to do is tattoo a pride flag on my forehead so it's obvious I'm family!"

"Why? Planning to pick up while you're home?" McCoy quipped, slipping her other hand around Abi's waist and wagging her eyebrows at her suggestively.

Abi giggled. "You wish, playgirl."

Out of her small group of friends, McCoy and her twin sister Sloane were by far the biggest flirts. McCoy had that overtly sexual "hella gay" vibe going, from her slicked-back chestnut brown hair with a disconnected undercut to her tight black jeans and striped vest over a sleeveless men's t-shirt. As hot as Coy was, Abi had never been the least bit interested. Despite repeated half-hearted attempts to get Abi into bed over the years, even McCoy understood their relationship would never be anything more than platonic. Their friendship meant too much to them both, and besides, Coy lived for the chase. As far as Abi knew, Coy never had real romantic feelings for her. Until recently, she'd been the only one Abi had ever confided in about Tess. Before Taunya had suddenly become okay with the idea of Abi dating her sister, it'd been McCoy listening without judgment. Abi would always love her for that.

Taunya came up to them, placing a hand on each of their shoulders and squeezing. "My loves! You guys are fucking adorable, and I mean that, from the bottom of my—" she belched, "—heart."

Abi snickered, turning her face into Coy's chest to hide her laughter. Coy's body shook under her palm as she guffawed. "Tauni, I think you mean the bottom of your *drunken* heart."

"Your water," the bartender announced from close by, and Abi looked up to see her sliding the unopened bottle toward her.

"Awesome, thank you." Abi stepped out of Coy's embrace, picking up the bottle gratefully. She twisted off the cap and took a long drink, enjoying the cool liquid wetting her parched throat after too much singing and screaming with the girls. The bartender still watched her, possibly to check her out, and it annoyed Abi. What, was she only gay enough if someone like McCoy was on her arm? *Now* she wanted to explore possibilities?

Krystal and Sloane approached the bar just as their bartender was lining up a row of vodka shots on the countertop. "I'm gonna be puking tomorrow," Sloane remarked, looking slightly green as she picked up hers. She handed one to Abi, clinking the glasses together.

Abi agreed, but it had been way too long since she'd let loose like this. Working for Margo had all but sucked the life out of her.

"You say that all the time, but don't you basically train your tolerance working at O'Rourke's?" Coy hollered to her twin, her grin unwavering as she grabbed her own shot.

"I'm a bartender, dumbass, not an alcoholic."

"Okay, on three," Taunya crowed, counting down as they each raised a shot glass to their lips.

Abi tossed it back, grimacing as the liquor burned its way down her throat. She slammed the glass back down, recognizing the remixed version of "Becky's So Hot" belting from the speakers. "I love this song! C'mon!" She grabbed McCoy's hand and led the way back into the mass of sweaty bodies. Taunya, Krystal, and Sloane soon flanked them, and together they danced to the next few tracks.

Abi got lost in the music, worries of the future fading away with her friends. She took her time studying them as they moved around the dance floor. First there was Sloane, who was significantly more feminine than Coy but equally attractive. Then Krystal, who Taunya had introduced her to some years before at a soccer game. Abi's gaze landed on her best friend, and their earlier conversation about Tess returned. Had Taunya truly given her blessing, if Abi was lucky enough to get another shot with Tess?

As if on cue, Taunya sidled up closer to Abi and pressed her lips close to Abi's ear. "Isn't that Dicky Vicki?" Taking Abi by the elbow, she directed her away from Coy and pointed across the dance floor. The lighting wasn't the greatest, but they were close enough for Abi to make out the two women cozying up on the stools at one edge of the bar.

"I don't know what she looks like!" Abi admitted, proud of herself for not stalking Tess's Instagram over the past year.

"It is! She's the curly blonde bitch with those ridiculously long tramp legs."

"Whoa, hold up!" It was Abi's turn to grab Taunya, but holding her still wasn't easy.

Coy's arm went around her shoulders. "What's going on?" she asked, sipping the beer she'd pulled out of her vest pocket earlier.

"I'm gonna rip off her eyelashes, that's what!" Taunya yelled, scrambling to break free of Abi's hold. When she slipped from Abi's grasp, Coy quickly removed her arm from Abi to sling around Taunya's waist.

"Come again?" Coy took another drink from the can, drawing Taunya in closer so they were hip to hip and going nowhere.

"She thinks that's Tess's girlfriend," Abi elaborated, pointing out the woman. She sat awfully close to the other woman, their foreheads practically touching, but it was loud inside the warehouse. Maybe they were having a hard time hearing one another?

"It is," Taunya insisted, craning her neck to see Sloane and Krystal had joined them. "Krystal knows!"

Krystal squinted, staring at the bar for several seconds before she began swaying again. "I'm drunk, but it sure looks like Vicki."

A fierce wave of protectiveness washed over Abi at Krystal's confirmation. Her gaze narrowed, and she focused on the two women with a fresh perspective. Even if they couldn't hear, if their conversation was that important, they could have left. She might not have been there for most of it, but Abi remembered how Chantelle's cheating had broken Tess. Taunya had said a few times over the years how the betrayal changed her sister. If Vicki cared about Tess at all, Abi didn't think she'd be a hair's breadth away from kissing someone else.

"C'mon," Abi said, grabbing Coy's vest and giving her a sharp tug. She didn't wait to see if anyone followed; she just let her legs carry her the short distance to the bar. Her heart slammed against the walls of her chest, but nothing felt more important in the moment. Tess deserved better.

Tess deserved *her*.

"Are you Vicki?"

The woman hardly spared them a glance until Taunya squeezed in between her and her lady friend. "Is your name Vicki, yes or no?"

"Excuse me? Who are you to interrupt—"

"Tess's sister," Taunya snapped, and Abi's gaze widened as her friend jabbed her index finger into Vicki's chest. She sneered, "I'm right, aren't I?"

To Abi's surprise, Vicki only laughed, completely unfazed. "*My* Tess? Wow, you're nothing alike."

"You would know that if you gave two fucks about Tess."

"Are you cheating on her?" The question left Abi's mouth softer than she'd rehearsed in her head, but Vicki flinched as if she'd slapped her. She sprang to her feet, knocking Taunya back in the process.

"It might come as a surprise, but I don't owe any of you a response."

"I know what I saw, bitch. I have eyes!"

"Tauni, take it easy," Coy added, grabbing Taunya again when she tried her hand at intimidation once more.

"You don't deserve someone as kind as Tess," Abi stated, continuing to glare until Sloane and Coy were pulling her and Taunya from the confrontation.

"Easy there, tiger," Sloane crooned, her arm around Abi. They followed Coy through the warehouse to the exit. Abi's pulse didn't begin to slow until they were outside in the misting night air.

"God," she groaned, lifting her face to the sky. Gentle rain dampened the heat on her cheeks, soothing her anger away drop by drop.

"What do we think? Is she cheating?" Krystal asked, her voice muffled from the loud ringing in Abi's ears.

She glanced among her friends, witnessing the various states of disbelief on their faces. Hysterical laughter bubbled from Abi's chest, and she clamped her hand over her mouth. A huge grin appeared on Coy's face, and before Abi knew it, they were all laughing at the sheer insanity of confronting Vicki.

"Such scrappers we are." Taunya giggled, swaying a little as she clutched her stomach.

"I thought she was going to deck you!" Sloane cackled, squeezing her legs together and bouncing around. "Oh fuck, I'm gonna piss myself!"

"'I *know* what I saw, *bitch*. I have eyes!'" Coy reiterated, gesturing to her face and laughing so hard, tears were rolling down her cheeks.

"Seriously, though," Abi said after she could breathe again. "What are we gonna tell Tess?"

Chapter Six

Abi

ABI TRUDGED INTO THE kitchen late the following morning, rubbing the sleep from her eyes and eager for caffeine. Although it had been a while since she'd stayed the night under the Moores' roof, it was practically a second home. No one batted an eye as she beelined for the coffee pot. When she remembered she still needed a mug, Audrey was already handing her one and pressing a kiss to her forehead.

"Morning, sweetie. Hung over?"

Abi muttered her thanks, filling her mug with liquid gold before reaching for the cream and sugar on the counter. "That obvious, huh?"

Audrey cupped Abi's chin, studying her face for a moment. "Your eyes are almost as bloodshot as that time Bobby and I caught you guys smoking up on Taunya's seventeenth birthday. And you smell like a bar."

Grinning at the memory, Abi took her coffee to the kitchen table. She scraped the chair back, wincing as the noise reverberated directly into her pounding skull, and sat down beside Taunya. Her friend looked like she'd been up for hours, not at all like she'd partied hard or almost got in a fight the night before. She was showered and dressed, mulling over a large binder of what looked like wedding list priorities.

"What's your secret?" Abi muttered, lifting the steaming mug to her mouth.

The pencil stilling through a half-written note, Taunya glanced up from her task and offered Abi a sly smile. "Switching to water about an hour before we left the warehouse."

"Seriously?" Abi deadpanned, groaning at the pressure behind her eyelids. Propping her elbow on the table, she let her palm hold her face up as she slurped back more coffee. Remnants of the night before flickered precariously through her mind like a light bulb shorting in its socket. She still couldn't believe they had gotten into it with Vicki. By the time Abi and her friends returned to the warehouse, Vicki was nowhere to be found. Now that morning had come, she would bet Tess was still none the wiser about her girlfriend's possible cheating.

Abi yawned again, the cause of her fatigue more than their excessive dancing and drinking. When she'd finally crawled into Tess's old bed at three in the morning, she couldn't fall asleep. No matter how much her body demanded the rest, it had been too weird being alone in Tess's domain. She'd spent the first hour or more replaying the exquisite way Tess had kissed every inch of her on said bed. By four thirty, she was so overstimulated that she'd had to get herself off just to relax. She'd fallen asleep thinking of Tess's crooked smile and gentle eyes. "What are you working on?"

Taunya pulled the cap off a pink highlighter, dragging the slanted tip across the top of the page. "Right now, I'm finishing the last details to mention to the caterer and photographer. Earlier, I had

Mom help finalize last-minute wedding guests to our seating chart. See?"

Abi's eyes widened when Taunya spread the poster-size diagram out on the table, careful to hold up one corner so it didn't dip into Abi's coffee. Two rows of round tables, along with cut-out guest names, were positioned around the chart. "Hardcore. I like it!"

Taunya scrunched up her nose, looking like such a spoiled princess that Abi laughed at the Kardashian vibes she was putting off. "Really? I think you're the first to say so. I've been driving everyone insane, or so they tell me. Even Tess avoids the house at all costs if she knows I'm here. McCoy flat-out said I had turned her off traditional weddings. She wants to go to the courthouse and throw a huge party afterwards. To be honest, her idea is tempting the hell out of me right now."

Abi laughed and immediately regretted it when the throbbing started all over again. She winced, gesturing to herself and mumbling. "Lipstick lesbian, remember? Trust me, I'm *here* for it, Tauni. You're planning my dream wedding. I only wish I could have been here from day one."

The exterior side door located right off the kitchen opened, and Abi turned in time to see Tess step through. She'd thrown her hair into a loose ponytail, drawing Abi's attention to her round face and neck. A thin gold chain hung loosely between her breasts. She wore a pair of denim jumpers, cut-off just above the knee, and the black t-shirt had short enough sleeves that Abi had no trouble admiring the full sleeve tattoo on one arm.

Aware she was staring, Abi reluctantly shifted her gaze back to Taunya. Her cheeks burned from embarrassment, but the only one eyeing her differently was Audrey over by the kitchen sink. As she stirred the bowl of pancake batter in her arms, she glanced strangely between Abi and her eldest daughter.

"Good morning, sweetie. Hey! Out of that bacon—Tessa Lily!"

Taunya and Abi both chuckled as Audrey swatted Tess's hand first before shooing her out of the cooking area. Appearing sullen, but with eyes twinkling with mischief, Tess grumbled her way over to them. She greeted first Abi, and then Taunya. Abi braced herself for another assault on her eardrums as she reached for a chair, but there was no need. Tess did all things with a gentle precision, and Abi watched as she slid the chair quietly from the table to sit down. "If it was a good morning, you'd let me have some of that."

"Don't be such a sulk," Audrey called, and a moment later she set a piping mug of coffee in front of Tess. She kissed Tess's forehead like she had done with Abi. "Unless you're going to help make the eggs, stay put."

Tess thanked her with a faint blush on her cheeks as she mumbled into her coffee, "I don't mind helping."

"Don't you usually have breakfast at your place, anyway?" Taunya speculated, giving up on her work for the meantime. She stacked the binders off to the side before facing Tess.

"Does the annex have a kitchen now?" Abi asked, glancing around the table.

When neither sister answered, Audrey spoke from her place at the stove. "A kitchenette at best, Abi. And anyway," she added, loud enough to gain her daughter's attention, "it's been a while since I've had guests, Tauni, not to mention this is more of a brunch. It's only polite that Tess makes an appearance."

"Makes sense. We're all benefiting from Abi being home." Taunya winked Abi's way, reaching across the table to clasp her arm. "Ohmygod! You and Coy slayed it last night on the dance floor. I wonder how many more nights we can fit in before you head back? It's been forever since we all went out."

"I had a lot of fun," Abi ventured after a minute. "But can we maybe hold off on the repeat? I'm dead today." When all three women laughed, she whined, "It's not funny. All of me aches. It's been forever since I went clubbing, not just with you guys."

"What do you usually like to do on weekends?"

Surprised by Tess's interest, Abi hesitated for half a second before replying, "Oh you know, clean my apartment, shop, read a book or watch Netflix. My roommates still go to the clubs, but I'm usually in bed by midnight."

"Are you serious right now?" Taunya sounded shocked, but Abi focused on Tess. A soft smile graced the edges of her mouth, and Abi's belly did a somersault. "Are you sure you didn't leave a wife back in Toronto? Because you sound hella boring compared to me, and I'm the one settling down."

"Hey, I'm exhausted when I get home. I clock in sixty hours a week." *Not anymore.* "And have an overbearing boss." Again, not anymore. Abi grimaced, hating the lie. She hadn't told anyone about quitting, not even McCoy. She didn't want Taunya distracted before the wedding, and Abi knew she'd go all mother hen on her.

"Well then," Taunya picked up her coffee mug, "I guess we're extra lucky you were able to come home for the wedding. We're going to have so much fun this week, right, Tess?"

"Yep, but it's on a need-to-know." Tess gave her sister a knowing smile before glancing in Abi's direction. "Top secret, and Tauni is so nosy it's driving her nuts."

"It truly is. Oh! You'll never guess who we saw at the club last night," Taunya exclaimed, reaching for her phone.

"Tauni, don't! She doesn't—" Abi closed her mouth abruptly, narrowing her eyes as she watched Taunya slide her phone down the table to Tess. *Shit.*

"Krystal got a picture. Vicki, sitting all cozy-like with some rando." Taunya arched an eyebrow, tapping her nails on the table's wooden surface as she waited for a reaction.

Tess frowned, studying the image taken in the semi-darkness. She lifted her gaze, confusion and hurt waging a war behind her eyes. Agony of her own stabbed Abi as she watched, and all she wanted to do was stand up and give her a hug.

Abi kicked Taunya under the table, hissing, "We need to work on your tact."

"What's that about Vicki?" Audrey wondered from in front of the stove.

"Was she..." Tess's brown eyes were luminescent with unshed tears. "How did it seem, Tauni?"

Sighing, Taunya at least had the decency to look apologetic. She placed both hands on the table, her voice softening as she took in Tess's noticeable deflation. Her entire body seemed to curl into itself. "I mean, we were all drinking, but it looked pretty damnable, Tess. Unless Vicki is super touchy with all her friends, the picture speaks for itself."

"We aren't positive, though," Abi quickly added, needing to comfort Tess, even though helping her see Vicki in a more generous light was the last thing she wanted. All Abi could think of was taking Tess's pain for her own. This time she did reach for Tess's hand, the one not clasped around her coffee mug in a death grip. "It'd be good to get her side of the story. Do you trust her?"

"I don't know, I ... I thought I did."

"Let me see that picture," Audrey demanded, carrying the phone to Taunya so she could unlock it once again.

"Coy had to hold me back from hitting her," Taunya confessed, catching Abi's gaze. The corners of her mouth twitched, a hint of a smile peeking through. "Abi too. You should have seen her. She was like a gorgeous lesbian knight swooping in to save you from Vicki."

Abi's face heated, but she didn't back down from the obvious opening, "'Swooping' is a bit of an exaggeration."

"If you zoom in, you can see the hand on Vicki's thigh," Audrey declared, stopping by Tess's chair to wrap both arms around her. "I'm sorry, baby. You could do so much better than her, anyway."

"I don't ... we don't know for sure what happened," Tess mumbled, and Abi watched a tear escape as she lifted her coffee mug to her lips. Now, Abi wasn't a violent person by any stretch, but beating on Vicki was sounding better and better the morning after. She wasn't perfect, but she knew hell would freeze over before she treated any girlfriend of hers the way Vicki was treating Tess.

It wasn't long before Bobby entered the kitchen from the basement, still sweaty from a morning workout. By the time they had helped to clear the table and brunch was served, Bobby had returned from his shower. Abi stole a seat again beside Tess, who rewarded her with a small smile. It was unnerving how such a gesture could liven up Abi in a way coffee never could. Attention from Tess was the equivalent of either downing a triple shot of wheatgrass from the barista near her Toronto office or binging on Red Bull and Skittles.

As soon as brunch was over, Audrey and Bobby thanked them for cleaning up before wandering outside to the back deck. Whether Abi visited or not, it'd always been that way in the Moore house, Audrey and Bobby disappearing after the meal while the girls cleaned up. It was honestly one of the most endearing aspects to being included in the family. Abi's parents were amazing as well, but there was something special about having siblings. Growing up, Abi had witnessed many water fights brought on by Taunya at the kitchen sink.

Taunya put away the leftovers and cleared the table before the ringing of her phone pulled her away. Two minutes into her conversation with her fiancé, she disappeared upstairs.

"I could finish up if you wanted to take off," Tess offered, her arm grazing Abi's as she placed a glass in the dish rack. "You're a guest, after all."

"I think me being a guest ended years ago." Abi's chuckle was light and teasing.

"Okay, well, you're on vacation," Tess reasoned matter-of-factly, taking a moment to fill that same glass with water and down a long drink. Her body language remained so neutral that Abi had a hard time grasping how she was truly feeling. Was Tess merely being polite because she thought that was what Abi wanted, or was she trying to get rid of her?

"Really," Abi said slowly, carefully watching Tess's reaction. "I'm not doing anything I haven't done in this house a hundred times before. It feels like I've come home."

"Fine, but remember the offer was there," Tess replied, her voice bordering on stiff. She'd been unusually quiet since Taunya had shown her the photo, and for good reason. What was with all Tess's partners cheating on her? Did they honestly not know how much of a gem Tess was? Maybe that was why Tess had run from Abi. She had a penchant for toxic women, by the looks of things, so maybe the idea of entering a healthy relationship was terrifying for her.

"Want to talk about it?"

Tess pressed the glass to her cheek, her eyes drifting closed. "Not really," she admitted, her voice low. Her eyes flashed open once more, and she peered up at Abi. "Why are you so nice to me? After what I did, you should hate me."

A soft laugh escaped Abi. She inched closer, wanting to get as near to Tess as she dared, considering Vicki was still in the picture. She settled for placing her hand on the countertop beside Tess's, so close that all Tess would have to do was move her finger and they'd be touching. Abi's gaze roamed over her small hands, remembering how they'd felt in hers, on her body. She memorized how strong and delicate they looked. The hand with a rose tattoo on the back was the starting point to her other tattoos, and Abi followed, appreciating the intricate floral designs and wild cats etched into the artwork. She reached Tess's face, and the other woman's hooded gaze was watching her intently. Abi blushed under that unyielding scrutiny, it slowly dawning on her that she hadn't responded.

"I could never hate you, Tess." *I love you, how can't you see that?* was what she wanted to say. But it wasn't the right time, and she had to face it, there might never *be* a right time. She couldn't *make* Tess love her. Abi bit her lip. "You weren't yourself that night. I know the kind of person you are, and I promise, I'll always be available if you need to talk."

"Thank you for saying that," Tess said, her voice husky and full of emotion. She turned to look out the small window above the sink. Her head hung low, and in that moment Taunya's worry came back to Abi. Tess *had* changed since they'd been together, and even though she should have a lot to be proud of in the past four years, her spirit was wasting away.

In a single sentence, Tess let out years of emotion. "She doesn't want kids."

Abi blinked, seconds passing before Tess's comment registered. "Vicki?" she murmured, scooting closer still. Her fingers found Tess's back, and she traced slow, comforting circles. She wasn't sure if it was for Tess's benefit or her own, to be honest.

Tess nodded, and her rigid posture slackened a degree under Abi's touch. "This is a sign, right? If she's cheating? I wanted to give things a try, even though..." She trailed off.

"You've wanted kids forever?" Abi supplied, offering Tess a wry smile. "Everyone knows that about you, Tess. Why would you be willing to try with someone who will only hold you back? You're better than that."

Tess shook her head. The movement was subtle, but Abi could still gauge her feelings. "Am I? I don't think so. I just wanted her to see me differently than Chantelle did," she whispered, reaching up to wipe a few stray tears away. She laughed, albeit dripping with sarcasm. "If I can't keep a relationship, how would I raise a child, Abi? Look at me, look at where I'm living. Vicki told me if she ever goes to my place again, it'll be when I'm not 'living with my parents.'"

Punching Vicki was quickly becoming a life goal for Abi. It was no wonder Tess's self-esteem was at an all-time low with a girlfriend like that in her life.

"I didn't go out with her last night, so she met someone else," Tess choked out, glancing over her shoulder at Abi. It broke her heart to see the tears slipping from Tess's eyes, and before she knew it, Abi was wiping them away with her thumb. "I hadn't seen the kids in a while, and I–I…wanted to see you."

"I saw you in the pool with them. Sierra and Zeke, right?" Abi murmured, using the hand on Tess's back to gently turn her around. Abi guided her into an easy embrace, just like any decent friend would do. She wasn't nearly as tall as Stacey, but Tess's cheek still only came to her shoulder, and she let out a silent gasp as Tess pressed her face into Abi's neck. She felt Tess nod, so she continued, "You're amazing with them. I think you'd make a fantastic mom one day, and I'm not just saying that. Any kid would be lucky to have you, Tess." Not to mention any *woman* would be lucky to have her, but Abi left that part out.

"Thanks," Tess whispered, pulling slowly away. She wiped her eyes again, averting her gaze from Abi's as she gestured to the door. "I um, I should go. Thank you, again. For the talk."

"Any time," Abi returned, pulling her bottom lip between her teeth as she watched Tess disappear outside. The door closed quietly behind her, and a heavy sigh escaped. This trip home was nowhere near what she'd expected.

CHAPTER SEVEN

Tess

IT WASN'T TOO OFTEN that Tess wished she worked on a Sunday afternoon, especially after a long week of standing and chatting with clients. But as she silently observed the others in her sister's bridal party taking up the better part of her parents' living room, she conceded it was perhaps the excessive talking getting to her. She sat alone in one of the two overstuffed suede armchairs, closer to the room's exit than the rest, but that was fine. She wasn't feeling particularly sociable since seeing Vicki in that photo. Vicki had messaged her once she'd gotten up, but Tess quickly let her know she would be busy for the day. Maybe she was a coward, but Tess hadn't wanted her failing relationship consuming her and getting in the way of the bridal party's official kick-off meet-and-greet. Not that it had worked anyway; when Tess's thoughts weren't plagued by a stranger's hand on Vicki's thigh, her conversation with Abi circulated in her mind. Opening up to Abi earlier had been both a surprise and a blessing. Admitting the fact Vicki didn't want kids was like a weight off her shoulders. She didn't *have* to stay with Vicki. She had choices, *dreams*. Had Abi spoken the truth? *Would* Tess be a good mother? Or would her future child grow up to resent her as well?

Letting her gaze wander around the bridal party, she paused when she landed on Abi. She sat curled up on the sofa with McCoy, a can of sparkling water in one hand. She must have felt Tess's eyes on her because she turned to smile. Tess's heart skipped a beat in response, and she could almost feel the saliva drying up in her mouth. Abi's smile was devastating. It lit up her whole face, making her more dazzling than ever.

Tess blinked, unsettled, aware of her quick inhale but unable to stop. There was still so much Tess needed to apologize for, so much she wanted to learn and rediscover when it came to Abi, but she was off limits; Taunya had made that clear long ago. Casual chats in public places were one thing, but nothing could ever happen between them. Even if Vicki wasn't in the picture, Tess wasn't a risk-taker. She couldn't live with herself if she hurt her sister over a what-if.

"Tess, hey, want any before it's gone? Coy's gobbling up the food in record time."

Krystal was in front of her, holding out a tray of various cheese cubes and crackers. Besides Taunya, she was the only other straight woman in their friend group. She also happened to be as quiet as Tess most days, so Tess was surprised by the effort.

She smiled. "No, thanks. I'm still stuffed from brunch, if you can believe it."

The gesture brought her back into the party's conversation, though, and away from thoughts of her pathetic excuse for a love life. Tess sipped her coffee, catching the tail end of Sloane's detailed night from hell working at O'Rourkes pub Friday night.

"I swear I'd never seen so many full bottles of the hard stuff smash to the floor all at once." Sloane was laughing so hard, a snort escaped, and when she covered her face in feigned horror, everyone else joined in the laughter. Sloane was the type of woman all the world would love to know. Unlike Tess, Sloane and McCoy were the life of the party. "I thought Frankie was gonna *die*. She was so pissed that she stormed out and didn't come back until closing."

"I bet she wanted to unalive the drunk who threw the bottle at you. She hates it when her authority is in question," McCoy commented, relaxing more on the sofa beside Abi. She reached for Abi, wrapping an arm around her shoulders before meeting Tess's stare. Coy's smirk as she took a drink of coffee sparked a jealousy in Tess she hadn't felt in a long time. It made no sense for her to be jealous, and that fact alone was infuriating. "*Especially* in the bedroom, if you catch my drift."

"Ugh, Coy! Twin or not, I do *not* want to think of you hogtied to my boss's bed!"

"How did we get so off topic?" Taunya arched a brow McCoy's way, the faint blush on her cheeks a semi-permanent fixture any time the two of them were in the same vicinity. Tess didn't get it, since her sister would swear up and down how straight she was. After a few too many drinks on her last birthday, however, Taunya professed to anyone within earshot that McCoy was the *only* woman she ever fantasized about. Of course, the morning after, a *very* hung over Taunya had been mortified beyond measure. Derek had a good laugh about it and still teased her occasionally. Tess liked the guy her sister had chosen to spend her life with. He had a sense of humor, worked hard, and treated Taunya like a queen. It was only seldom that Tess let her jealousy run rampant, but when she did, it was usually over how blissfully happy Taunya was.

"Tauni's right. There's still a lot to go over for the wedding." Abi clasped her hands, glancing around the room to each one of her friends before landing on Tess. There was hardly any trace of her hangover, and the quick flare of heat in Abi's gaze set Tess's insides on fire. She downed her remaining coffee, wishing like hell it was spiked. Silently, she ran through all the reasons she should have been turning tail away from Abi.

She was with Vicki ... because ... because, well, sometimes she couldn't remember the reasons why, but Abi was her *sister's best friend*. Hell's bells, Tess still remembered Taunya's idle threats after Abi came out as a lesbian years ago. She'd been her bratty, overprotective self and bombarded Tess during one of her visits home. She'd been living with Chantelle across the city at the time, but Taunya had still felt within her rights to ward off Tess by informing her, "*Just because you're both gay doesn't mean...*"

Her benign threats had stung, Taunya's teenaged accusations making it seem as if Tess was a predator. Hell, Abi had been fifteen! At twenty-one years old, Tess hadn't been scoping out underaged lesbians. In fact, it wasn't until Abi's going-away party that Tess had looked twice. And damn had she ever looked twice.

And now you have a girlfriend.

At least, she thought she still did.

"Tess?"

Shaking herself from her daze, Tess was sheepishly aware of the five sets of eyes watching her from around the room. Running her fingers through her hair, she hoped her cheeks weren't as rosy as they felt. "Sorry, what?"

"Can you reveal this week's itinerary for the girls?" Taunya asked, sounding hopeful. It was as if they hadn't already addressed the same conversation that morning. "Please? I know you wanted it to be a surprise, but I'd love to know what to wear tomorrow. You've been so hush-hush."

"And this was all part of your MOH duties, right?" Abi's question stirred others into guessing what events Tess had chosen from Taunya's insane list of possibilities. With a modest budget and tighter timeframe, Tess had only squeezed in six activities for the upcoming week. Six out of the hundred or more initially on Taunya's list. A bachelorette party would conclude Taunya's dream bridal party bucket list week from hell. Tess was footing the bill, like the fool she was. It would be an extremely costly gift, one she certainly couldn't afford, but when Taunya had brought it up months ago, all Tess could do was say yes. She loved Taunya, and if organizing these events gave her a lifetime of lasting memories to go with her wedding day, Tess wanted to do that for her.

Before Tess could reply, Taunya nodded, excitement sparkling in her brown eyes. "Of course! She planned the whole thing, right down to the bookings. Tell them, Tess."

An uncomfortable chuckle escaped Tess, and she sat straighter in her seat. "Where is everyone's sense of adventure?"

"Oh, we lovvve a sense of adventure."

"Seriously, knowing the deets will just make it more exciting."

"I bought a new waterproof camera for this week, so I'm ready for anything," Sloane added.

"C'mon, Barber, spill," Coy taunted. "Abi needs to know if she'll be wearing a lace push-up bra, a bikini, or a sports bra and jersey shorts."

"Coy!" Abi protested, her cheeks flaring red as she smacked the mechanic in the arm.

Tess closed her eyes and expelled a long breath, ignoring McCoy's laughter as she silently prayed for self-control. To get through the next two weeks, she'd need it all, and then some.

Her hands were clammy as she stood outside Vicki's condo. Was she always nauseous like this when visiting her girlfriend? She stared down at them folded tightly in front of her, the echo of Vicki's voice behind the door kicking up her heart rate. *Was this a flower occasion?* Tess thought out of the blue. Should she have bought some at the supermarket on the way? Vicki's last text had been cryptic, after a series of abrupt one-liners that could have been perceived as apologies. *I wish you were with me last night,* or *I missed you,* or Tess's favorite, *Whatever your sister told you, it's not true.*

The deadbolt turned over, and Vicki swung the door inward, ushering Tess inside. "Hi, thank you for coming," she said, leaning into Tess and waiting for a kiss. Vicki's top-shelf Alghabra perfume saturated Tess's senses, the comforting scent of what she imagined a Greek goddess would smell like, wrapping around her. Tess breathed a sigh, surprised at how stiff her shoulders were as she looped her arm around Vicki's neck and closed the gap between them. A burst of longing exploded inside Tess, and emotion clogged her throat as they kissed. Why couldn't it be like this all the time?

"I missed you last night," Vicki husked, tracing the outline of Tess's face with one finger. Her smile was softer, even repentant, but her pale blue eyes were nothing like Abi's striking glacier ones.

Where had that come from?

Tess gave a hard swallow, forcing out, "It doesn't sound like you did." Her gaze dropped, unable to keep eye contact. Again, her stomach twisted in knots. Her hands trembled around Vicki, so she backed away, taking in a deep lungful of air. Had it always been so damn hot in Vicki's condo? Tess reached for the rubber band on her wrist. After so many years, just knowing it was there gave her a sense of security.

"Baby, there's nothing going on between Natasha and me any-more. You don't need to worry."

"She's your ex?"

Vicki breached Tess's space bubble once more, reaching out to touch her arm. It did nothing to squelch the unease brimming to the surface. Vicki sighed when Tess backed away. "For a quick minute, we had a fling. It wasn't serious, Tess."

Fuck it.

The rubber band was pulled back, and seconds later the sharp snap of the tension band meeting flesh was the only sound in the room. Vicki's eyebrows went up, but she silently observed where the rubber band rested. Tess shot Vicki a doubtful look, snapping the rubber band again as she considered Vicki's side of what happened. Her throat ached at the possibility of another betrayal. She studied the sincerity in Vicki's eyes, her bottom lip trembling when she found herself back in Vicki's arms. "I told you about Chantelle."

"I know, and it's not like that. I swear," Vicki murmured, tilting Tess's chin to give her another kiss. This time it was longer, deeper, and in no time, Vicki had her pressed against the closed door. "Trust me?" she breathed against Tess's lips. Their eyes met, and for a moment Tess stared back at the woman she'd met months ago.

"I want to," she admitted, and Tess's breath caught when Vicki ran her tongue up her exposed throat.

"I cooked supper for us, but it's in the warmer, so..." Vicki winked, her hand slipping into Tess's. She tugged her toward the bedroom, pushing Tess down on the bed before straddling her.

It wasn't long before Tess was wrapped up in Vicki's world, and all her earlier worries were put to rest.

Chapter Eight

Abi

ABI CHECKED HERSELF OVER in the full-length mirror, assessing the potential outfit just as she had the last five she'd tried on. When she'd finished modeling all the clothing she'd brought for the trip and still wasn't happy, Taunya generously offered Abi free rein of her own closet. So, there they were, in the downtown apartment Taunya shared with Derek and their roommates, getting ready for their first bucket list adventure.

"What do you think?" Turning slowly, Abi studied the way the ripped boyfriend jeans hugged her butt without giving up the baggy aesthetic in the legs. The simple gray crop-top showed off her belly button piercing nicely, and if she remembered correctly, Tess had loved her body jewelry. Not that she was solely dressing with Tess in mind. She definitely was *not* doing that.

Taunya stuck her head out of the bathroom, still in her bra and panties. She frowned at Abi's shirt, crossing her bedroom to the closet. "Wrong vibe, babe. Last thing you want is to raise your bow and flash everyone. It's cute, though. Maybe wear it tomorrow? Tess is keeping this week as a need-to-know just to annoy us control freaks, but..." She paused, pulling a flannel shirt from her closet and handing it to Abi. She grinned. "She did say tomorrow will be out of town. Try that on."

"And here I thought anything plaid made you cringe," Abi deadpanned, reluctantly pulling off her top. Holding the plaid shirt at arm's length, she noticed the worn material with a bleach stain on one cuff. "This can't be yours."

Taunya smirked, still rooting through her closet. She selected skinny jeans and a casual, burgundy weekend blouse for herself, sitting on her bed to dress. "You're probably right, and it's too small to fit Derek. Could be one of the girls left it behind. Seems like Tess's style, no? Wear it anyway; whoever it belongs to can't have been missing it much."

The thought of Tess's *anything* clinging to her skin had Abi breaking into a goofy smile. She slipped her arms through the sleeves, trying unsuccessfully to reel in the giddiness spreading warmth through her. Facing the mirror once more, Abi bit her lip, loving how the shirt looked on her. She looked hot, and there wasn't any doubt in her mind that Tess would be thinking the same thing.

It was crazy how life turned out. Abi had come home for Taunya's wedding at the expense of her job, never considering Tess would be in a relationship. Now she was here, craving Tess's attention and love as if she'd never left. The feeling was a little more mature, less frenzied in lust and more selfless, but just as all-encompassing. A part of Abi wanted to try her hand at breaking Tess and Vicki up, and knew she was awful even for thinking it. She had no right to crash land into Tess's life four years later and expect Tess's feelings for her to have awakened. It was unrealistic.

Derek appeared in the open doorway. "Hey, what are you two doing here? Thought you were headed to a group thing this afternoon?"

Abi opened her mouth to reply, but Taunya cut in. "We are. Abi was late getting back from visiting her parents. What are you doing at home?" She crossed the distance to plant a kiss on his lips.

"Late lunch break. I came home to grab my gym bag. You smell nice."

Abi watched them kiss, the pang in her chest returning as Tess sprang to mind. Generally speaking, Abi deluded herself into thinking everything in life happened for a reason, that she was alone and suffering unrequited love for some grander purpose, but damnit, she really wished she knew the answers sometimes.

"You guys look so happy," she said once Derek had disappeared again.

Taunya smiled, sighing dramatically as she practically floated about the room. "Is it cheesy that I still get butterflies when he enters a room?"

"A little." Abi let out a soft laugh but couldn't disguise her wistful tone. "It's supposed to be that way, though, right? Otherwise, why bother?" Lack of magic was exactly why she'd broken things off with Margo. While she'd cared for her, Abi's heart didn't speed up when she entered the room. Not the way it did whenever Tess was close by.

Speaking of Margo...

Her ex-boss had texted twice that morning and called once, practically begging for Abi's return. And with the groveling came an abundance of incentives if Abi signed a new contract with MT Marketing; on the table so far was a generous pay increase, her own assistant, an extra paid vacation, and a yearly bonus. Margo certainly knew how to play hardball, but Abi would need more reassurances if she were to go back. It was about more than money to her, although she needed that too.

"Now that I've gotten over myself, I can see how you and Tess vibe together," Taunya stated, keeping her voice casual as she slipped on her high heels. She watched Abi for a moment, and then a smile appeared. "It's kind of beautiful witnessing how much you love her. Even sitting across the room from one another yesterday, I picked up a connection between you."

Abi inhaled deeply and smiled a little. It was nice to finally have someone else notice what she had for all these years. Not that she could do anything about it, but she and Tess belonged together. When Abi responded, a gush of air left her lungs in a sigh. "Thanks."

"Now, if *Tess* could get on board the Abi love train and quit being so clueless, life would be peachy," Taunya added with an eye roll.

"Did you send it?"

Abi looked up from her phone to see Taunya whizzing her car through traffic, already thirty minutes late. Luckily, Taunya's apartment in South Main was only a ten-minute drive from Commercial Drive, where Lykopis Archery was located. "I did, but she's probably busy getting ready. Tess doesn't live on her phone like we do."

"Still, when she sees it, she'll know you're thinking of her."

"I didn't even have her number. I had to hit her up on Insta like some run-of-the-mill stalker."

Taunya laughed hard, missing the correct turn-off completely. "Fuck," she wheezed, unfazed by how late they were. At the rate they were going, Abi hoped Tess had thought to book the entire afternoon. "Babe, you are nowhere *close* to run-of-the-mill. There should be awards out there or something for how dedicated you are. I'd nominate you."

Abi buried her face in her hands and groaned. "You're dead to me right now. I'm serious," she added when Taunya continued to laugh. "You could've given me her number."

"You could've asked," Taunya volleyed back, still giggling.

Her phone dinged, snapping her up in her seat like an elastic band. Her pulse quickened when she saw the Instagram notification and she immediately clicked on it.

Tess – 1:47PM

> Things are okay, I think. We talked... thanks for asking.

The happy emoji sitting at the end of Tess's message brought Abi a boatload of muddled feelings. Tess replying with a smiley face brought a twinge of happiness and excitement, but her and Vicki patching things up had Abi's shoulders slumping in defeat. Why had she thought Tess would break up with Vicki and then turn around and ask Abi on a date?

So stupid.

"It's hard to believe you were shaking your ass so confidently the other night with the way you're blushing now," Taunya teased, completely misreading the reason for Abi's flushed cheeks. The car came to a stop at a red light.

"I am not!" Another incoming message lit up her phone and squelched her disappointment as she read it. "Apparently, Coy's getting antsy. Tess wants to know when we'll be there."

"Pulling up now, babe," Taunya affirmed, flicking on her blinker and deftly sliding into a free parallel parking space.

The rest of Taunya's bridal party was waiting when Abi and Taunya arrived inside Lykopis Archery. The building was a lot more spacious than it looked from the street, with a couple of sofas and chairs set along one wall. Tables were set up with multiple types of bows and arrows. Most were crafted on-site, and Abi only knew that because McCoy had been a tad exuberant when she called her that morning. Within five minutes of Tess dropping the Lykopis name, Coy was on Google, refreshing her knowledge of the archery business and filling Abi with random details.

Once Sloane noticed them, she nudged her twin, a wide grin spreading. "Pay up."

McCoy, deep in conversation with Krystal, paused, glancing up to see Taunya and Abi heading toward them. An exaggerated groan left her lips before she grudgingly retrieved her wallet. She handed a five-dollar bill to her sister before returning her attention to Krystal.

"Who do you think they were betting on?" Taunya whispered. "You or me?"

"Maybe both, since we're late?"

Abi felt the intensity in Tess's gaze before she saw her. She was leaning against the back of an old leather sofa on the outskirts of the bridal party, hands shoved into jean pockets and her gorgeous hair tucked behind her ears. Her lips parted when she noticed Abi watching her and quickly shifted her attention to Taunya. "Since you're the bride-to-be, we won't mention you're forty minutes late."

Taunya quickly quipped back, "You literally just did, Tessa." Hand on her hip, she frowned at the twins. "And what bet is this?"

McCoy chuckled, absently toying with the collection of handmade bracelets on her left wrist. Her thumb rings were back on as well, Abi noticed. "Sloane bet that you and Abi would show up wearing unsuitable footwear. I assumed at least one of you would know better. I was wrong."

Abi huffed, "Ruuude, Coy. Have you seen this shirt? Totally appropriate. I was going to wear a…" She trailed off when she noticed her laced-up high heels. Her jeans had covered them when she'd slipped them onto her feet, so as a compromise she'd rolled her pant legs to capri-length. She glanced at her friend's footwear, noting Taunya doing the same to her. Their eyes met and held briefly before they broke into a fit of laughter.

"It's funny how they're only just realizing," Krystal commented, looking up from her phone to grin.

"I think going with a good versatile pair of shoes would be best for this week. And maybe bring along a pair of sandals," Tess suggested, the corners of her mouth twitching.

Still giggling a little, Abi sidled up beside her. She leaned against the sofa as well, standing as close to Tess as she dared before copying her stance. "Good advice, thank you." She cocked her head, giving the other woman a small smile before breathing in the delectable perfume Tess wore. She'd been arming herself with the Gender One brand for as long as Abi could remember. Subtle hints of bergamot, cardamom, jasmine, and something delicious and musky; it was sensual and unassuming, much like the wearer.

"I umm … you look terrific today." Tess's voice was so low, it took Abi a moment to grasp her compliment. She stared straight ahead as if simply looking at Abi would be crossing lines. Abi tugged her bottom lip between her teeth, glancing down to where their hands rested. Their fingers were so close to touching that Abi could feel Tess's heat emanating from her sun-kissed skin.

"Thank you. And I think I'm wearing your shirt," she practically purred. One of the archery instructors had come over and was now talking things over with Taunya, but Tess made no move to get up. As discreetly as possible, Abi closed the last half an inch separating them and touched Tess's hand.

"Abi ... what are you doing?" The question tumbled out in a choked whisper, and the slow blush spotting Tess's cheeks made Abi pause.

She blinked, clearing away the cobwebs surrounding her, and immediately pulled back. "Right, yeah. I'm sorry, I wasn't thinking." Her friends talking in the background faded out as all the blood rushed to Abi's ears. *What was she doing?*

"V swears I have nothing to worry about," Tess added, almost as an afterthought. "She knows I always overthink things, and she promised me there's nothing going on anymore with her and Natasha."

"That was her ex?" Abi's brows furrowed as she considered this new development. She didn't want to argue with Tess, but seriously, *clueless* was an understatement. Tess had to be in denial. She pushed off the sofa, needing to pace.

"Abi?"

"Natasha's hands were on your girlfriend, Tess," Abi exclaimed, wheeling back to face her. Tess met her gaze with a shuttered expression, and Abi shook her head. "Like, way more than my little finger graze a minute ago. It took a long time to realize Chantelle was cheating, so how do you know for sure?"

"She loves me."

"So did Chantelle!" Abi clenched her fists, suddenly *furious*. "You were going to marry her, have babies, and she *still* slept with someone else."

The moment Tess's face fell, Abi regretted her words. She didn't want to hurt Tess; that was the *last* thing she wanted to do. A sad realization dawned on Abi, and she bowed her head in dismay. "This is why I can't ever move home. Watching you, time and time again, pass up what is right in front of you ... honestly, Tess, I think it would kill me."

Chapter Nine

Tess

"Watching you, time and time again, pass up what is right in front of you ..."

Abi's emotive speech had tormented Tess for the better part of the day. She'd hidden her pain behind a smile, rehashing Abi's parting words until they were an unwelcome soundtrack reverberating through her mind. Her sister had asked three times during archery if there was anything wrong, but Tess couldn't talk about it with her. She'd thought that after their conversation the day before, she and Abi were on the same page. Four years had passed; surely Abi didn't still think she was in love with Tess?

"I vote we make archery a regular thing."

"Hell, yeah! It was way more fun than I'd expected."

Tess smiled, listening to Taunya's friends discuss their afternoon in detail. Krystal was right, their archery lessons had been a success. It made months of anxiety over planning the bucket list worth it, Tess supposed. Knowing everyone came away from the first event happy was rewarding. Even Abi seemed happy, and the way she could forget their earlier tiff boggled Tess's mind. She'd been *sick* from the nerves ever since.

Coy chuckled any time Abi and Taunya's entrance that afternoon was brought up. They were by far the most femme women in the bridal party, but showing up in heels? It had surprised everyone when they'd not only held themselves upright while holding a bow, but they'd also *slayed* archery.

"I'm not the craftiest person around, so I had Mom help plan this one," Tess clarified, setting three bags in the center of the living room. The furniture had already been pushed back or stacked away to create a large enough space for the next pre-wedding activity. "Please, knock yourself out. There should be tons of options, since Mom went crazy in the craft store."

Abi, Krystal, and Sloane all made a grab for the bags, squealing when the one filled with glitter and glue packages spilled onto the hardwood floor. McCoy was content to watch the chaos, not in any rush to stake her claim on a t-shirt. Neither was Tess, honestly, and if she didn't take her maid of honor duties so seriously, decorating bridal party t-shirts would be the last thing she'd be doing that evening. Her biceps and shoulders were strained from archery, not used to holding up so much weight for long periods of time. If she could do her own thing tonight, a hot soak in a bubble bath would be the first to check off her list. Afterward, if she felt up to it, she'd go for a bike ride. The weather was gorgeous, and she was certain her Ducati felt neglected. It'd been two weeks or more since Tess had taken her for a ride out of the city. Since Vicki didn't like her Ducati, they often traveled in her Prius.

Once they'd taken seats with a plain white tee in front of them, Sloane and Krystal began organizing the crafts into piles. As an exuberant kindergarten teacher, Krystal quickly called dibs on decorating Taunya's shirt. Gossip and indie rock music filled Tess's preferred tranquility, but she had to admit the company was nice for a change.

Coy eventually made her way to the floor as well, taking position beside Abi and reluctantly unfolding a t-shirt. As they decorated, Abi caught everyone up on her visit to her parents the night before.

Tess's attention stayed trained on Abi, losing herself in the compelling way Abi told her story. She had a voice Tess could listen to for hours. A small smile formed at how she had set up shop on the floor. The younger woman sat with her legs folded underneath her, the pale flesh of her knees teasing through rips in her jeans. Her silky, caramel-brown hair was haphazardly braided to one side, falling over her shoulder as she leaned forward. She still wore that blasted shirt, the aged red and black plaid long-sleeve hugging her torso in all the right places. The top three buttons were left open, drawing attention to the swell of her breasts. Tess was ashamed to admit she'd fallen victim to that cleavage more than once that day, even after reprimanding Abi over her flirting. She deeply regretted the rift she'd caused between them at Lykopis, but it was important for Tess to establish boundaries. It was difficult, though, knowing she still had a reaction to Abi when she was trying so hard to make things work with Vicki.

She headed into the kitchen to pull the two sheet pans of nachos from the oven. Then she grabbed the sour cream and salsa out of the fridge before eyeing up the drinks on the top shelf.

"Tauni's missing all the fun."

Tess jumped at the sound of Abi's voice, banging her tender shoulder into the fridge door in the process. She winced, retrieving a few cans of Molson beer and Bubly sparkling water. "She was actually okay to miss it," Tess gritted out, sucking in a sharp breath as her shoulder began to throb. "Tonight was the only time her hairdresser was available, and she asked Krystal to decorate hers."

"Are you okay?" Abi asked softly, lifting the cans out of Tess's arms and placing them on the island.

"Er ... yep. Yes, sorry, the stupid door hit me. Maybe I should start working out, you know, so I can take a punch." A nervous chuckle slipped out, and Tess blushed, massaging her shoulder to make her point. She shifted on her feet, unable to meet Abi's eyes. Even without heels on, she stood an inch or so taller than Tess, her sheer existence imposing, sucking Tess in with some kind of freakish gravitational pull. With her hair, flawless skin, tight figure, and kissable lips, Abi was a sensual goddess. And sometimes, when Tess looked at her, Abi's beauty literally stole the breath from her lungs. The two of them alone, in the kitchen? Horrible idea, but that didn't stop Tess's imagination from running rampant.

"I know you want me," Abi crooned, closing the small gap until Tess was intimately sandwiched between the island and the warmth of the other woman's curves. Tess sucked in a breath, her pupils dilating as she caught sight of Abi's mischievous grin. Slender hands made their way to Abi's plaid shirt, and as Tess zeroed in on the next two buttons falling open, a deep desire unfurled low in her belly.

"A–Abi, fuck," she rasped, her own hands landing on Abi's hips. She kneaded Abi's supple flesh, gently squeezing and relishing how right it felt to touch this woman.

"I know you want *this*," Abi continued, her gaze smoldering on Tess. She bit her lip and allowed the shirt to slip off her toned shoulders. Tess's gaze raked over the exposed skin, already acutely aware of the gush of warmth trickling between her legs. Abi took her hands in hers, leaning forward to place her tongue against the base of Tess's throat as she led Tess's hands to her breasts. Abi licked a languorous path up Tess's throat, and Tess couldn't hold back her moan any longer. Her legs buckled at the sound of Abi's seductive voice in her ear. "So *take* me, Tess."

"You're perfect just as you are," Abi said, and the fantasy causing Tess to salivate abruptly snapped like her trusty rubber band.

Tess's knees wobbled — in real life this time — and she felt her pulse skyrocket when she noticed Abi was in fact standing only inches away. Tess squeezed her eyes shut, shifting awkwardly on her feet to relieve some of the ache emanating from her core.

This is bad. This is so, so fucking bad, she thought, turning away from Abi in shame. *Pot, meet kettle.*

"I'm sorry about earlier," Abi continued in the softest voice Tess had ever heard. Her hand slipped into Tess's. "I know you must think I have selfish reasons for not liking Vicki, and you'd be right, but I also know Tauni would agree with me on this."

Tess swallowed, silently urging her pulse to calm the hell down. What were they talking about again? Oh, right, *Vicki*. Possible scenarios of her girlfriend cheating hadn't consumed Tess like they probably should have that day. Honestly, up until about two minutes ago, arguing with Abi was what had nagged at her the most. Now, with the R-rated fantasy she was having of Abi, it was difficult to think of anything else.

Abi's gaze dropped to Tess's mouth, and her tongue swept out to wet her lips. Tess's breath hitched all over again as she stared, entranced. When she was certain she was about to be ravished, Abi took a few steps back. She cleared her throat a few times, obviously feeling whatever sexual pull was happening in the kitchen. "So, um, Tauni doesn't let you cut her hair?"

Her question was baffling, and Tess stared at her like an idiot. She was a hot mess, turned completely to mush in a matter of seconds by a younger woman, so out of her league, it was criminal. Tess understood why she was attracted to Abi, but she'd never understood how the feeling was reciprocated.

Abi cracked open one of the beers on the counter, offering it to Tess. The tension in Tess's shoulders eased up, and she finally grinned a little, gratefully accepting the bottle. Abi watched as she took a drink, murmuring, "So cute," before gathering up the other drinks and leaving the kitchen.

Bashful, Tess ignored her comment and hurried to catch up. They were entering the living room when she remembered she hadn't answered Abi's question. "Tauni's let me at her hair a few times, but she likes her highlights and extensions. I'm a basic barber."

"Basic?" McCoy echoed, accepting the beer Abi handed off. "Thanks, Abs. And there's nothing basic about you, Tess! You make my undercut look killer, and somebody's always coming into the shop with a design etched into their scalp. And yeah, I ask them where they go for their cut."

"Thanks, I appreciate you saying so." Tess was flattered that someone as self-absorbed as McCoy would offer her such a well-meaning compliment. The surprise must have shown, because Abi gave Tess one of those heart-stopping smiles. The softness in her eyes made Tess feel like she was drowning in a calm ocean. How was that even possible? She turned away, silently chastising herself for becoming so unraveled.

Chapter Ten

Tess

"Hey, what's that song called?" Sloane's voice was pitched higher than the stereo's volume inside the rental van, and Tess winced. Her temples throbbed in tune to whatever grunge song currently played, and it was a wonder she could hear anything with the multiple conversations happening. She gripped the steering wheel a little tighter as they sped down the highway toward Langley.

"Coy!" Sloane hollered, twisting around in the passenger seat. "What's the name of that song with Girli and Elliot Lee?"

Tess rolled her shoulders, the growing tightness in her chest a sure sign she'd forgotten to take her medication. This bridal party week had her feeling like she needed a dose increase.

I should've taken my bike.

Her attention slipped from the road once more, and her brow furrowed as she noticed Sloane playing with the stereo settings. Seconds later, the bass in the Caravan increased to a dull thud. Sloane caught her eye and gave her a thumbs-up. "You don't mind, do you?"

Tess wetted her lips with a strong desire to speak her mind, but she just shook her head slightly, turning back to the road. One hand left the steering wheel, reaching to snap her rubber band hidden beneath the sleeve of her raincoat. A pair of hands squeezed her shoulders from the middle seat, and Tess glanced in the rear-view to see her sister smiling.

"Thank you," Taunya mouthed before raising her voice to add, "I know the week is just getting started, but it's already more fun than I've had in years!"

"The Fab Five reunite!!" Coy crowed from the back of the van, where she sat with Krystal. They were sharing a bag of chips.

"Horseback riding won't be great in the rain," Krystal complained, and Tess saw her craning her neck to look out the window.

She did the same, squinting at the glooming gray clouds overhead. She reached to dial back the volume on the stereo before saying, "I'd rather it come now and clear up later. I planned a vineyard tour and outdoor dinner for tonight." The trail ride and tour had been the first two things Tess chose from Taunya's bucket list of ideas. She'd wanted at least one of the five days to last into the night, so she fit the two together. Locating accommodations for six turned out to be a chore, however, since none of the vineyards or genuine trail ride businesses had cabins to rent. After weeks of headache and her credit limit almost maxed out, Tess had soon discovered how valuable her barbershop connections turned out to be.

"You outdid yourself, Tess." Abi's compliment hit Tess right in the chest, making her feel all warm and tingly. She felt her cheeks heating.

"All at the same ranch?" Taunya asked, sounding equally impressed.

Tess shook her head, watching as the first raindrop splattered on the windshield. "About a twenty-minute drive from the ranch. And then we have accommodations back at the ranch for the night."

"Rain or shine, I'm hella excited, not gonna lie." Coy laughed.

"'Kay, bitches, lemme get another picture!" Sloane waved her phone back and forth. "Squeeze together."

"Sloane, how many do you need from the driveway to the ranch?" Abi asked, smirking from her place beside Taunya.

Tess flicked her blinker on, checking for blind spots before merging into the center lane. She was only half listening to the group's conversation, so when Coy mentioned their vlog, she asked Sloane to clarify.

Sloane settled back into her seat, pulling her shades down over her eyes before replying. "Yeah, we post a lot about mechanics and mountain biking, but there's other stuff too. Basically, whatever we're doing in the week. I'm compiling all the footage I've taken of this week and will edit it later." Then Sloane talked about their audience and views, and she mentioned something about their "handle." Seconds later, she was cranking the volume on the stereo again.

While Tess had understood most of what she said, one thing remained, and she called out over the music, "What's a 'handle'?"

That got Sloane's attention, and even with her sunglasses on, Tess caught her dubious expression. She turned down the volume yet again. "Dude, you don't know what a handle is? Just how old *are* you?"

Tess squirmed in her seat and faced the road again. Her ears felt hot. "Social media isn't my strong suit."

"Clearly. Man, how do you have your own business? Networking on social media is huge, Tess. Tauni!" Sloane exclaimed, twisting in her seat once more. Tess groaned. "Your sister doesn't know what a handle is."

Taunya merely waved off the concern. "Believe me, it's not for lack of trying. She can barely operate her Facebook, let alone any other platform."

"Oow!" Tess complained when Taunya tugged the ponytail secured in her baseball cap.

"If you want, I can always take a look at your setup," Abi offered, meeting Tess's gaze in the rear-view mirror. Her blue eyes sparkled, drawing Tess in until she was visibly gulping.

Tearing her gaze away, she had to clear her throat before stuttering a reply. "S–sure, I mean, yes, please, that would actually be great. Thank you."

"Is it just me, or did Abs somehow make that sound sexual?" Coy's cackle all the way from the back had the hairs on Tess's neck standing up. She ducked her head, wishing the Caravan's floor would transform into a portal and take her back home. She'd jump through that so fast, Sloane would have to grab hold of the wheel.

"Just you, playgirl!" Abi shot back.

"Coy, I think you're the only one out of the six of us who obsesses over sex," Taunya added.

As soon as they entered Langley, Tess turned into the first Tim Hortons she came across, grateful the parking lot wasn't busy. Her hands were trembling as she reversed into a parking space and shut off the ignition. She placed them in her lap and took a deep breath, letting her eyes drift closed as she got her bearings.

"Damn, Barber, it's like you read my mind!"

Tensing, Tess didn't offer up a reply to the *mechanic*. God, she hated that stupid nickname. She sat and waited, listening to the van's door open and Taunya's friends clambering out, already discussing which type of caffeine they'd refuel on. It wasn't until she heard the doors click shut again that she finally exhaled. Light-headedness came over her as oxygen rushed to her brain, but the tightness in her chest eased dramatically.

"You okay, Tess?"

The unexpected voice made Tess yelp and swivel in her seat, coming face to face with Abi. Her forehead was creased in concern, and she looked so damn cute in her bridesmaid t-shirt and old jeans that Tess immediately felt herself relax. "I didn't know you were still here."

A small smile appeared. "I see that. Do you need your medication? I can grab your bag from the back."

Tess's lips parted, and for several seconds she just stared at the other woman.

"Tauni told me you take meds," Abi supplied, leaning closer, "but I've known for years about your anxiety."

"Oh."

Oh? That was the best she could come up with? Abi knew things about her that Vicki wasn't even privy to. Tess had always felt so ashamed about her anxiety that she had made a point not to tell people unless it was unavoidable. "I ... um, I don't have it. I forgot it at home."

"Ah, that makes things hard." The trill of Abi's cell phone startled them both, and Tess watched as she rummaged through her purse for the device. She pulled it out, looking at the caller before muttering, "She's relentless, I'll give her that."

"Hmm?"

"Oh, it's nothing, sorry." Abi flashed her a small grin before dropping her phone back into her purse. She stood up, gesturing to the passenger seat. "Think I can climb over?"

Tess eyed the console between the seats, then looked back at Abi. "P–probably." She angled out of Abi's way as she climbed into the front but still managed to get knocked on the shoulder with her ass. Tess caught a whiff of whatever sensual fragrance Abi had on and couldn't help but inhale it in. "What are you wearing?"

"Gucci Guilty Absolute. You like it?" Abi inquired, locking gazes with Tess again. A sheepish grin curved her mouth.

"I don't think I should be driving," Tess said instead, knowing how scatterbrained she got when she was like this.

"This isn't your thing, is it?"

Tess dropped her gaze from Abi's, landing instead on where the snug t-shirt hugged her breasts. She blinked slowly. "Hmm?"

"This, the bridal party, the bucket list. It's not you at all."

"It's important to Tauni, though."

"Do you always do everything she wants?" Abi asked in a tone full of curiosity rather than ridicule.

"She *is* getting married, Abi."

"I know," Abi said softly, her gaze roaming over Tess's face, "but just don't forget to take care of you. Tauni would want that."

Would she? It was difficult to get in the right mood needed for these events. It was *go go go*, and quite honestly, the fastest thing in Tess's life on the daily was her motorcycle. The epitome of an introvert, she would happily live in a small town where the most exciting thing that went on was the annual blossom festival. She loved Vancouver, loved the neighborhood where she grew up, but it'd always been a bit too busy for her. And loud.

"Do you love Toronto?" Tess asked out of the blue.

"Toronto?" Abi wrinkled her nose. "What's to love? It's freezing in winter, suffocating in the summer, and it lacks some of the best things about Vancouver."

"Which are...?"

"The scenery, nature." Abi pulled her bottom lip between her teeth, watching Tess watch her. She smiled, shrugging one shoulder as if the answer should be obvious. "All the people I love are here.

Don't get me wrong, my roommates are great, but I haven't heard from them since I landed. It's not the same."

"It must have been hard to move to a city where you didn't know anyone."

"It was." Abi nodded, her eyes still locked on Tess. Besides her mom, Abi was the only one who gave Tess their undivided attention. With others, she often felt like she spoke too slow or what she was saying was irrelevant. It stemmed from her own insecurities, she knew, but it was nice not to feel that around Abi.

"Tess, I—"

Coy's childish slap on the hood startled them both. It broke the charged moment inside the van, and Tess blinked, only just recognizing how close they were sitting. She quickly backed away, reaching for the van's door and exiting the vehicle. The smell of fresh rain filled her nostrils, and the farther she got from Abi, the less she could smell her lingering perfume.

As they continued on to the ranch, Tess was already breathing a little easier, sitting in the middle row with her sister. Well, at least until she began answering the several texts from Vicki over the last hour.

Vicki – 6:10AM

> Missed you last night.

Vicki – 7:59AM

> Where are you?

Vicki – 8:30AM

> Tess???

Vicki – 8:35AM

> Your bridal party week is taking up too much of your time.

Vicki – 8:50AM

> Your sister is a selfish bitch. I could tell as soon as she walked up to me the other night. Why can't she have a normal bachelorette party?

Vicki – 9:13AM

> I changed my mind. You're selfish too! It's no wonder you were single for so long since, you can't even text your gf back.

Vicki – 10:11AM

> I shouldn't have said that. I'm on my break. Call me.

Tess clutched her phone, rereading Vicki's words until she noticed her fingers turning white. Relaxing her death grip, she was aware of her shallow inhales and exhales as they attempted to keep pace with her racing heart. She pulled her hat lower over her eyes as if that would be enough to shield her from view. It fucking hurt, but there was truth in what Vicki said. Tess was a crap girlfriend. She'd never had women flock to her, and the rare time it happened, she managed to screw things up. If it wasn't her anxiety, it was—

"Wooow, Tess, she's really escalating," Taunya said after staring at her big sister's phone.

"What?" Tess licked her lips, and a tear escaped as she glanced to where Taunya hovered over her shoulder.

Taunya must have seen something in Tess's expression, because her angry features softened, and she pulled Tess in for a comforting hug. "Your girlfriend's crazy," Taunya murmured against her ear. She pushed Tess back a little, and Tess caught the fire still in those brown eyes. "*Please* tell me you're breaking up with her."

"I..." Tess hesitated, her eyebrows creasing as she frowned. Break up with Vicki? She couldn't. She would be alone again, another failed relationship she'd have to tell her mother about.

"I think we're here," McCoy called out, and Tess looked to see her turning the van onto a long, paved driveway. Hanging overhead was a sign saying *Welcome to Carter's Country Stables.*

"Looks to be right. I–I know the owner is Liz Carter," Tess mumbled, her tongue thick with emotion. She ducked her head to hide the sting of unshed tears.

"You guys go on ahead. Tess and I'll be right there." Taunya bobbed her head, a smile hiding the obvious tension between the two of them.

"Don't be long. Looks like someone's already on their way out to meet us," Abi said, shooting them a smile from the passenger side. Her gaze lingered on Tess a moment longer before she climbed out with everyone else.

Once they were alone, Taunya ran her fingers through her long black tendrils, letting out a heavy sigh. "Now, where were we? Right, you were about to tell me how you plan to break up with Dicky Vicki."

Tess's lips parted, but she didn't comment on the hateful nickname. Instead, she blurted the first thing that came to mind. "Vicki didn't mean what she said. She gets like that sometimes, that's all."

"She's a bully, and yes, she did. The same way she meant to be that close to another woman Saturday night."

"She *loves* me." Tess swallowed, aware of the slight tremble in her bottom lip. Who was she trying to convince at this point?

Taunya reached for the cell phone still in Tess's death grip. Their eyes met, and with her free hand, Taunya reached up to catch a fleeting tear. "*I* love you. Vicki's a piece of shit. She's a manipulative, lying, emotional abuser. Put in your password."

"She was upset. I should have texted her this morning. I always do." Tess stared absently at her cell now in Taunya's hand, not registering what her sister expected of her.

"Please, put in your password." Taunya snagged Tess's hand, pushing it toward the lock screen. Her movements were jerky, like she was still trying to keep a lid on her temper. Tess did as she asked, not clueing in until Taunya was video-calling Vicki.

"Tauni no, please!" Tess grabbed for the phone, but Taunya only held it farther away.

"Well, you aren't Tess," Vicki stated the moment she appeared on screen. She was sitting in her office an hour's drive away, but the bottom of Tess's stomach dropped out when a scowl appeared. "Where is she?"

"Right here," Taunya supplied, angling the phone so Vicki could see Tess sitting behind Taunya. "I'll cut to the chase, since we're in the middle of something. My sister is *literally* the sweetest person alive, but I have no qualms in telling you to go fuck yourself."

Vicki's flinch was almost indiscernible, but Tess noticed, and the shrill tone that ensued had her shrinking farther into her seat. She reached for her rubber band.

Snap! Snap! Snap!

"*What* did you just say?" Vicki snarled.

"Did I stutter? This is a breakup call, Vicki. Forget Tess exists, or you'll be dealing with me. And I'll *gladly* spend my wedding night in jail." And with that, Taunya calmly ended the call and handed Tess back her phone.

"I–I can't believe you just did that! You don't–you don't just breakupwithmygirlfriend, Tauni!" Tess was frantic, her words all blending into one another, and she made a mad scramble to unlock her phone. After messing up the code a fifth time, security locked her out. An anguished wail escaped her, and she tossed the phone into the front seat. Her chest squeezed, and she placed her hand against it over her jacket, shuddering at the lack of air in the van. "This is all my fault! She's going to hate me!"

"No, it's not, and good riddance. Think of it this way," Taunya relented, and seconds later her hand was rubbing slow, comforting circles over Tess's back, "Now you're free to let in someone who truly deserves you."

Tess could only shake her head. Her sister wasn't faulty. She could do no wrong and was good at everything. Taunya would never understand what it felt like to be worthless.

But Tess did.

CHAPTER ELEVEN

Abi

"Our papa used to say places like this were God's country," Coy said, looking out into the distance as they followed behind their trail guide. She was loosely holding the reins of a gorgeous Appaloosa, and despite the rain dripping from her eyelashes, she looked so peaceful that Abi was almost jealous. Outdoorsy stuff wasn't exactly her thing, but she had vowed in front of the mirror that morning not to complain. Rain or shine, through potential bee stings, mosquito bites, or the rare chance of a sunburn, complaining was something she would not do. For Tess and Taunya's sake, because she loved them dearly.

"It's pretty," Abi conceded, her gaze zeroing in on the flies buzzing around her horse's head. She rode a chocolate-brown horse named Puddin', and according to their surly trail guide, she was the tamest companion they had. So far, Puddin' had surpassed Abi's expectations.

"Pretty? Abi, it's sooo beautiful here," Sloane said for the third time. She was in complete awe as she soaked in one of Langley's picturesque valleys. The well traveled grassy path was soppy in areas from the ongoing bursts of rain, but with the forest ahead and the sounds of a stream close by, it *was* rather soothing.

Abi sensed the remaining bridal party coming up behind them, and she smiled over her shoulder at Tess. Whatever had happened in the van between Taunya and Tess, Abi got the feeling it was over Vicki. Curiosity had questions on the tip of her tongue, but she held back. The usual warmth in Tess's brown gaze was empty, even tired, with red-rimmed eyelids. Abi didn't want to say anything that might have her upset all over again. It was hard to ignore the desire to comfort her. It wasn't as if she and Tess had ever been a couple. In fact, while they'd known one another for what seemed like forever, they'd never really had the chance to spend time alone. Abi would have to change that before the week's end, because being around Tess was easily the best moment in her day. She was already dreading having to return home to Toronto.

"It's good we brought our rain jackets," she offered, opening up possible conversation.

Tess only grunted in response, looking ahead of them at the scenery as she took a sip from her water bottle. Even in old jeans and riding boots, her understated beauty caught Abi's eye. Her ash-blonde hair was fastened inside a Boston Red Sox cap Abi knew had belonged to her father.

"I think it's wonderful what you're doing for Tauni. For all of us," Abi tried again, wishing that Tess would open up to her.

"Um, thanks." This time Tess blushed, and it pleased Abi to no end. Girlfriend or not, Tess wasn't immune to her.

"Okay, listen up," their trail guide barked, shifting in his saddle to take them all in. His penetrating deep brown eyes landed on Abi, and she shivered under her raincoat. The owners' grandson, Kris, was one scary SOB. "We're about to cross the creek. Don't rush your horse, and you won't get bucked. Understood?" His lips twisted in what might have been a smile, but with the scar slashed into his bottom lip and down his jaw, it came across as threatening.

"Where did you find him?" Abi muttered to Tess, sliding single-file behind Taunya's horse, Maverick. Puddin' stepped easily into the creek, but Abi still held her breath as they crossed.

That evoked a small laugh from Tess. "He lives here with Liz. She's one of my best clients."

"Oh, really? Well, it was nice of her to help arrange all this."

"So, um ..." Tess's voice trailed off, and once the horses were safely on the embankment, Abi glanced behind her to catch the blush darkening her cheeks. Abi bit her lip at the sight, her own heart speeding up. She watched as Tess scratched her nose, avoiding her knowing gaze. "God, emotions are messy. And confusing."

"You're telling me," Abi agreed, waiting for Tess's horse, Jackal, to catch up to her and Puddin'. They walked side-by-side for a distance, and when Tess didn't offer up anything more, Abi added, "I took a page out of your book and slept with my boss. It didn't work out so well for either of us."

Tess groaned, no doubt remembering what a mess it was in the end with Chantelle. Abi still couldn't grasp how anyone would cheat on Tess. Abi knew she'd been younger and watching Tess with rose-colored glasses, but she and Chantelle had seemed genuinely happy for a long time. Taunya told her about the ring Tess had bought, which of course had twisted Abi's insides.

"What happened?"

Abi pursed her lips. Rehashing her failed relationship with Margo wasn't a highlight for her, but she'd do it if it meant taking Tess's mind off her own troubles. "She wanted me to move in. I tried so hard to get there emotionally with her, but I just couldn't. I broke it off, and she became a world-class bitch practically overnight."

"I'm really sorry, Abi."

Abi shrugged. "It happens. I'm not making excuses for Margo, but I did make it harder than it needed to be. Unfortunately, love isn't a switch that can be turned on or off, otherwise the last four years might have been easier."

That had Tess wincing, and she lowered her gaze. "Abi, about that night..."

"No offense," Abi cut in, giving Tess a small smile, "but maybe we can have that talk when we get back to the city?"

"I'd like that." Tess's return smile sent heat shooting straight to Abi's core. Damn, her feelings were all over the map during this conversation! "Abi, your emotional maturity is..." Tess let out an awkward chuckle, "well, way beyond mine. Your self-awareness is one of your best qualities. I hope you never lose that part of you."

Tess's compliment washed over Abi like a gentle breeze on the sunniest of days, and her wide grin would have made even her fifteen-year-old self cringe.

"Come on, slow-pokes!" Taunya yelled out ahead of them. They were a fair distance away, but neither Tess nor Abi picked up the pace. They rode side-by-side in silence for a time, enjoying the scenic views and listening to distant conversations from the rest of the girls. Sloane and Krystal were fawning over Kris, drilling him with questions, and Taunya was giving Coy updates on her honeymoon destination. It was wonderful to spend a little time with Tess, relatively uninterrupted, and even nicer knowing they could enjoy each other's company without feeling the need to fill the quietness. Tess had been that way for as long as Abi had known her. She was the calm after the storm, the "five o'clock somewhere" after a hard day.

Knowing Tess was like this in spite of her anxiety made her all the more special to Abi.

"I think … I'm single again," Tess said in a low voice, breaking the silence. There was a faraway look on her face as she stared off into the meadow. "Is it awful how … conflicted I am about it?"

"You broke up with Vicki?" It was impossible to keep the elation from her voice, and she covered her mouth to cough. "I'm sorry. When did it happen? "

Tess shrugged, peering at Abi under thick lashes. "I'm upset, but I think mostly because of how it happened. I don't love Vicki, I just…" She shrugged again, helpless. Her lips parted and then closed before she softly added, "I just hoped the feeling would come, you know? I want what you talked about the other day, what Tauni and Derek have."

"Oh, Tess," Abi whispered, fighting her desire to haul Tess off her horse and onto hers. Her body craved what she knew only Tess could provide, and hearing the other woman voice the exact same things Abi wanted was almost more than she could handle. She leaned over to grasp Tess's hand. "You can still have that."

"I–I can't. Abi, you know I can't." Their eyes met, and the despair in Tess's brought on her own. She pulled her hand free from Abi's, gesturing to her sister. "Tauni means too much to the both of us. I'd never want you to jeopardize your friendship over a passing crush."

Abi couldn't help but flinch at those words. "A *crush*?" she sputtered. Fury rose in her throat at the way Tess repeatedly dismissed her, and she snapped out, "God, Tess, you're such an idiot sometimes."

Frustrated and not wanting to be around her anymore, Abi took off with Puddin', leaving Tess in their wake.

Abi had been doing so well on this trip, being mindful of things she said. It had been, what, four days? Near Tess, that could be considered a lifetime. No other woman made Abi cycle through her emotions at jet speed like she did. Abi was used to going from one to one-sixty in the span of seconds around Tess, but today's outburst had been a first. And there were no take-backs when it came to matters of the heart, not that Abi necessarily would if there were. Tess needed a wake-up call, and if Abi could help her see the situation for what it was, great. That stubborn, hot mess of a woman could take from it what she wanted.

How could she not see how great they could be together? Tess obviously still considered her too young to take seriously. A friend of her sister's with a silly crush rather than the woman she could be for Tess. After Abi's humiliating walk of shame out of Tess's life years ago, she'd spent so many nights alone in Toronto, sometimes wishing she'd never gone to Tess in the first place. While Shannon and Millie went out to enjoy the nightlife, Abi would cry herself to sleep, replaying Tess's disbelief and Taunya's anger in her mind so often that she started to doubt herself.

She had been young. What could she have possibly known about love at twenty years old?

After a couple of weeks, she'd picked herself up and put her broken pieces back together. She had then spent the next six months sleeping her way through the lesbian community. Some of those women she'd even dated for a week or two, but eventually she got tired of not feeling anything more than lust. It wasn't until she met

Margo that she genuinely tried a committed relationship. It had been wrong of her to get involved with her boss when she had so much baggage, but in a way it'd helped Abi understand something important.

Tess was wrong.

It wasn't a passing crush for Abi. She'd loved Tess long before she snuck into her bedroom that night. It happened somewhere between talks with Tess behind closed doors as she helped Abi understand her sexuality at fourteen, to developing a huge crush on Tess and embarrassing herself not long after. Abi had fallen head over heels for her best friend's sister. Any time Abi had a heads-up Tess would be home, she'd invite herself over to hang with Taunya. From afar, she'd watch Tess going about her life oblivious to Abi's feelings.

She'd fallen for her casual beauty and her compassionate personality. Tess always had an innate kindness and respect for the people around her. Her smiles were as bashful as they were crooked, and even now at thirty years old, it took almost nothing for Tess to blush. She was reserved, choosing to play her cards close to her heart, but only because she couldn't see how incredible she was.

It wasn't like Abi was asking for marriage or a U-Haul. She asked only for a *chance* to prove how good she and Tess could be together. It wasn't thoughtless or selfish; she knew Tess's feelings for Vicki would take time to fade. All Abi wanted was an idea of what her future might hold. Her return to Toronto factored into any possibility with Tess. She'd asked Margo to email the tentative contract for her to consider; if nothing else, it gained her more options than she'd have had otherwise.

"You're quiet," McCoy said in a suspicious tone. "Why?" she asked once they were piled into their rental van and headed for their next destination.

Abi shrugged one shoulder, peering out the window at the scenery racing past. She was spent from earlier, unable to think anymore of her conversation with Tess and the deafening silence that had answered her until she'd ridden ahead. There were only so many ways a person could relay their disinterest.

"Hey," McCoy murmured, her calloused fingers ghosting over Abi's cheek. "Come 'ere, babe." They were in the back seat, Tess and Taunya up front, so Abi relaxed into McCoy. Their clothes were damp from the rain, but Abi didn't mind. Strong arms wrapped around her, free of judgment, comforting her just as they had for years. "I don't know what's happened, but you're incredible, okay? I love you."

"Love you too," she whispered, grateful always to have McCoy to lean on.

CHAPTER TWELVE

Tess

CHABERTON ESTATE WINERY WAS a fifty-five-acre vineyard only a ten-minute drive from the Carter ranch, rich in French history and providing succulent, authentic cuisine for even the most stubborn palate. Tess had contacted them in record time when she'd stumbled across their website. Taunya loved fine cuisine, and when she explained to the owners it was for a wedding party, they agreed to the tour.

Smelling faintly like Jackal, the horse she'd ridden, and in desperate need of coffee, Tess wished they'd had time to freshen up first. That was one of the downsides to cramming so many things into one week. After her whirlwind of a day with both Vicki and Abi, it was hard to be in the moment with her sister. She couldn't understand how Taunya compartmentalized so well. It was only hours earlier that she was telling Tess's girlfriend off via video chat, and now she, Krystal, and Sloane were listening intently to the tour guide and *oohing* and *ahhing* over the different types of wine. Tess chose to hang back, her mind elsewhere, rehashing the day and wondering how it'd gotten so out of control.

Abi's parting words before she'd rode off on her horse nagged Tess. She'd thought of their one night together a thousand times over the last four years and had questioned if she'd made the right decision pushing Abi away. She'd never wanted Abi to be a rebound, and it pained Tess to this day that she'd treated her as such. It was overwhelming, and *humbling*, how Abi could still feel so strongly, no matter how misplaced her crush was. That's all it was, an infatuation, and Tess would be a fool to think otherwise. Vicki hadn't even attempted to text since their unofficial breakup; what did that say about Tess? That she wasn't worth fighting for? There was a reason her partners mistreated her, and she never wanted it to happen with someone like Abi.

Tess watched her now, staving off futile jealousy over McCoy. The mechanic's hands or lips always seemed to find a way to touch Abi, whether it was an arm around her shoulders or a chaste kiss somewhere on her face. Tess hated to admit it, but McCoy and Abi would make a handsome couple. Even *if* Tess wanted to punch Coy in her smug face. Confidence and strong will oozed from the younger woman, and if Coy and Abi ever broke up, at least it wouldn't personally affect Taunya.

McCoy noticed Tess's glare and grinned, giving her a small finger wave as she kissed Abi's hair. Tess looked away, her hands beginning to shake. For the life of her, she couldn't figure out a way to get it together this trip. She rubbed her arms, slowly backing farther out of the room to avoid drawing attention to herself. Her breaths were ragged as she finally made it outside, and as she inhaled, she was grateful for the moisture in the air from all the rain.

God, I wish I could go home, she thought, closing her eyes. If it weren't for Taunya, she'd have been gone two hours ago. She'd be pouring her heart out to Stacey by now over a bottle of cheap wine, not taste-testing the decadent bottles they offered here at Chaberton Estate.

"Hey."

Tess turned to see Abi perched on the last step of the winery; she must have followed her outside without Tess realizing. Abi looked crestfallen, like she too could give in to the torment engulfing them. Tess didn't know when it happened, but something between them had shifted again. Whatever it was, it felt as tangible as the raindrops now pelting their cool cheeks.

"Abi, hi."

Abi wrung her hands, indecision warring in her eyes. She bit down on her bottom lip, and when she didn't move from her place on the stairs, Tess took a tentative step toward her.

"Stop," Abi ordered, but her voice was so soft, Tess barely heard it. Abi held up her hand, halting Tess's footsteps. Her chest was rising and falling in rapid succession under her purple raincoat. Their eyes met, and Tess watched her struggle to find the right words. "I want you to listen *very* carefully to what I'm about to say," she continued after a long moment. She finally took that last step so she was on level ground with Tess. A small gasp escaped Tess when Abi's soft fingers grasped her chin. Her lips parted, and although it was probably the worst time imaginable, the memory of Abi's mouth on hers popped into Tess's head.

"It was *never* a passing crush for me. I loved you, Tess," Abi gritted out, her voice hushed as she met Tess's gaze head-on. Tess paused, unsure if she'd heard right, but the certainty in Abi's words was unwavering. Abi scoffed, "You know, I tried so hard to put that night to rest. I've been in relationships, I've *been* loved, but ... never by you. Tess, you are all I've ever wanted."

"Abi..."

Abi brought up her other hand to cup Tess's cheek. "Damn you for not seeing it. *Damn* you for not realizing that I would never stray from you," she said, dipping her face to capture Tess's lips in hers. Tess froze, shocked by the abrupt kiss, shocked at how *right* it felt to have Abi's mouth moving sensuously over hers. She melted into Abi, sinking her fingers through Abi's silky, soft caramel tendrils of hair. For a moment, all of Tess's uncertainties washed away. For a moment she could just enjoy being wrapped up in the other woman. Abi's tongue slipped between Tess's parted lips, deepening the kiss until her head spun, and delicious, throaty mewls infused the evening air.

A door shut loudly in the distance, but Tess was so caught up in Abi, she didn't realize they had company until she heard several throats clearing behind them. She tore her lips from Abi's, dropping her hands away so fast, she might as well have been burned. The entire bridal party and the tour guide were standing there, staring, but it was Taunya's slack jaw that had Tess stumbling back.

"T–Tauni, I'm sorry!" she stammered. "It's not what it —"

"Looks like?" Abi cut in, her face twisting as she squinted at Tess. She turned away, but the measure of despondence in her voice was insurmountable. "Of course it isn't, because I'm the only one who would think that *that* passionate kiss fucking meant something!"

Tess bounced her curled knuckle against her mouth, fighting back tears as she watched Taunya and Coy run after Abi. She was trembling, *gasping*, and all she wanted to do was run after Abi as well. *Why* had she said that?

"Oh, snap," Krystal exclaimed, finally breaking the awkward silence. "I didn't see *this* planned for the week. Sloane?"

"I've heard rumors, but," Sloane laughed, looking over at Tess and letting out a low whistle, "*damn.* You guys are scorching hot together."

Tess just shook her head and walked away, reaching for her rubber band.

There was a reason Tess refrained from drinking more than a glass of wine in one sitting. Any more, and it took the express lane to her head. As bottles of Pinot Noir and Chardonnay circled their table at dinner, not even the extravagant entrée of pan-roasted Columbia River steelhead she'd ordered soaked up the alcohol. She was, quite admittedly, very drunk. What was worse, it had begun to show.

"I'll be paying this meal off for months, but it was worth it, right?" she exclaimed, nudging Taunya sitting to her left. Drops of red wine sloshed from her glass and onto the sheer white tablecloth, and she giggled. "Whoops! Sorry!"

Conversations around the dinner table quieted, and Tess had a sinking suspicion she'd spoken louder than she'd meant to. She was dizzy, and a tipsy, utterly sheepish grin appeared. "Yo," she greeted her sisters' friends, her lips forming a circle as she drew out a long 'o' sound.

"*Yo?*" Sloane echoed, shock quickly turning to glee. She smirked, and out of nowhere her phone appeared in her hands. "Dude, I'm so filming drunk Tess!"

"I'm serious," Tess continued, raising the glass to her lips again. She took a long sip and glanced around the table. Abi sat farthest from Tess and had barely looked at her since their kiss. She was probably already regretting those precious moments together, but it was whatever. Tess was too drunk to care how much the constant rejections in her life hurt. "Can I throw a kick-ass bridal party or what?"

"This week's been unreal," Taunya said, stilling Tess's hand holding the wine glass. Tess frowned as her sister carefully dislodged the glass from her fingers. "Thank you so much. You're too generous. I didn't expect all this."

"We already talked about it, and we're gonna help pay for some of the costs," McCoy added, gesturing to everyone but Taunya. "I know I never expected you to foot the entire week, Barber."

"Pssh," Tess said, waving her off. She gave Taunya a cheeky grin, reaching for her wine glass again. "I aim to please." Taunya stopped her progression, making Tess pout, and she squinted at the younger woman. "You *are* happy, right?"

"I'm so happy, Tess. It's you who's not happy." Taunya kept her voice low, but since no one else was speaking, it was obvious it wasn't a private conversation. "Talk to me."

"I am fine. *So* fine." Tess ducked away from Taunya's concerned gaze and swiped up her glass of water. Her hand shook as she lifted it to her lips. She could feel Abi's eyes on her, no doubt judging, and humiliation burned her cheeks worse than the alcohol did. Drunk Tess was sloppy and loose-lipped. She set her glass down roughly, seconds before she dropped it, and patted Taunya on the back. "Where's your crown? Did I not get you a crown? I'm so sorry, Tauni! I'm a terrible maid of honor."

"Relax, Coy and Sloane picked one up. It's at home," Taunya replied, raising her hand as one of their servers walked by. "Can we get my sister some coffee ASAP, please?"

"Certainly, miss."

"Who'd have thought my baby sister would be getting hitched before me?" Tess was on a roll and had no notion of stopping. It was as if every thought she'd so carefully buried in her work or bridal party planning over the past year had come forth in a messy, jealous slur of emotion. "I should be married with kids by now. I'm happy for youuu, though, Tauni. So sooo happy. *Delirious*."

"Your 'happy' is dripping with envy," Krystal noted, and Tess paused to frown across the table at her.

Abi appeared at her side, a hand on her shoulder. "Walk with me?"

Tess dropped her gaze to the inviting hand, noting the plum purple polish on Abi's fingernails. Her tongue felt thick as she angled her face up to Abi's pensive blue eyes. "I'm not that drunk. *You*," Tess expressed, tapping her finger into Abi's chest, "Abigail Young, are mad at me."

Abi caught Tess's finger easily, twining their fingers together with the hand not resting on Tess's shoulder. She chuckled. "What can I say, you're hard to stay mad at."

"Are you two gonna make out some more? Sloane, you still recording?"

"Seriously, dude, what do you take me for? I'm not passing up an opportunity to film an angsty lesbian drama."

"God, I'm surrounded by melodrama," Taunya tutted.

Tess pushed herself off the chair but swayed as soon as she was upright. "*Whoa*, I've got you." Abi's arms went around Tess, and she heard her say, "I think we should just head back."

"Agreed," Taunya patted Tess's back. "Let's get you to bed."

"Wow, you're a lightweight, Barber," McCoy grumbled as she, Abi, and Taunya helped Tess into the van some time later.

"She's never been a big drinker," Taunya replied, her voice muffled as Tess covered her sister's mouth.

"I can hear youuu," she sang in her best, *loudest* country drawl, *"I ain't deaf y'all, jus a lil' tipsy now, lil' tipsy now..."*

"Oh my god, someone get the radio on. I can't take it!"

"On it, twinsie," Sloane said from the front seat. Tess swung her head in Sloane's direction, squinting as she saw the phone in her hand.

"Hey!" Tess exclaimed, swatting Taunya's hand away when she started digging in her pockets. She giggled when someone poked her in the ribs.

"I'm driving," Krystal said, appearing before Tess. "Keys. I've only had one drink."

"Gotta find them first. How many pockets can a pair of cargos hold, Tess? Fifteen?" Taunya joked.

Tess momentarily quieted to gape incredulously at her sister. "Fifteen?" she echoed, bursting into giggles once more. "Micro teensy-weensy pockets maybe. Oh! I wish I had my guitar! Then we could have a bonnnfire!"

Abi's laughter was a bridge in Tess's favorite guitar solo, filling her with warmth and a longing she had no right to feel. She looped her arm through Abi's, refusing to let go until they were seated together in the van. Exhaustion claimed her, and when she found her head resting against Abi's, she couldn't be bothered to worry about what her sister might think. She closed her eyes, smiling a little as the entire van sang at the top of their lungs to the pop mashup Sloane controlled on her Spotify. It was almost as lively as a good bonfire.

"Looks like Liz went to bed already," Tess stated once they arrived back at the ranch. The lights were off in the main house, and Tess watched as Krystal drove to the group's designated cabin. As Abi and Taunya climbed out of the van, Tess noticed a familiar figure headed their way.

"Kris, right?" Abi greeted the man, reaching back to help Tess from the van. Tess's perception was off, and she stumbled, almost falling on her ass.

Kris nodded, grimacing as Tess stifled back more laughter. It was completely out of hand tonight! "Howdy, Cowboy," she greeted, complete with a terrible southern drawl and finger salute.

"Tess," Kris grunted in return, fishing out a set of keys to unlock the cabin. The scar on his face was distracting, and Tess watched as he rubbed at it numerous times until he'd found the correct key. When the cabin door swung inward, Kris stepped away to let Sloane through.

"I've gotta pee!" Sloane squealed as she raced past.

Kris narrowed his dark eyes on Abi and Tess, backing farther away, but he didn't leave. He was a tall man, and when compared to Tess's short five feet, it made her look like she'd been zapped with a shrink ray. He was broad-chested too, like he did a lot of pull-ups in his spare time. It was hard to tell what else he looked like with the sweatpants and hoodie he had on, but he sure as hell didn't seem like any cowboy Tess knew. Not that she personally knew any.

"Thanks, Kris!" She grinned, rocking back and forth on her heels.

"Yes. Thank you, Kris." Taunya winked on her way past with her backpack.

"You're getting married next weekend, so you can't have him!" Tess reminded her sister in a singsong voice.

"And you're gay, so I guess neither one of us will!" Taunya was laughing, glancing back at Tess like she hadn't just screwed up the entire day.

"I know that, *duh*," Tess teased back, smirking at Abi as Taunya headed into the cabin. She slapped Abi's ass, causing her sister's friend to yelp in surprise. "Gay for you, that is."

As soon as Abi's eyes widened, Tess grasped too late what she'd done. What she'd *said*.

Damnit, she breathed, squeezing her eyes shut and wishing she could disappear. McCoy coming up behind them made it more humiliating. A disgruntled snort left the mechanic's lips, and she wedged between Abi and Tess. "Tess, drunk or not, I'll put you in the van to sleep if you can't respect Abi. She deserves a helluva lot more than a drunken come-on. Dust off your lady balls and do better tomorrow."

Kris scoffed, leveling his intense eyes on Tess. Unease floated off him in waves. "Liz failed to mention we'd be putting up a bunch of drunk women for the night."

"*One* drunk woman, but okay." McCoy snorted, sizing him up like she must have done to morons a thousand times at work. "Liz also failed to mention we'd be dealing with an uptight asshole, so..." She shrugged.

"I ain't uptight. I'm a fucking alcoholic," he bit out, expelling a frustrated breath. Scraping a hand over the black stubble on his scalp, he cut his gaze to the ground. "Recovering alcoholic. A heads-up would've been nice. Even the smell is too much some days."

"Sorry," Tess lamented, sober enough now to be genuinely sympathetic. She should have acted more responsibly tonight.

"Shit," McCoy muttered when Kris left them to head back to the main house. "That dude is intense, am I right? Abs, you coming?" She looped her arm around Abi's waist, gently untangling Tess in the process. She caught McCoy's guarded look and reluctantly let go of Abi, swallowing down the ball forming in her throat.

Abi hesitated, looking back at Tess as McCoy guided them into the cabin. "You coming?"

"In a little bit." Tess teetered on her feet before taking a seat on the steps. She didn't want to be crammed into a small space with the five of them. Not when the weather was finally agreeable or when she still had so much to think about. She'd keep them all up. She swallowed several times as she fought for control. "I'll just sit out here ... for a little bit. If that's okay."

"Of course."

The longing in Abi's softened gaze had Tess's heart squeezing in agony. Unable to take it any more, she tore her gaze away.

Chapter Thirteen

Abi

THE LOW VIBRATION OF someone's cell phone ringing pulled Abi out of a restless sleep. When her eyes fluttered open, it took a moment to remember she was still in the cabin on the ranch. Moonlight glinted through the window, casting Sloane into its silhouette of radiance and intrigue. She had taken up camp on the sole recliner, a thin blanket pulled up to her neck as she slept like a baby.

Not wanting to wake McCoy snuggled in behind her on the sofa, Abi carefully lifted the arm pinning her down. Slowly coming to a sitting position, she froze when McCoy mumbled in her sleep. Abi waited a beat or two to make sure her friend was still conked out before standing and immediately sought Tess. The cabin was ridiculously small, more of a home for a stable hand than properly suited for guests. The fact they'd spent the night in such rustic accommodations emphasized just how much Tess must have been spending on some of their other activities. It was a smart move on Tess's part to pay less where she could, but after the swanky dinner the evening before, Abi worried how much this week would set her back. When Coy had pulled them together to talk it over, Abi had jumped at the chance to help pay. It was only Taunya who seemed all too happy about the arrangement, and it had to be the spoiled brat coming out. Also, Abi knew how Tess operated. Taunya was almost impossible to say no to, and she imagined it was especially difficult for a people-pleaser like Tess.

Taunya and Krystal were asleep in the only bed in the open concept, and after a good look around, Abi didn't see Tess anywhere. Had she not come inside the cabin after all? Apprehension clenched at Abi's insides, and as she double-checked the bathroom, she tried not to worry. Earlier, McCoy had spoken of Tess sleeping in the van, so maybe that's what happened. Abi tiptoed through the cabin, locating an abandoned sweater on the coffee table and pulling it over her head.

As soon as she creaked open the cabin's door, she spotted Tess leaning against the railing on the small deck, fast asleep. She still wore yesterday's clothes, most of which had been rained on and dried several times over. Most of her blonde hair had escaped its ponytail, framing her rounded face and naturally dark eyebrows. The laces of one boot had come undone, and every few heartbeats, Abi watched Tess shiver. She bit her lip, her forehead creasing. It pained her to see Tess this way, and yet a part of her hoped like hell Tess would come away from her storm and see the world differently.

Abi snuck back inside the cabin, tiptoeing past Sloane to where the extra blankets were piled in a beige tote bin. After selecting the warmest one, she carried it outside and draped it carefully over Tess. She smiled when Tess snuggled into the added comfort, and it took discipline on her part not to cuddle into the smaller woman. Instead, she kissed Tess softly on the cheek and returned to the couch.

When Abi opened her eyes the next morning, Coy's meadow green gaze stared back at her. Abi sucked in a sharp breath, her eyes widening. "How long have you been watching me, creeper?"

Coy broke into a shit-eating grin, her near-perfect pearly whites dazzling from two years with braces. "A minute or so. I don't make a habit of waking beautiful women unless it's for sex."

Abi rolled her eyes. "Uh-huh."

Coy was a huge flirt, so when her ringed fingers reached between them to trail along Abi's jawline, it was no surprise. She leaned closer until Abi felt the slight friction from her septum ring tickling the shell of her ear. "After the display yesterday, I take it you still don't want what I'm offering."

Abi playfully poked Coy in the ribs. "I don't, and besides, we both know I couldn't handle you."

"Me, or my strap-on?"

Abi pushed away, rolling her eyes again at Coy's teasing laughter. "Is there a difference with you? Pretty sure your strap-on selection is as legendary as you."

"Coy, quit being so cringe!" Sloane groaned, walking past them from the bathroom. She threw a pillow at her twin, but it hit them both. "No self-respecting friend of ours wants to be another notch on your headboard."

"Aww, don't tell me you're still pissed about Ash," Coy volleyed back, sitting up on the couch with Abi. Unlike Abi's sleep shorts and t-shirt, Coy had slept in a pair of form-fitting boxers and ribbed tank top. As she sat there rubbing the sleep from her eyes, her muscled arm flexing with the movement, she looked ready to film a Calvin Klein underwear commercial. When Abi lived in Vancouver, she'd seen her friend's charm work on multiple women at different clubs or parties, but she'd never once felt that irresistible pull with Coy. Not like with Tess. Like Supergirl and her alter ego Kara, Coy and Tess couldn't be any more different.

"Am I pissed that Ash had their eye on me for weeks, and after meeting you once, you fuck them in the public washroom at my work?" Sloane asked dryly, her voice husky from sleep. Another pillow sailed through the air, but Abi was far enough away not to get hit this time. "Gee, I wonder how I'm not jumping for joy over that."

"If it helps salt the wound, Frankie wasn't happy about it either." Coy chuckled, bending down for her jeans piled on the floor. Frankie was a name Abi had heard often through the last four years, and she cringed as scenarios came to mind of what the dominatrix might have done to Coy.

"I didn't hear about this; did she hurt you?"

Coy shot her sly smile, winking. "Only in the best ways."

"You couldn't sit down for a week without ice packs and a chair doughnut under your ass, McCoy." Sloane shook her head, her features the epitome of disappointment. "That should teach you not to upset Frankie. Part-time domme or not, she's terrifying."

"Why are we talking about something that happened a month ago?" Taunya complained, throwing her blankets off a few feet away. She slipped out of bed, scowling at them as she made her way to the bathroom. "You're all lucky I don't carry around ammunition for later use, or we'd never get anything done for all the bickering!"

A knock sounded on the door, and Abi's breath caught as Tess popped her head in. She looked a lot better than when Abi had seen her at night, physically, but mentally... Abi had a feeling it would take more than a few hours of shuteye to work her shit out. "Um, good morning," she rasped, doing a quick scan of faces in the room before focusing on Coy's state of undress. She blinked, a low blush creeping onto her cheeks as she cleared her throat. "There's brunch up at the main house. My head's pounding, so I'll just be in the van. No rush. I don't have anything planned until the spa this afternoon."

Tess left as quickly and quietly as she'd come in, leaving Abi to wonder if she should go after her.

"Leave her be," Taunya said, coming up beside Abi and giving her a knowing look. A small smile appeared. "She's got a lot to work out, and no offense, but I could use less of what happened yesterday. Let's just get through this week, okay?" Upon Abi's nod, Taunya draped an arm over her shoulders, adding, "Besides, there's no rushing my sister."

"You're not lying." Abi laughed, and the tightness in her chest eased a little. She backed up, jerking her thumb over her shoulder. "I'll pee, and then we can head over."

While she washed up in the bathroom, she heard Taunya's booming voice. "Will someone get Krystal up?"

Abi chuckled to herself, smiling into the small bathroom mirror at her reflection. She was lucky to have friendships that picked up easily where they left off when she was home. Not many people could say the same.

By the time she'd returned to the main part of the cabin, Krystal was awake, and most of their belongings were packed. "Just peed, huh?" Coy arched an eyebrow, smirking.

Abi flicked her brushed hair, twirling around. "Perfection takes work, playgirl."

"Can't perfect what's already perfect, Abs."

"Mmm, let's roll before your sister hits us with another pillow."

"Heard that!"

Deciding to leave their bags, they left the cabin and walked down the path to the main ranch house. Liz had the front door open and was waving them in by the time they'd reached the large wraparound deck. "Come on in, you're just in time for breakfast."

"Morning," Abi greeted her with a smile.

"Thank you for having us," Taunya added, shaking Liz's hand as they stepped inside.

"It's no trouble at all. I'm used to cooking for the ranch hands, so what are six more mouths to feed?" The older woman shut the door behind them. "Take off your footwear and come on through. Tess gave you the heads-up, I presume? She was here a bit ago, but the poor girl spent more time in the bathroom than anything."

Coy began to laugh, but Abi's glare quickly had her smothering the sound with a cough. "Yes, she had a few too many glasses of wine last night, unfortunately," Taunya informed Liz with a grimace.

"Kristopher told me." Liz looked as if she'd say something more, but she just showed them to the dining room.

"Are we eating with your family?" Krystal asked, glancing around at the several place settings.

"Yes, I hope you don't mind?"

"Not at all." Sloane's grin had Abi rolling her eyes.

Brunch got under way, and it was about ten minutes later when Kris and three other men walked in. One must have been Liz's husband, because he kissed her before taking a seat beside her. Polite conversation started while they ate the typical staples of a large farm style breakfast: eggs, pancakes, sausages, toast, and fruit, and Abi filled up on as much coffee and fruit as her stomach allowed. It was nice and peaceful, and she felt a little guilty that Tess wasn't there to enjoy it.

"Just 'cause she helps run Cairns Corp doesn't mean she should have unlimited access to Cadence. She doesn't rule the world."

The company name Kris was quietly hissing in conversation with Liz was familiar to Abi, and she perked up in her seat. She didn't make a habit of eavesdropping, but when one of her business icons got casually dropped in conversation? All bets were off.

"This feud between you two is exhausting. Bury the hatchet already, Kristopher. Courtney is practically Cadence's aunt. Of course, she should get to see her."

"Are you talking about Courtney Cairns?" Several heads turned Abi's way, and she blushed. "Sorry, it's just, I know that name."

"So do I." Coy shrugged. "She and her girlfriend partied at our place once or twice."

"Lexi?" Okay, that was definitely a snarl. Kris got to his feet, picked up his plate, and left the room.

Abi was too excited to let his abrupt departure faze her. "You *know* Courtney Cairns and never told me? Coy, she's like, *huge* in the business world right now. I've been following her since she joined the company at twenty-two. She's ... she's like—"

"Your celebrity crush?" Krystal guessed, chewing on a piece of apple.

"Super successful and a feminist?" Sloane threw in.

"Super hot and badass?"

Abi frowned at Coy, who only laughed. "What? I'm not blind."

"How could we explain it in a way you'd understand?" Taunya pondered, tapping her chin. She snapped her fingers. "Courtney Cairns in the business world is like ... you getting a chance to look under the hood of a say … a Mercedes-Benz." She glanced between Abi and Coy for confirmation. "Right? That's a fancy brand, right?"

"Well, Benzes are no supercars, but I get it."

"Do you work in business … Abi, is it?" Liz asked, pushing her plate away and folding her arms on the table. She seemed intrigued, so Abi took it as a good sign to continue.

"I do! Marketing, actually, although I may be looking for a fresh start at home here in Vancouver." The statement was out before Abi could stop herself. Since when had she changed her mindset on moving home? Surely not after *one* kiss with Tess?

"For real?" Taunya's eyes widened, and she grabbed Abi's arm.

"Courtney's like family," Liz said with a slow smile. "Let's keep in touch. Maybe I can connect the two of you over lunch someday."

Abi nodded, sure her eyes were sparkling. "I would seriously love that, Liz. Thank you."

"Just hit her up online." Coy shrugged. "Or I could text my friend Naz. Lexi freelances in her tattoo shop sometimes."

"You know nothing about networking," Sloane said, shaking her head.

Abi just smiled, a warm feeling filling her chest. She didn't know what came over her, but something about this felt *right*. More than right. Maybe moving home could be a possibility after all.

Chapter Fourteen

Tess

"Stay close to your brother, Sierra. And Zeke, make sure you've got eyes on her!" Stacey called out as her kids ran off to the playground. She huffed, lifting one of the iced coffees out of the takeout tray and passing it to Tess. "Here you go. You still take whipped cream on top, right?"

"Yeah, this is great, thanks." Tess took the plastic cup from her friend gratefully, not wasting any time sucking back some of the much-needed caffeine. She relaxed into the park bench, closing her eyes with a sigh.

"Long day?" Stacey chuckled, and a moment later Tess felt the bench dip as she sat down as well.

Tess nodded, silent as she took another long drink. The sugary syrup in the iced coffee was slowly working its magic, giving her sleepy brain the boost needed to get through the evening. "Mhmm, long week, Stace. Long, looong week."

"And it's only Wednesday! The rest of the bridal party getting to you?" Stacey nudged her shoulder, "That's a lot of chatty extroverts working against your introvert tendencies."

Tess cracked one eye open, canting her head to the side to take Stacey in. She was carding her fingers through her pixie cut and giving Tess a knowing smirk. Giving her the stink-eye, Tess returned to her earlier position, indignantly slurping her straw as she pouted. "You're making fun of me."

"No, never." Stacey let out a derisive snort. "It's more of an 'I fucking told you so' comment, because I did, didn't I?"

Tess heaved another sigh, opening both eyes and sitting up straighter. "You told me I was a shoo-in for the world's craziest sister award, not that I would *literally* feel my life draining away in their presence."

Stacey cracked up, nudging Tess again and jostling her nearly empty cup so much, it almost overturned. "God," Tess whined, but she was stifling back depleted laughter. "You're one of them, an-an ... *extrovert*! Stop!" she jokingly whisper-shouted, craning her head past Stacey for added effect. "Someone help! Stacccey, you're sucking out my sooooul!"

"At least I make you laugh while I do it." Stacey sported a silly grin, her blue eyes full of affection as she wrapped an arm around Tess. She planted a kiss on her cheek. "*Mwah*! I love ya, girl."

"Right back at ya." Tess leaned into her embrace. Her shoulders still shook with the occasional burst of silent laughter, but neither one said anything more for several minutes. Tess scanned the handful of children using the playground equipment, satisfied when she came across the two troublemakers she knew so well. "Sierra's sure growing fast. Is she tall for her age?"

"For six, yes, and strong too. She treats the monkey bars like her own personal playroom. I swear if Zeke did half the shit she does at that age, I would've been having a heart attack every day."

"I believe you. Zeke was so chill; still is. He's good to look out for her, though," Tess murmured, watching as Zeke chased his little sister around the playground. They were great kids, beautiful and kind, but maybe she was biased. Even when Zeke sassed her, Tess adored him. Stacey liked to tease that neither one of her kids could do any wrong in Tess's eyes, and perhaps she was right. After all, she took her role as cool auntie seriously.

"So, what's been going on? Your call came as a surprise," she asked, holding her hand out for Tess's empty cup. Tess handed it to her, watching as she tossed both cups in the trash before returning. "I figured it'd be September before I saw your gorgeous mug again. Your texts have been sporadic, but that's understandable given the current bucket list from hell."

"Yeah, sorry about that. It's been a time, for sure." Tess grimaced, filling Stacey in on the last few days. Her friend got angry and surprised in all the right places, but honestly, it was draining having to retell the drama regarding Vicki. Bringing up the few sexually charged moments with Abi put a familiar fire in her belly, and her knowing blush had Stacey crowing with excitement.

"Dayum, where do I start on this?" she exclaimed, placing her fingers against her temples and mimicking an explosion. "Seriously, my mind is blown right now. First, for an introvert, you sure get around with the ladies." Stacey wagging her eyebrows suggestively had Tess rolling her eyes. "And second, how come I didn't know how badass your sister was? And thirdly," she paused, her brows furrowed in concentration, "thirdly? Is that a word? Fuck it. Abi! You'd think you'd text a bitch when the woman you haven't stopped thinking about for four years sticks her tongue in your mouth."

An image of Abi doing naughty things to her with said tongue flashed behind Tess's eyes, and her body blissed out in response. She squirmed in her seat, trying to relieve the pressure between her legs.

Stacey was right about one thing. Having sex with Abi the night of the party had cracked open Pandora's box. She'd managed to hurt Abi, betray Taunya's trust, and develop a connection so deep, it terrified her to this day. She'd spent the last four years longing to feel with someone else what she'd had with her sister's best friend.

"C'mon, you know I don't overshare. Not everyone feels the need to text what they ate for breakfast while in the bathroom," Tess mumbled, rubbing her left eye. It'd been driving her batty since she'd somehow gotten massage oil in it that afternoon. Must have been leftover clumsiness from her hangover, but she'd been the only one in the bridal party to trip over the masseuse's massage oil, coat her fingers in it while picking it back up, and then stick those same fingers in her eye shortly after. Sometimes, she boggled her own mind.

"Oh, burn," Stacey replied, laughing. "And *you're* deflecting."

"I'm not, it's just…" Tess shrugged, not knowing fully what she was experiencing, just that it was happening at a whirlwind pace. She'd been single for a little over twenty-four hours and had already spent half the night thinking about another woman. Shouldn't she be on some kind of dating hiatus? Getting quality "Tess time"?

After waking up for the second time that morning, in the van, she'd spent the rest of the day actively avoiding the bridal party as much as possible. She was ashamed for how she'd acted the day before, and, most importantly, ashamed for whatever drunken comments she'd made to Taunya and Abi. "It's not important, because it can't happen again."

"Oh no, nope." Stacey shook her head, waving Tess's comment off like it personally offended her. "We're not doing this again, T."

"Tauni doesn't want us together," she tried to explain. "I need to respect that."

"The hell you do!" Stacey turned incredulous eyes on her, her cheeks blotting as anger spilled from her lips. "You're turning thirty-one in November and still in the same mindset you were when you were twelve!"

"No, I'm not."

"You are! Remember when Taunya snuck into the neighbor's backyard after school to use their trampoline and ended up in the ER for a broken leg? You told your parents she tripped down the basement stairs."

Tess smiled a little at the memory. Six-year-old Abi had been the one to run back to the Moore residence to seek Tess. She'd lied too that day, taking blame for the idea to sneak out while Tess babysat.

"You and Abi both covered for Taunya that day."

"That's different."

"How so? It boils down to the same issue: your inability to tell someone to fuck off. Taunya's spoiled to death because no one stands up to her. If you and Abi want to pursue a relationship, it's no one else's business."

"Damn, you're salty tonight," Tess muttered, drawing her hand back and adjusting her sunglasses. She would need more eye drops before her drive home.

Stacey chuckled, not at all offended. "Salty, Tess? Is that a word we're using now? What's it even mean?"

Shrugging, she grinned. "Pissed off, I'm guessing. Taunya and her friends use it a lot. And the slang word 'slay,' which apparently is some kind of compliment."

"Jesus. Soon you'll be twerking to an Ariana Grande song on a TikTok video." They laughed and sat in silence for a while, just watching Sierra and Zeke play. "I meant what I said, though. Don't turn down something good just because it makes certain people uncomfortable. Fuck 'em."

Their eyes met. After all these years, Tess could anticipate how her friend would reply, and it made her smile. "Fuck 'em, huh?"

"Fuck 'em," Stacey repeated, smiling as well. She chucked Tess affectionately on the cheek with her knuckle. "And that, little Tessa, is my motherly advice for the day."

Tess was fighting to keep her eyes open by the time she pulled into her parents' driveway. It had been nonstop all afternoon for the bridal party. The only moment she had found time to breathe was when she'd been dozing on the massage table at the spa. When they were finally back in the city, Tess, Taunya, and Abi had dropped the other girls home before heading to the Moore house. Once there, they'd left Abi, and Taunya had followed Tess to drop off the rental van. By the time they reached home again, Tess had been running late to meet Stacey. Now the sun was setting, and she hadn't eaten anything since early afternoon. The sweetened, iced coffee churned in her empty stomach, but as she trudged into her tiny one-room home, all she wanted was a shower and nap. Didn't matter which came first.

As soon as the door closed to her sanctuary, she tried kicking off her boots unsuccessfully, hobbling around as one foot got stuck at the heel part. The cozy, queen-sized mattress across the room practically beckoned to Tess, which only made her attempts more frustrating. With her sock feet finally free, she all but collapsed onto the unmade bed. *I'll close my eyes just for a minute...*

Tess woke to the heavy strumming of her mom's acoustic guitar that was already hooked up to the PA system. Audrey must have been on the mic, because Tess heard her country twang as she belted out Terri Clark loud and clear. No doubt it was another party outside of Tess's tightly wound bridal events for that week, and Tess was glad for the brief reprieve she'd snatched.

Yawning, she took her time rolling out of bed, and her empty stomach growled when she didn't immediately head to the mini fridge. Instead, she grabbed a shower first, the cold water doing wonders in waking her up. Her eye felt better too after the rest, no longer watery and itchy.

Abi's melodic laughter could be heard from the backyard. Tess smiled as she dressed, adoring the sound, adoring the woman it belonged to. She kept returning to Abi's declaration the evening before, and every time she thought of Abi's tears, or that slight tremor in her voice as she professed her love once again, Tess felt a crushing weight barrel into her chest: turmoil, confusion, fear, unrest, absolute wonder. Wonder at the unyielding power of Abi's affections. Never had Tess believed someone would fall in love with her in earnest. Not after Chantelle. Vicki's declaration hadn't sounded like Abi's. Perhaps it wasn't fair of Tess to compare them, but their words hadn't touched her the same. Abi made Tess feel naked and whole at the same time, raw and desperate to be seen, and yet her praise and promises were balms to Tess's fragile heart. She was caught in some kind of treacherous limbo, half dying to give things a shot with Abi while her other half was terrified of the many potential consequences. Besides the obvious of upsetting Taunya, Tess didn't know how she would cope with another failed relationship. And that scared her. She didn't want to risk falling in love just for Abi to break her heart down the road.

Choosing a pair of her favorite black and red two-tone sweats and a loose-fitting white t-shirt, Tess inspected herself in the mirror hanging on her bathroom door. Her eyelid was still slightly puffy, and the black roots on her scalp needed touching up, but at least the dark circles under her eyes weren't as prominent. Her outfit was on the baggier side, however, and with her short stature it easily came off looking homely. She frowned, debating if she should change. The sweatpants were cozy, and that was what she was going for. After the week she'd had, she *needed* the added comfort. Still, there was a crowd tonight, if the commotion outside was any indication, so Tess opted to go with a little makeup. Nothing crazy, since that wasn't her style, but enough to bring out her eyes and maybe add some life to her cheeks.

Jitters accompanied Tess as she pulled out ingredients for a PB&J. The restlessness of her hands had her dropping her slices of bread on the floor. "Nothing's stopping you from turning off the lights and pretending you're not here," she muttered, except she knew that was a lie. Her bike was parked out front for everyone to see, and if she was honest, a huge part of her was on pins and needles with thoughts of seeing Abi. Unfortunately, if her mother saw her, Audrey would be talking Tess into a jam session. When they were alone was one thing, or when they performed for seniors and half of them didn't remember her, but in front of Taunya's entire bridal party? In front of *Abi*?

Tess shuddered, her fingers finding the edge of her rubber band, but she didn't snap it.

She took her suppertime meds and ate quickly, preferring to get the night over rather than drag it out. The longer she waited to go out there, the steeper her anxiety usually climbed. She slipped on her Converse sneakers and walked over to where her Gibson acoustic rested on the wall beside her bed. Her lips twitched as she glided her fingers softly down the strings before lifting the instrument off its base. She didn't know why, but feeling the power in the strings centered her; it was an odd quirk she'd had since she was young. Clearly, she hadn't figured out how to break the compulsive habit.

"Let's do this," Tess murmured, straightening her shoulders. She headed for the door, grabbing her jacket on the way out.

CHAPTER FIFTEEN

Abi

LOUNGING WITH FRIENDS AROUND a backyard fire, listening to Audrey sing, easily made for some of the best memories Abi had of her old neighborhood. When she'd lived down the street growing up, she and her parents would often come over on Friday nights. They'd play board games or watch movies, or sometimes Audrey would invite her jam partners over, and Abi's family would catch a free concert. It had always been a lot of fun, and when Abi and Taunya had grown "too cool" for those Friday nights, her parents would still go. Taunya would usually talk Abi into going to a party and have a full cover story waiting for their parents. Those nights were memorable in their own right.

Tonight, most of the wedding party was present, Derek's groomsmen included, and it was a relaxing change from the last few days. As much fun as Abi was having with the bucket list, it was good not to have a required outing to prepare for. Tess had already informed everyone she was working in the morning. Thursday's adventure was planned for the afternoon, but Tess refused to tell them what it was until an hour before. It was so unfair.

"So, I have to know," Taunya said, pulling Abi away from her thoughts. She stood before her with Derek in tow and a Mike's Hard lemonade in one hand.

"What do you *have* to know, Tauni?" Abi lifted one eyebrow, her voice teasing. She watched in silence as Derek sat down in the lawn chair beside Abi, and then Taunya took a seat in his lap. "Incredible," she marveled, shaking her head. What would it be like to have a relationship where they still openly cuddled whenever possible, *years* later? Catching Taunya's confused expression, Abi gave her a wistful smile. "You guys are cute together; goals for the rest of us."

"We're about to get married, so I should hope so." Derek laughed, and the sappy glint in his brown gaze only cemented the situation laid out before Abi.

"Not goals for me," Coy spoke up from Abi's other side. She took a swig of her beer, adding, "I'm gonna keep riding my solo train, making pit stops at every exotic destination I see along the way. A new vay-cay every day, know what I'm saying?" She raised her arms in front of her and pumped her hips in her chair in what Abi could only guess was her acting out some fictional sex scene.

"And then you wonder why I won't 'board' you," Abi deadpanned and smirked when their friends cracked up.

"You're gross, Coy." Taunya was wrinkling her nose, looking like she might go find a can of Lysol spray to disinfect Coy with.

"Seriously, I don't know how you keep track of everyone," Derek added, gripping Taunya a little tighter in his arms. "Vancouver isn't *that* big; surely you run into a disgruntled ex now and again?"

"Oh, sure."

"Most of them are good with just a night after Coy explains she's in an open relationship," Sloane cut in, casting an exasperated look in her twin's direction. She was loading a marshmallow onto a long roasting stick.

"Sloane," Coy warned, her body tensing beside Abi.

"What? You said it yourself; Frankie scares off anyone who stays around too long."

"I'm not *in* a relationship with Frankie."

"Riiight. She just owns your pus—"

"Can I talk to you for a minute?" Coy was already out of her seat, baring her teeth at her sister. She grabbed Sloane by the wrist. "*Alone?*"

"I'm getting hitched in T-minus ten days, so we absolutely have zero time for bullshit sibling rivalry," Taunya declared, pointing her finger at the twins. "*Play nice.*"

"No fighting, promise." Coy flashed her small grin, and Abi glanced back and forth between the twins, wondering what she was missing.

"I get the feeling Sloane doesn't like Coy with Frankie," she mentioned after they'd disappeared into the house.

"You're not wrong," Krystal replied, speaking up for the first time. She was often so quiet, Abi sometimes forgot she was there unless they were facing each other. She glanced behind her where Krystal was watching Audrey strum the guitar.

"What's the story there?" Honestly, Abi was surprised she hadn't heard Coy's version. Her friend usually told her everything.

"Stuff with Frankie is always hush-hush around us, but from what I've seen, she seems very closed off from her feelings," Taunya answered with a shrug. "I just know that when Coy pulls one of her stunts, Frankie gets a little unhinged. From jealousy, no doubt. Sloane's said in the past how possessive she can be."

Abi grimaced. She could only guess how at a disadvantage Sloane was, sharing a face with Coy and having to work for Frankie when the older woman was angry.

"So, were you serious about maybe moving home?"

Taunya's question made Abi pause, and she pulled her lip between her teeth. The possibility of going back to work for Margo's company was just that, a possibility; she was keeping her options open. Truthfully, she'd love nothing more than to move home, but only if she could be with Tess. She'd decided a long time ago that until her feelings faded, it wasn't productive or healthy to be in the same city. All it would do was leave her hopeful and broken, and no one wanted to live in limbo like that.

"I always think of moving home," Abi admitted, turning to face Taunya with a shrug. "I just don't know if it's in the cards for me." Her best friend knew her better than anyone, though, and Taunya's sympathetic smile informed Abi there was no disguising whatever feeling festered behind her eyes.

"Well, I hope if you ever land a job offer with Cairns Corp., you take it. All the other stuff can be worked out."

"I will." Abi wasn't confident about the latter, but she'd be foolish not to take a job with one of the leading investors in the country. "It's just hard when—" She went still, trailing off the moment Tess appeared in the backyard. She was drinking from a reusable water bottle, and in her other hand she held her acoustic guitar. She was dressed for comfort, but it in no way hindered her sex appeal. Abi's hand fluttered to her chest, the effect Tess had on her almost enough to make her forget how she'd ignored Abi all day.

"If you think that's something, wait until you see her in a dress."

Abi flushed at the sound of Taunya's low chuckle, and she tore her eyes away from the woman who had garnered all of her attention the last few days. Geez, the last several years. She inwardly groaned, raking her fingers through her caramel waves as she tried to appear casual.

"Tauni's right," Coy said, apparently back from whatever tiff she'd had with Sloane. She flung her arm around Abi's shoulders. "The barber cleans up well. With any luck, you'll be the one taking off her dress the night of the wedding."

"Ew, that's my sister you're talking about!"

"Hey, Tess. You playing tonight?" Derek asked as Tess approached the group. Abi had always loved how sweet he was with her. They genuinely cared for each other, and Abi could tell it meant the world to Taunya.

A strained chuckle escaped Tess. "Yeah, um, I don't think I can avoid it, unfortunately." Her hands were empty now, Abi noted, so she must have left her guitar with her mom. She couldn't take her eyes off Tess, and she studied her telltale signs of nervousness as she caught up with Derek. Tess didn't take a seat in the empty chair beyond Krystal, instead busying herself either by wringing her hands or putting them to her face. Abi itched to reach for her, to take those small hands in her own and kiss away the worry drawing fine lines across her forehead. More than anything, she wanted to pull Tess aside and talk things out. They were both adults; there was no reason to avoid each other, and since they had to be in close proximity until at least the following Sunday, it was quickly becoming unbearable.

"Go and play. I promise we won't laugh," Taunya encouraged, reaching up to squeeze Tess's hand just as Abi was dying to do.

"Have fun. I bet you'll be great," she added, holding her breath as Tess finally glanced her way.

A tremulous smile appeared seconds before she broke eye contact again. "Thanks." She bit her lip, looking like she might say something more, but must have decided against it.

"My *gawd*," Sloane breathed as they watched Tess walk away. She fanned herself. "Am I the only one affected by the sexual tension between you two? The lead-up is pushing my sanity, Abi. It's making my kitty—"

"Again, that's my sister," Taunya wailed, covering her ears.

Thankfully, the distinctive twang of Tess's guitar quieted the uncomfortable conversation. Abi stood and walked away, wanting to be closer to the music, closer to Tess. She'd never been one for gossiping about her sex life, and it was especially so when it came to Tess. What she felt for her best friend's sister went beyond sex, beyond reason. It was special, even sacred, and like hell would Abi sit and listen to what it was doing to her friend's nether regions.

Abi gave Tess a little wave when she noticed her watching. Her lips twitched with Tess's responding blush. Even under the soft glow of the Chinese lanterns fastened to strings around the backyard, that blush was indisputable. It was adorable, and face it, that blush was all for Abi.

She had to be doing something right.

The following day, Abi woke with the early morning sun shining through the gaps in the curtains and the delicious smell of coffee wafting up from the kitchen. She threw off her blankets but didn't immediately get out of bed. She found herself staring sleepily at the rainbow-colored musical notes painted in sporadic sections on the bedroom wall, remnants of Tess's teenage artistic side. When she'd moved in with Chantelle so long ago, all the posters and pictures had come down, her dressers emptied, but those stylish musical notes remained.

Abi seriously considered getting up for the day when her phone rang, a little too close to her head on the mattress.

"Shit!" she exclaimed, fumbling for the device. Her heart was thumping so hard, her hands were jerky as she pressed the call button. "'Lo?"

Soft laughter sounded on the other end. "Are you just waking up?"

Abi grunted. "Is this your pitch, Margo? Job or no job, I'm on vacation, remember? I was up late, ergo, sleeping in. And," she checked the alarm clock on the nightstand before rolling her eyes, "it's only seven thirty."

"Relax, I'm teasing, Abi."

"You don't tease, ever."

"I used to tease you," Margo argued, her voice filled with a kind of longing Abi would rather stub her toe over than dissect.

With another sigh, Abi slipped out of bed, heading to the bathroom down the hall. "If you're aiming to rehire me, there needs to be set ground rules, Margo. Can we discuss them now, or do you need to reconsider having me in the office again? I can't have you hitting on me, for one."

"No, you're right, I'm sorry. Let's talk it out and see if we can't come to an agreement."

When Abi reached the kitchen ten minutes later, Bobby was packing lunches for work and had fresh cinnamon rolls out of the oven. "Morning," she greeted him, padding to the coffee pot in her socked feet.

"Good morning. Help yourself, Abi. Taunya and Derek are still sleeping, and Audrey's in the shower."

"Okay. You headed off?"

"Yep." Bobby zipped up his lunch bag before giving Abi a quick hug. "Enjoy your day," he said, and chuckled. "Tess has something ... entertaining for you girls this afternoon."

"Sounds dubious," Abi joked, watching as he picked up his briefcase. "Have a great day too, Bobby. Knock 'em dead."

"Don't I always?" Bobby's grin was contagious, and he ruffled Abi's hair just like he used to when she was a kid.

"Oh," he added, turning back to Abi when he was almost to the door. He winked. "You can find Tess in the garage."

Abi had to bite her lip to hide her grin. "Thank you."

When she was alone in the kitchen, Abi waited all of two minutes before grabbing a circular serving tray from the lazy Susan. There she placed two mugs of coffee and two of the cinnamon rolls on the tray before carefully carrying them to the garage. As she juggled the tray on one hand long enough to open the door, she tripped over the lip of the door frame as she headed inside.

"Oh!" her eyes widened, and she quickly regained control of the tray but grimaced as she noticed the spills. "Saved most of it."

"Abi?"

"Good morning," Abi greeted Tess, crossing the short distance to where she sat on the floor. The garage door was open, and for once the weather looked perfectly agreeable. The sun cast a warm glimmer on the flowerbeds running down both sides of the Moores' driveway, and the distant chirping of birds immediately put Abi in a happy place.

Today, Tess was dressed in old jeans and a sweater, and her hair was thrown up in a rushed ponytail. Her bike was beside her, and it appeared as if she was cleaning the Ducati's chain with some type of brush. Abi gave her a soft smile. "I come bearing gifts. Can you take a break?"

"Yep, sorry, I was just doing a little maintenance before work."

Abi arched her brow. "No need to apologize, Tess." She watched as Tess picked up the rag near her on the floor, wiping her hands before she climbed to her feet.

There were dark circles under Tess's eyes, but she managed a weak smile as she accepted one of the coffees. "Thank you."

"You're welcome; when do you need to leave?" Abi asked, looking around for a place to set the tray.

"I'll head out by eight thirty. Thursdays are usually pretty good for walk-ins. Oh, um, here," Tess said, scrambling to clear a spot on the tool bench behind her bike. Abi set the tray down, grabbing her own coffee to lift to her lips. She sighed as the first sip went down. Bobby had always made the best coffee.

"And how are you doing? You look..." Abi wetted her lips, gesturing to Tess as she tried to find the right words. It could have been her lingering fatigue, but Tess looked a little worse for wear. Worry was etched into her features, and her disheveled appearance made it seem like she hadn't slept in days.

"I..." Tess set her coffee back down, even though she hadn't yet taken a sip. She fidgeted with the strings on her hoodie, avoiding Abi's gaze.

"Hey. Hey, you," Abi murmured, setting her drink down as well. She reached for Tess, her breath catching in her chest as she noticed the unshed tears in the other woman's eyes. The back of her hand grazed Tess's cheek, her own tension dispersing as she slipped her fingers languidly along her jaw. "It's fine, Tess. We're fine, okay? I just want you to be happy. Please, don't cry."

"I'm so tired," Tess rasped, closing her eyes just as tears spilled out. She turned her face into Abi's touch, nuzzling her palm. Her laugh was strained, her voice thick with unspent emotion. "I haven't been able to sleep. The crap with Vicki, and me hurting you, I..."

Abi reached for Tess's hand, tilting her head to the side. "Come with me?"

Tess resisted for only a second before she allowed Abi to guide her out of the garage. They headed to the annex in silence, still holding hands, and when Abi intertwined their fingers, Tess didn't pull away. Abi resisted the urge to puff out her chest.

This was happening. It was possibly the worst timing imaginable, but it was real, and it was happening.

Once outside Tess's home, Abi opened the door for them and gently pulled Tess in behind her. She looked around at the chic minimalist furnishings. "This is lovely, Tess."

"What are we doing here?"

Abi kicked off her slippers, waiting for Tess to do the same with her sneakers. "You're dead on your feet. You need rest."

"I need to work," Tess protested, her shoulders slumping as she caught Abi's determined look.

"You need to take care of yourself first," Abi said, still holding Tess's hand as she guided her to the bed. "Lie back, and I'll tuck you in."

"There's so much to do, Abi," Tess mumbled but did as she asked. Abi's pulse sped up as Tess pulled off her hoodie, flashing a tantalizing tease of creamy midriff in the process. She lay down, watching in silence as Abi draped the bedcovers over her. Her eyes were bloodshot and watery as she finally muttered, "I'm so sorry for how I've been acting."

Abi's eyes widened, and her gaze flew to Tess's just as a bubble of laughter popped out. "About which part?" she asked, only half serious. She knew the last couple of days had been especially hard on Tess, but she couldn't help but tease her a little. She wagged her eyebrows. "Drunkenly claiming to be gay for me?"

"No." Tess surprised her with a laugh of her own, the sound coming out hoarse and gritty. "I am definitely gay for you."

"Really? Do tell." Abi's heart was slamming against her chest as she climbed onto the queen-sized bed as well. Moments like these, she could quickly forget about life outside Tess's home or her earlier conversation with Margo. It was just Abi and Tess, alone in their bubble.

Abi's knees pressed into the mattress, but she didn't straddle Tess. Instead, she leaned over the other woman until their noses were almost touching. "Last I heard, I was too young for you."

There was a sharp inhale, and Tess's long eyelashes fluttered up toward her. She swallowed, drawing Abi's attention to her slender throat. "T–that was then. We're older now and ... things with you are ... different, Abi. I'm different now."

"And?"

"And what?"

"What else are you trying to say? I mean, we're talking four years worth of explaining, not just the last two days."

Tess frowned, and just like that the moment was once again rife with melancholy. Abi edged away, not wanting Tess to think she'd brought her into the annex for sex, but Tess caught her hand just before she slipped off the bed. Abi watched as obvious pain locked Tess's jaw. She clearly struggled to relinquish even an ounce of control. Abi waited in silence as she picked at a hangnail on her thumb, noticing the angry laceration on her wrist from the rubber band she kept there. Abi's heart went out to her.

"I should never have let you go that night. At the party. Not like that," Tess finally murmured, glancing at Abi. Her eyes were wide and glistening once more, fresh tears begging for release. "I am ... *ashamed* for how I acted, for the things I said. I–I wasn't in a good place, and when you told me…"

"That I loved you?" Abi softly added. She leaned over and brushed the runaway tears from her cheeks. Tess stared past her, unable to make eye contact, but her head bobbed in response. She chewed her lip again, the skin already chapped and cracking from the ongoing abuse from her teeth. Abi's heart sank as it dawned on her. "You didn't believe me then, and you don't believe me now, that's it, isn't it, Tess? It's not about how young I am anymore, it's that you genuinely don't believe I could love you. It's why you were putting up with Vicki. You knew she didn't really love you, and that was less scary."

Tess remained quiet, but the "deer in headlights" expression on her face told Abi all she needed to know. She sighed, sadly, her heart breaking for the other woman. This time she did straddle Tess's thighs, reaching for her arms and tugging her into a sitting position. When Tess still wouldn't look at her, Abi grasped her chin gently between her thumb and forefinger. "Look at me, please?"

When Tess lifted her face to meet Abi's gaze, Abi whispered, "I hate those bitches for hurting you. For all the scars they left on your soul. Tess ... I could seriously name a million reasons to support all the things I feel for you, but it would still mean opening your heart enough to believe them. To believe *me*."

She smiled, her vision blurred with tears as well, but she moved her hand to trace her fingers over Tess's eyebrow. "It kills me you can't see how incredible you are. How thoughtful, how calming. I love how you always bring in the groceries for Audrey, or how you apparently still go fishing with Bobby, even though hurting the fish always makes you cry afterward. I love that even though you're shy, you get up in front of people and jam with Audrey because you know how much it means to her. I love how fiercely you love Taunya, even when I wanna punch her for not appreciating you more."

A ghost of a smile appeared before Tess murmured, "Is that all?"

Abi laughed in surprise. She gave Tess a light shove but quickly snaked her arm around her waist, pulling her closer still. Their noses touched, and Abi's eyes drifted closed at the intimacy. She heard a soft sigh escape Tess, and she smiled. "No," she husked, nuzzling her nose over Tess's. "I could fill a journal." She had, when she was younger, but it was probably best that she left that out.

"Thank you," Tess whispered. Then, "You must think I'm an idiot."

"Mmm. Sometimes." Abi laughed softly. She went to pull away, but Tess snagged her arms around her waist.

"Can we just sit like this for a while?"

Abi studied her for a moment. Exhaustion plagued Tess, from her heavy-lidded eyes to her slumped shoulders. She looked ready for sleep, not sex, but as Abi leaned forward to kiss away a runaway tear off her cheek, she asked, "Why?"

She felt, more than saw, Tess's smile. "Because," she reasoned, emotion thick on her tongue as Abi kissed up another tear. "I realize I never have. You love a woman who has never even held you. Seems rather tragic, if you ask me."

Abi pulled away an inch, giving Tess a tremulous smile. "It's a tragedy."

"McCoy holds you and acts like she's won the lottery, so I figure I'm missing out."

"Oh, yeah?" Abi's voice cracked as she chuckled, her heart pounding at the glimpse of Tess's possessive side. She wrapped her fingers around Tess's neck to tug her closer, her mouth hovering over Tess's so close, it felt like Tess was breathing air back into her lungs. She hesitated for only a second before brushing a soft kiss onto her lips. "Jealous, were you?"

"Evidently," Tess breathed, a shaky sigh leaving her when their lips met once more. Abi wanted to ask what this meant for them, but she didn't. It was obvious Tess still had doubts, and she meant too much to risk scaring her off again. There would be plenty of time for emotive confessions. All Abi could do now was care for Tess when she so obviously needed it.

She slid off Tess and got under the covers. Tess didn't need to be told; as soon as Abi's head touched the extra pillow, Tess was lying back down as well. Abi wrapped her arms around her, sighing in contentment as Tess snuggled into her chest. "Sleep," she instructed softly, hooking her fingers in Tess's.

It didn't take long for Tess's feather light snores to fill not only Abi's ears, but her heart as well.

CHAPTER SIXTEEN

Tess

NORTH VANCOUVER WAS HOME to so much natural beauty, including some of the most resplendent temperate rainforests in the Pacific Northwest. For an outdoor enthusiast such as Taunya, Tess would have been remiss not to include a nature walk this week. She chose only the best with Lynn Canyon Park, knowing it would be an ideal spot to swim and picnic. Despite the logging done in the past, with massive tree stumps just off the constructed paths, Lynn Canyon was still a magnificently luxuriant forest.

"Did you know this park is what they call a second growth forest? That's why a lot of the trees here aren't much older than a hundred. Stunning, though, aren't they?" McCoy announced a few feet away. She was off the wooden path and leaning against an enormously tall tree as Krystal took a picture of her. A small cluster of similar-sized Douglas firs surrounded McCoy, some so towering and with leaves casting a veil over her view of the sky that they were the high-rises of the forest.

Out of the six of them, who would have thought McCoy would become their unofficial botanist guide to all things green? She posed proudly wearing a baggy pair of camo cargo shorts, hiking boots with flashy rainbow Pride socks halfway up to her calves and a black bandana fastened around her neck. Despite the fact that it had been raining on and off all day, she had stubbornly worn a matching camo long-sleeve rather than a raincoat. Tess honestly didn't know what to think about the other queer woman. McCoy came off as a bit of a womanizer, forever hooking up with women and, after six years, still trying to sleep with Abi. For some reason, Tess always imagined her as one of those dumb jocks who got all the women, yet here she was, passionately giving them a history lesson and looking like she could wrangle a croc.

Maybe I've been too judgmental, Tess thought. It was possible she'd disguised a lot of her misconceptions with jealousy.

"You're not just a handsome face after all," Taunya cheekily replied, swatting McCoy playfully on the ass as she rejoined them on the boardwalk.

"No, that would be Sloane." Coy laughed, earning a second, harder swat from her twin.

"Fuck you. I am plenty smart!" Sloane laughed good-naturedly. In her baby blue windbreaker and black leggings, she looked nothing like McCoy, despite being her identical twin. Today, she'd plaited her chestnut hair down her back in a low-maintenance yet attractive style. She currently had a sleek video camera secured to a headband. The design had the camera nestling snug against her ear. Knowing she'd likely be filmed the better part of the day had Tess more nervous than usual. She just hoped Sloane had the sense enough to remove any embarrassing footage before airing it on her vlog.

"Am I the only one who hasn't been here before?" Krystal paused in her picture-taking, lowering her phone just as a young family was approaching them, heading in the opposite direction. Krystal moved to one side of the path to let them pass.

"No, it's my first time too," Abi admitted, smiling at the adorable baby as the family went by. They were walking in a single file on the path now, and as usual she hung to the back of the line to be closer to Tess. Or at least that's what Tess presumed was the case. She wasn't at all surprised when Abi reached behind, her fingers outstretched for Tess as she casually added, "I can't get over how magical this place is. The forest feels so alive, like something out of a fairy tale."

Tess closed the gap between them as best as she could without kicking Abi's heels and silently grasped her hand. Their cloak-and-dagger act was ridiculous and excessive, but as her fingers dangled in Abi's, Tess found she loved their secret romance. Since their conversation and ensuing nap the day before, their time together had been rife with sexual tension. She had taken them all to their first pole dance group lesson for Thursday's bucket list activity, and after, since Sloane had to work, Coy suggested they do trivia night at the pub. The day had turned out better than Tess had imagined, but she hadn't been able to steal Abi away to talk — or anything else that might occur.

It was no longer an *if* that Tess would sleep with Abi again. It was a *when*, and the anticipation had her nerve endings standing at attention. She'd woken that morning with newfound purpose, determined at least to kiss Abi before the day got crazy busy. Things didn't go as planned, and by the longing looks Abi had sent Tess's way, they were clearly on the same page.

It began misting again, the light dew billowing near the forest floor and enhancing the lustrous greens of the plants and leaves. The scenery *was* captivating, and Tess had come here so many times with her family just for that reason. Today, however, something equally stunning held her attention. The prelude the day before had lit a ravenous fire in her belly, teasing her with thoughts of a sequel to their night together so long ago.

Up ahead, Tess watched as McCoy merged to the front of the bridal party, once again taking the lead as the pathway veered around a bend. A long flight of steps awaited the group, and they had to make room for several other tourists walking past. While McCoy nattered on about the history of the park and how often she'd hiked the available trails, Krystal and Taunya — today wearing her tiara — snapped pictures. Sloane was complaining about Coy — Tess didn't care enough to learn the specifics — while she rummaged through her backpack. Seconds later, Sloane pulled out an apple.

Abi laughed softly, tossing a sly look over her shoulder at Tess. "What?" Tess grinned, her eyes widening slightly when Abi turned to plant a quick kiss on her mouth. She wheeled back around before Tess could process and gave her fingers a light squeeze. Her pulse speeding up, Tess swiped her tongue over her bottom lip, an inaudible moan escaping as she savored the taste of Abi's coconut lip gloss.

Uneven breathing laden with desire washed through Tess, and before she had a chance to analyze things or shy away, she pulled Abi with her off the trail. Abi allowed Tess to lead her into the denser brush, both women eager to steal a few moments alone together. As soon as they came across a tree thick enough to suggest a little seclusion, Tess pushed Abi up against the rough bark. Abi's icy blue eyes blackened as Tess watched her, her chest heaving with ragged breaths. Like McCoy, Abi hadn't bothered with a jacket, and as a result her indigo blue tank top clung to her breasts and tight abdomen. Her nipples were hard as rock through her thin layers, and Tess's mouth watered for a taste.

"Hurry up and kiss me," Abi said, sounding frazzled.

Aware she'd been caught ogling, Tess's eyes flickered to Abi's once more. She yanked her closer, crushing their lips together in a blinding kiss. They groaned in unison, lips parting to delve deeper. Abi gave as much as she took, boldly gliding her tongue over Tess's at the same time as she pressed her hand into her torso. Abi's heady coconut and shea butter lotion melded with muskiness from the rainwater, engulfing Tess, somehow suffocating and breathing air into her lungs all at once. She wanted more, wanted everything Abi was willing to give. She slid her arm around Abi's waist, her hands coming to rest on her ass. Tess palmed her cheeks, giving them a firm squeeze and loving Abi's throaty moan.

"Tess!"

"Abi!"

Calls rang out in the distance, familiar voices shouting their names and effectively waking Tess up. Reluctantly, she gave Abi one last kiss before coming up for air. "God, you're beautiful," she panted, offering Abi a wide smile. She reached up, her fingers ghosting along Abi's rain-slicked cheekbone as she got lost in those sparkling blue eyes.

Abi took Tess's hand, kissing her fingers before kissing her lips once more. She grinned, happier than Tess had ever seen her. "We better go, or they'll be calling a search party."

"Where the hell did you two vanish to?" Taunya demanded once they were back on the trail's wooden path.

"Yeah, Tess. Did Abi need help with something? Or was she helping you?" McCoy's devious look had Tess blushing again, and she tucked her chin down. A knot formed in her stomach, and regret over kissing Abi was quick to rear its ugly head. Tess hadn't had time yet to talk to Taunya about ... well, whatever it was that she and Abi were doing. What had come over her? It was selfish of Tess to chance ruining Taunya's bridal bucket list over a what-if. Her goal these two weeks had always been to get through the wedding unscathed, but now...

What if Abi is the one I'm meant to be with?

"I, umm, I thought I saw an injured rabbit, so I had Tess come with me," Abi explained as they kept walking. Tess had to hand it to Abi; she thought fast on her feet and could spin a lie easily if needed. Tess was grateful for the explanation, because she wasn't much help.

"Uh-huh." Taunya sent Tess a disbelieving look but didn't say anything more.

Once they'd reached the suspension bridge crossing over Twin Falls to the other side of Lynn Canyon, Abi backed up so quickly, she stumbled over a rock. "Oh, no. Nope, not fucking happening."

"Abi, I thought you knew we'd have to cross a bridge." Taunya sounded concerned.

"You know I'm terrified of heights!"

"It's been four years, and since you never complained, I thought you were over the fear!"

Tess frowned, feeling like an ass. How could she not have remembered something so significant about Abi? And then she reprimanded herself. It wasn't as if she'd occupied her time growing up by shadowing her kid sister around. There was still plenty she and Abi needed to learn about the other.

"I don't remember you telling me either, or I would have mentioned the suspension bridge." McCoy grimaced, and once again they moved to the side to let people pass. A steady influx of tourists traveled back and forth on the bridge, quite a few pausing to take pictures at the waterfall below.

"It's not something I tend to brag about."

"Why don't you guys go on ahead?" Tess suggested, catching the pure panic in Abi's eyes. Tess's wisdom for offering comfort was rusty, but she was prepared to turn Abi's mood around however she could. "I'll hang back with Abi, see if we can't come up with a solution."

"Are you sure?" Taunya pursed her lips, clearly indecisive.

"Just leave me here. I'll head back to the car," Abi grumbled.

"We can all head back. Or we can go around the long way." McCoy glanced around for confirmation. "For Abi, we could do that. Right?"

"No, you guys go. But, Coy, could I borrow your bandana?"

McCoy cocked her head Tess's way, understanding slowly dawning. She quickly unfastened the material around her neck, sniffing it before handing it over. "Doesn't smell too bad."

"Thanks. We'll meet you on the other side."

"You can do this, Abs," Taunya encouraged her friend, bending down to give Abi a quick peck on the forehead. She squeezed her shoulder before running to catch up with the rest of the girls.

"Short of sedating me, I don't know how you think I'll get across that bridge," Abi admitted when they were alone. She gnawed at her lips, her gaze flitting around them like a caged bird already plotting an escape. Light wisps of hair in her ponytail had come loose, framing her angelic features and making those intense blue eyes pop. Tess knew she was scared, but she also knew Abi would be kicking herself later if she didn't at least try. Abi's tenacity was one characteristic Tess *was* familiar with.

Taking hold of Abi's hand, Tess led her to one of the concrete pedestrian-only blockades. She leaned against it, spreading her legs wide enough to tuck Abi between them. Tess rested a hand on Abi's hip and looked up at her. She'd never been one for PDAs, but holding Abi like this, it was perfect. She reached up to tuck the runaway strand behind Abi's ear, trying for a smile. "Two things: one, I'm sorry and wish now that I'd talked this bucket list out with you guys. I feel like shit how I just assumed all would be on board with whatever I came up with. But I'm hoping there's something I can do to help. An incentive, if you will."

"Bribes, huh?" Abi smirked, bending to graze her lips across Tess's ear. She whispered, "Does it involve you naked?"

Tess flushed at her bold question. They hadn't gotten that far yet this time around, and honestly, Abi being disappointed over her body fell in around Tess's top five worries of the past two days. She was just so ... average, and Abi was ... well, *Abi*. The last four years hadn't necessarily been kind to Tess, unlike Abi's striking features. Still, Tess swallowed down the lump forming in her throat and croaked out a reply. "Whatever it takes to get you moving, Abi."

Abi pulled back to look at her. Apprehension over the bridge was still present in her visage, but the roguish grin was new. Tess's insides churned and heated at the unspoken innuendo in that one look. "You planning to blindfold me? Kinky," she asked, slipping her hand in Tess's. Tess led the short way back to the entrance of the suspension bridge, paying due diligence to Abi's physical reaction. When her skin paled and slight tremors began in her legs, Tess rubbed her back in slow circles.

"Do you trust me?" Tess murmured, reaching into her back pocket for McCoy's bandana. Shaky breaths left her, but Abi nodded. Sweat dotted her upper lip, and she kept licking them incessantly until Tess halted the action with a kiss. Warmth and adoration for Abi blossomed in Tess's chest like a rose in full bloom. Tess wasn't sure she could explain the fireworks bursting in her heart. She'd never felt anything *remotely* like this with Vicki.

Vicki who?

Tess's smile was slow. She was way too happy to bother feeling guilty over her ex. "Close your eyes."

"This takes a trust exercise to a whole new level," Abi commented but did as Tess asked. Tess rolled up the black bandana, taking her time securing it around Abi's eyes. She was anxious about getting halfway over the bridge before Abi balked, but she tried not to let it show. Better to try to project positive vibes than her usual anxiety.

"Talk to me, Abi. Tell me what you want for us," Tess said in a way of distraction, standing behind Abi and placing her hands firmly on her hips. She waited for more tourists to enter ahead of them, and then she carefully guided Abi over the threshold.

Abi's knees buckled, and Tess's arms quickly slid under her armpits to hold her upright. "I've got you. I won't let anything happen to you." Her voice was gentle, and she pressed her face between Abi's shoulder blades to prove it. It would be so much easier to steer Abi if their heights were reversed, then Tess would be tall enough to look over the younger woman's shoulder. "Talk to me."

"W–what do you want me to say?" Everything there was to Abi trembled in Tess's grasp, from her limbs to her question. Concern overshadowed Tess's determination to get across the bridge, but when she slowed to turn back, a low gasp escaped Abi.

"I'm not sure." Tess considered the future. Would they be facing it together? "It sounds like you miss it here, but would you ever move back?" While she liked to think she was adaptable in relationships, Tess didn't think she could start over in her career again. She'd worked far too hard and for too long to sell her shop and start anew. She also wasn't certain it was wise to jump into a new relationship. Whatever she pursued with Abi, Tess wanted to make sure she didn't repeat the same mistakes. She tended to bend over backward for girlfriends who refused to meet her halfway.

Abi's not like that.

"If the situation presented itself, I'd move to Van again in a heartbeat. It's my home," Abi replied, sounding as though she'd considered her options a great deal.

Tess tilted her head in acknowledgement as two older men gave Abi's blindfold an odd look before settling on her. "Tell me about your ideal future. What's it look like for you?"

"Well ... I'd be home. Not like home-home, but living somewhere in Van. Preferably with you," Abi declared, making Tess smile, once again admiring Abi's straightforwardness.

"I like that," she admitted, pressing another kiss to Abi's back. "What else?" Peering over the railing of the bridge as they slowly crossed, Tess marveled over the mystical beauty of Twin Falls. Who would want to live anywhere *but* B.C.? She couldn't fathom leaving all this behind.

"By this time, we'd be married. Or at least engaged, and you'd have repeated the 'L' word for the thousandth time and meant them all." Abi was wistful, lost in a fantasy of what she envisioned for them. She wasn't shaking anymore, and Tess was thrilled to see the bridge's end approaching. "We would both be our own bosses, me running a lucrative marketing and design company and you with your quaint barbershop."

"You haven't even seen it yet, but I like where this is going."

"You're right, I haven't! I'm sure Instagram pictures don't do it justice. And I love the name you chose. Simple to remember."

"Ah, yes. Tess the Barber." Tess chuckled. "As original as a box of stale crackers."

Abi giggled. "I've seen worse names for small businesses. And I meant what I said before. I'd love to see about getting you set up with a website or on TikTok something. Social media can often help get your name out there."

Her support was incredibly touching, and Tess immediately felt guilty for even thinking Abi could turn out like Vicki or Chantelle. She'd always been one to wear her heart on her sleeve. She'd never hidden the fact that she was Tess's biggest cheerleader. Emotion clogged her throat. "I wish you would. I'm terrible with all that crap," she managed thickly. When they reached the end of the bridge, Tess's relief was paramount. "We made it, Abi. Watch your step," she announced, helping Abi over the threshold once again.

"Solid ground feels amazing!" Abi helped Tess remove the eye covering, and then she was throwing her arms around Tess for a bruising kiss. She pulled away to look at Tess, lovingly taking her in for a moment. Her eyes narrowed as she noticed the unshed tears, but something on Tess's face must have halted the question pursed on Abi's lips, because she closed them. She squeezed Tess's hand. "Thank you. I fully plan to claim my reward tonight, so leave your door unlocked."

Another slow grin worked its way onto Tess's face. The tightness in her chest slowly eased off, and before she knew it, she was laughing. "Yes, ma'am."

Chapter Seventeen

Abi

THE GROUP REACHED THE lake by one pm, carefully walking down the narrow slope to reach the water. The scenery was like nothing Abi had seen before, utterly majestic in its vibrance. The green of the trees and bushes reminded her of Katniss's secret hunting grounds in *The Hunger Games*. She had heard the waterfall while on the suspension bridge, listening to the satisfying sound of the water spilling down the rocks to the swimming hole below, but with the blindfold on this was her first time seeing it. Laughter and cheering rang out around them, and Abi spotted people above them taking turns jumping off the cliff into the water.

"As soon as we eat, I'm climbing that cliff," McCoy announced from up front. She was the only one carrying an oversized wilderness pack strapped to her shoulders with enough food to last all six of them at least two days. While Abi had known both Coy and Sloane were quite outdoorsy, this was her first time seeing them in action. She had to admit it was equal amounts of impressive, adorable, and annoying. All morning, Coy had answers for just about *everything*. And when Krystal slipped and cut her leg, it wasn't nurse Taunya who whipped out a Band-Aid — it was Coy.

"Do you have Subway or McDonald's hidden somewhere in that backpack? Yes, please."

"Very funny, *Abigail*," Coy hollered back with extra emphasis on her name. "You guys laugh, but I can bet I'm the only one who thought to bring lunch."

Tess let out a snort from behind Abi seconds before Sloane threw in, "We were in charge of the picnic, dumbass."

"Exactly my point," McCoy drawled as they reached the clearing. She headed for the first set of vacant boulders closest to them and wriggled out of her backpack. "*We* were in charge of food, yet *I* did everything."

"That's it, I'm moving home," Abi gushed, eyes widening as she took in the swimming hole for the first time. It was all lush greenery of moss and ferns and jagged boulders etched into the landscape. The calm of the lake and the fresh spring smell in the air was serene, and the sound of the waterfall only added to the effect. With the transparent blue-green water, it was as close to a tropical paradise as one could find, and the fact that Tess had planned *this* for an activity? Lounging about this hidden oasis for the afternoon? She definitely deserved a kiss.

"You keep saying that like you're waiting for someone to stop you." Taunya grabbed Abi around the waist, spinning her around so they were facing each other. Taunya's wide grin mirrored her own, and for a moment it was as if they were kids again. They knew what the other was thinking, and when Taunya darted to the boulder where Coy was, Abi knew they were on the same page.

"Food. Food first. Awe, c'mon!" McCoy complained as Abi and Taunya started stripping off their clothes. The light rain hadn't let up all day, but nothing would ruin this day for them.

"Lunch can wait! This girl cannot!" Taunya piled her clothes on a wide patch of rock and headed for the water, calling over her shoulder. "Sloane and Krystal, get your sexy asses in here!"

"Race you!" Sloane said, laughing as Krystal, not at all fazed, took a much slower approach to undressing.

"Am I not invited?" Tess muttered a few feet away.

Abi was just taking her pants off to stack on her sneakers and wet tank top when she glanced over at her. "Sweet baby Jesus," Abi exhaled, and her mouth went dry as she took Tess in. Her gaze traveled her body leisurely, appreciating the lean muscle of her bare legs and arms and the slight pooch of her stomach. A tattoo she hadn't seen before adorned her upper left thigh, directly below her black swim shorts. She wore a simple, no fuss, matching black sport bikini top, but Abi hadn't seen a woman look so naturally beautiful. Her shoulder-length ash-blonde hair was down, and the way she stared at Abi...

McCoy sidled up beside her, nudging Abi in the side. "You and Tess trying to keep things low-key?" she wondered, a snort of laughter escaping as she added, "'Cause your jaw legit hit the ground a few secs ago. And the way she's checking you out? I dunno, Abs."

"Don't know," Abi repeated blankly. She blinked, eyeing Coy. "Don't know what?"

"Abi, c'mon in!" Taunya called out.

"Maybe it's 'cause I know you've already hooked up," McCoy began, reaching for the hem of her long sleeve. She pulled the camo top over her head, exposing a tattoo sleeve and a half on her muscular arms. The motion ruffled her topknot hairstyle, but she didn't make a move to fix it. She was grinning like a Cheshire cat as she winked at Abi. "But it *looks* like you're banging each other."

Tess stepped up to them, a slight blush reddening her cheeks as she tried not to look directly at Abi. "Abi, you l–look..." She trailed off.

McCoy groaned. "This is painful to watch. Jesus, Tess, just tell Abi how gorgeous you think she is!"

Abi and Tess fell into step behind Coy, who was moving precariously onto the slippery stones toward the shallow water. The lake was cool and clear right to the bottom. Abi found it hard to believe she'd lived in Vancouver most of her life and never come to Lynn Canyon with her family.

"Took you long enough," Taunya remarked. She was treading water several feet away, a short distance from Sloane and Krystal, who were splashing one another.

Tess grabbed Abi's hand when she started to slip. "The surface drops off pretty quick, so just be careful."

Abi flashed her a grateful smile, not missing out on Tess's protective streak. It was something she could certainly get used to. "Jump together?"

"Yep."

Just when they were about to leap, McCoy appeared in behind and tackled them into the water. Abi's shriek drowned out Tess's seconds before submersion, and for several seconds the surprising coldness of the water assaulted her senses. When they resurfaced, Tess still held her hand. She grinned sheepishly and let go, swimming a few lengths away.

"Who's climbing to the top with me?"

"I'm sure Frankie would love to top you," Sloane answered casually, not quite hiding a smirk.

"What top? To that cliff?" Krystal asked Coy, and pointed to a high drop-off point where a few other people were getting ready to jump. She shook her head incredulously. "I wanna live a long life, my friend."

Sloane glanced sideways at her twin with a shrug. "It's a hard pass for me, too, Coy. Sorry."

"You used to do it!" Exasperated, McCoy glanced around the group, her eyes landing on Tess. When Tess shook her head, Coy threw up her hands. "Seriously? You too?"

"I don't mind heights, but cliff jumping is a different bag, Mc-Coy," Tess explained, her gaze landing briefly on Abi.

Abi ignored her body's response to her and shook her head at her friend. "Don't even look my way, playgirl. I barely survived the suspension bridge."

"I'll jump," Taunya declared, her determined gaze daring anyone to argue. Her jaw was set in a hard line, like she'd taken the last few minutes to think long and hard about it. If that was the case, Abi knew there would be no stopping her now.

She frowned. "Tauni, don't feel like —"

"It can't be that bad, right, Coy?" Taunya continued, splashing McCoy. Her laugh sounded shaky, but she was smirking. "Can't be worse than the time we bungee-jumped."

"You're both adrenaline junkies," Krystal called out as they watched Taunya and McCoy climb out of the water.

Taunya sent them a thumbs-up, looking giddy now as she followed behind McCoy.

"Wanna swim for a bit?" Abi suggested, pushing forward into a front crawl. She swam four or five strokes before turning around. Tess caught her eye, and Abi quickly swam in her direction again.

"Hey," Tess greeted her, that sexy crooked grin appearing as Abi swam around her.

"It's too bad we didn't think to bring a ball," Sloane said, swimming with Krystal a few feet away.

"That would've been fun," Abi agreed, stopping to tread water in front of Tess. They were close, almost touching, but still not enough for Abi's liking. She could see the faded scar above one finely shaped dark eyebrow, the desire in Tess's brown eyes, the way her thin top lip twitched under Abi's scrutiny. Her gaze dropped lower, taking in Tess's shoulders before slipping to her cleavage below the clear lake water.

"I really wanna kiss you right now." The huskiness in Tess's voice had Abi raising her face to meet hers once more. After a week of close proximity and years of pining, she wanted to do a hell of a lot more to Tess than kiss. Abi wanted to be all over Tess, her lips and fingers and tongue finally exploring in all the ways she never had before. Tonight couldn't come soon enough.

"What's stopping you?"

Tess's lips parted in surprise, and Abi giggled as she bobbed her head around in search of their friends. "Just kiss me, beautiful." She snaked an arm around Tess's shoulders, pulling her closer until their bodies were as flush as possible while treading water. "Much better," she murmured, a hair's breadth away from Tess's lips. Tess was the one to seal the gap between them, a throaty noise escaping her as she hungrily captured Abi's mouth in hers. Abi sighed, closing her eyes as she melted against Tess, momentarily forgetting the need to kick her legs. Tess held her up, deepening the kiss, one hand clasping the back of Abi's head and the other with a firm grip on Abi's ass.

Abi heard the blood rushing to her ears, and the sensation of Tess's silken tongue exploring her mouth as she took control of their kiss made her dizzy. Here they were, openly making out with each other. God, how long had Abi dreamed of this? *Yearned* for this?

The entire day so far seemed monumental somehow that Tess would be so openly affectionate with her.

"Nice to know you two aren't camera-shy." The smugness in Sloane's voice was as effective as a cold shower. Abi felt the immediate change in Tess seconds before she broke away.

Her cheeks had a gorgeous rosy tint to them as she scowled in Sloane's direction. Sure enough, Abi noticed Sloane's camera still hooked around her ear. "You'll delete that, right?"

"Maybe, maybe not." Sloane wiggled her eyebrows, her cheeky grin broader than Abi had ever seen it.

"If you don't, and it goes viral on YouTube or whatever, you owe Tess every cent you might profit." Abi reached for Tess's hand, observing how the other woman immediately softened. She stared pointedly at Coy's twin. Moments like this, Sloane and Coy weren't much different.

"I don't think going viral is Tess's biggest hang-up, but I'm invested in this conversation. So please, continue." Krystal laughed.

"God, here they go," Tess muttered, pulling everyone's focus away from Sloane and pointing to the cliff behind Abi. Abi turned to see Taunya and McCoy in the distance, both peering over the steep embankment to the water below.

Sloane cupped her hands over her mouth, shouting, "*Whoop, whoop*! You got this!"

"Go, Tauni!" Abi cheered, Tess chiming in as well when she called out a second time.

Krystal was the only one with a hand over her eyes as she tried not to look. They kept cheering their friends on, watching as they backed up and disappeared. Abi held her breath as, moments later, they hurtled toward the edge, screaming as they jumped off.

Sloane laughed, letting out another whoop. "I should've gone. The anticipation is worse than the drop. The footage would have been epic, too."

McCoy resurfaced first, boasting in a way only Coy could, and Abi exhaled loudly. Her heart was pounding erratically, and she realized she had Tess's hand in a death grip. She instantly released it, giving Tess an apologetic look. "Sorry."

"Something's wrong with Taunya. Fuck, McCoy!" Tess screamed, taking off after them.

Abi saw it too. Taunya was above water and moving but wasn't at all coordinated. It looked as if she was struggling to remain conscious. "Coy, help her!"

They watched as Tess swam toward her sister, pumping her arms and legs as fast as she could. Coy reached Taunya first, wrapping an arm across her torso. Abi was once again holding her breath.

CHAPTER EIGHTEEN

Tess

"SHIT, I THINK IT'S broken. Does it look broken to you? Tessa?"

Tess took a deep breath, unable to stop her eyes from rolling as she drove them to the hospital. She peered into the rear-view at her sister sprawled out in the back seat. Taunya's head was resting on the windowpane, her mouth set in a grimace, and her eyes were closed. The gash on her face from the fall was temporarily glued shut and covered with gauze — all from McCoy's first-aid kit. Abi had helped dress Taunya in the clothes she'd worn earlier, and with Taunya's direction, McCoy had done a stellar job securing Taunya's ankle with a medical wrap. Out of everyone in the bridal party, it hadn't come as a surprise that McCoy's take-charge attitude would swoop in and save the day. She'd helped Taunya out of the lake and carried her over the treacherous rocks before running to get her hiking pack. Tess hadn't realized how strong McCoy was until she was piggybacking Taunya the entire way back to the car. A simple thank-you seemed inadequate after a two-kilometer trek back. Tess would have to drop over at some point with a case of beer or offer a free haircut or something.

"I dunno, Tauni. I can't see much with the wrap in the way, but it was already swelling. You're the nurse. Can't you tell if it's broken?" Tess let out an uneasy laugh, deciding it was best not to bring up the time Taunya broke her leg. Wouldn't the pain be similar if her ankle was broken? Taunya was acting like the same, melodramatic younger sister Tess had had to calm down her entire life.

"I should be able to, yes, but I can't think straight."

Tess winced. "Sorry." She shifted her gaze back to the road, feeling her own anxiety prickling the edge of her chest and pinching at her stomach. She hadn't fully recovered from the scare earlier. She hadn't swum that fast since her last swimming test eons ago.

By the time they'd reached the emergency room and Taunya was registered to see a doctor, she was fighting back tears and updating her status on social media. Tess was raiding the vending machine for something to aid in her raging migraine. She'd already slipped back out to the car for the travel-size Ibuprofen Taunya kept in her glove compartment, but it was only diminishing the effects a little. The fluorescent lights were too bright, the waiting room too busy and loud for Tess. Her nausea lingered like a bad cold, and the sound of her sister's voice was quickly becoming needle pinpricks to her brain.

"This better do the trick," she muttered, squinting as she selected a few packages of almonds. She paid and watched them drop down. Like any good big sister would do, she also bought a Snickers bar for Taunya. Tess was sick and hungry, and it was almost tragic they never got to enjoy the effort of McCoy's picnic lunch. Hopefully it was something the mechanic could take for lunch over the work week.

"You're wearing sunglasses. Inside." Taunya pouted, taking the offered chocolate bar from Tess.

Tess mumbled in agreement, all out of talk until food was consumed. Afterward, maybe the pounding in her head would ease off and she could go back to being Taunya's lean-to. She was sitting in a wheelchair, looking the worse for wear. Her black hair was tangled and loose, and bits of dried blood had crusted around the gauze on her cheek. No one knew for certain how it happened, but Taunya claimed she'd rolled her ankle seconds before the jump. It must have altered the fall, landing her in a shallower body of water than McCoy. She'd scraped her face on a branch or rock and was lucky the fall didn't kill her. While hundreds of people went ahead and did it, cliff jumping claimed a few lives a year at Twin Falls.

"I'm sorry you had to leave your bike. Told you driving with me and Abi this morning was a better idea."

"I'll get it later."

McCoy had offered to drive Tess's bike back to Kitsilano, but she wasn't as comfortable on a motorcycle and didn't have a license. Apprehension of someone crashing her baby or McCoy killing herself on it had Tess politely declining.

"Well, thanks for coming with me, Tessa."

Tess straightened up in the hard plastic hospital chair, greeting the pressing fatigue in her sister's brown eyes. Eyes so like Tess's and yet their personalities couldn't be more different. She watched Taunya take delicate bites of her bar, waiting to see if she had more to say. Tess dumped another handful of almonds into her mouth, sighing between chews and wishing she'd bought a drink to go with it.

"Of course, Tauni," she murmured after swallowing. Her hand found the back of her head, and she absently kneaded her fingers into her scalp. "Did you let Derek know you're here?" Tess had sent a group message to their parents letting them know what happened but not to worry.

"Yeah. I had to convince him I was fine with you here and to stand down. He's worried. He didn't think I'd jump, even though he and Matt have." Taunya's smile was pinched, the discomfort from her ankle radiating off her.

"I didn't think you would either. Cliff jumping is different from skydiving or bungee jumping. You're not even a strong swimmer."

"Coy said it was safe."

Tess rolled her eyes and instantly regretted the movement when those invisible needles stabbed her with the effort. "Coy is a contradiction. She'd say anything was safe so long as she brought along her emergency pack."

"You barely know her."

"I know enough." Tess sighed, taking out her cell phone. There were three new messages from her mom, Stacey, and Abi, all wondering how Taunya was doing. "Stop ignoring Mom and text her back," she told Taunya after reading the text.

"All she'll do is rip me a new one for being so stupid. I hate how overprotective they are," Taunya grumbled. Tess glanced from her phone to see her folding her arms across her chest.

"You're almost twenty-five, living life. You'll figure out what's stupid or smart along the way. They know that." Tess rubbed her eyes. She needed a little lie-down or a cold cloth. She looked over to the nurses' station, wondering if she'd be able to track someone down who would give her a cool compress.

Another message came through, this time from ... Vicki? Tess frowned, wondering what her ex could want. Perhaps Tess had left something at her apartment and she wanted it picked up. Or what if she was reaching out with a desire to reconcile things between them? Tess's frown shifted to a pained grimace with that thought. Getting back together with Vicki was the last thing on her mind lately. Her thumb hovered over the unread message, and after a moment she sighed, curiosity getting the better of her. She opened the SMS thread.

Vicki – 2:33PM

> Call me, Tess, please? Let's work this out. I miss and love you.

Tess stumbled over the tail end of the message. There was that word again, but seeing and hearing Vicki tell Tess she loved her didn't feel quite right. Not like when Abi had said the same words, and they certainly didn't affect Tess in the same deep, resounding way. She pondered the reasons, wondering how she could feel more connected to Abi after such a short time in proximity to one another. Or had their connection stemmed from long ago, the night of Abi's going-away party?

"Mhmm, maybe." Taunya let out a strained chuckle, reaching over to push at Tess's shoulder. "I saw you and Abi kissing right before the jump."

Tess stilled, a handful of almonds frozen halfway to her mouth. She blinked, slowly, thoughts of Vicki fleeing as she stared wild-eyed at her sister in what must have been a deer-in-headlights expression. A slight quiver began in the pit of her stomach. Faint recollections of the last time they'd discussed Abi in detail rushed through Tess's frazzled mind. She felt her fingers reach for her rubber band, only to remember she'd taken it off at the lake.

"You should see your face right now." Taunya smirked, her audacity in teasing Tess knowing no bounds. Tess caught the mischievous gleam in her eyes. "I already apologized to Abi over what happened, but since you're trying to hide it from me, I take it she didn't talk to you?"

Tess's face felt tight. In fact, her entire body felt tight, and she narrowed her eyes suspiciously at her sister. "I don't understand."

Her gaze dropped down to where Taunya's hands were clasped together. Nothing about her nonverbal signs indicated her previous hostility toward Abi and Tess as an item, and when she finally spoke, Tess couldn't believe it. "I'm not the same person as four years ago, and I'm sorry I threw a wedge between you and Abi. I had no right, and ... to be honest, it's been super adorable watching you skirt around her this week. She really loves you, you know."

Tess averted her gaze, staring straight ahead as Taunya's words sank in. Her heart clamored in her chest at what this might mean. She popped an almond in her mouth, chewing slowly, aware of the increasing tightness in her chest. "It might be the migraine affecting my processing, but... Are you giving us your blessing?"

Taunya's laugh was loud and boisterous, and it had Tess wincing, "You don't need it, but sure. I love you both, and just want you to be happy."

For the first time since they'd arrived at the hospital, Tess grinned. And then she laughed too, which caused her to impulsively drop the last few almonds and clutch her pounding head. "Oww," she groaned, but not even a migraine could stop her beaming smile.

CHAPTER NINETEEN

Abi

ABI'S EYES DRIFTED CLOSED, her hand stilling on the door handle to Tess's place late that night. The haunting voice coming from inside the small building as Tess sang resonated intimately with her. For a moment, she just stood there, savoring the private moment, relishing those parts of Tess she was so often too shy to show off. Long-ago memories of standing outside Tess's bedroom door the night of the party crept over Abi, and for the first time she questioned if she was making the right choice.

Showing up out of the blue like this hadn't worked out for her the first time. What made tonight any different? A younger, equally vulnerable Tess had used Abi as a rebound and left her crying not long after. She'd always meant more to Abi than a casual fling, and now they both had too much to lose. Tess was just coming out of yet another failed relationship; who was to say she wouldn't treat Abi the same way as before?

She took a deep breath, letting it out slowly, before checking Tess's last text message on her phone.

Tess – 10:28PM

Door's unlocked if you're still awake.

Abi bit her lip. Tess had *hours* to back out of their promises tonight. She knew from Taunya that they'd finally talked in length, so Abi had to believe Tess genuinely wanted this too.

Standing a little straighter, she knocked on the door to the annex twice. When Tess didn't stop playing, Abi slowly pushed the door open. Tess was sitting cross-legged on the floor, her guitar perched on her lap as she effortlessly strummed a classic Dolly Parton song. Not wanting to disturb her, Abi quietly clicked the door shut and padded over to sit beside her.

"Abi. You came." Astonishment colored Tess's words, and she immediately paused in her playing. Her crooked smile was genuine, if not a bit shy as her eyes met Abi's.

"Sorry I'm late. Fell asleep watching *The Princess Diaries* with Tauni." Abi's gaze trailed over Tess, watching as she stood up and returned the guitar to its clip on the wall.

"Oh? How was it?"

"Funny, angsty, but a little too hetero for my mood tonight." Abi was blabbering. She *never* got anxious around Tess. Getting to her feet as well, she clenched her hands together, uncertainty casting an uncomfortable ambiance in the room. Her gaze followed Tess as she tidied up loose sheet music off the floor. Her ash-blonde locks were damp and loose, almost reaching her shoulders. Like Abi, she wore a tank top, but hers was a plain black one, unlike Abi's kitten pattern pajama set. Her boy shorts were also black, showcasing a slender pair of smooth, tanned legs. Though they'd spent a good chunk of time in bikinis while at Twin Falls, seeing Tess in her panties felt a lot more intimate. Abi cleared her throat. "Um, how are you? You weren't staying up just for me, were you? I'd feel even worse than I already do."

"Why?" Tess paused in her task, glancing over in confusion. "You don't think you're worth waiting up for?"

"No, that's not it." Abi's heartbeat quickened as Tess crossed the small space toward her. "I'd feel bad if you thought I stood you up."

Tess reached her side, and her movements were jerky as she took Abi's hands. She leaned in close, and Abi could feel the slight quiver of her lip as she scraped her teeth lightly over Abi's earlobe. It was obvious she was trying hard to be confident in the moment, and that made Abi love her all the more. "You're here now." The sensuality in Tess's voice caught and held Abi's attention.

Don't make the same mistake, don't...

"We don't have to have sex," she blurted, backing away slightly, catching Tess's eyes. Surprise and bafflement shone on Tess's face, but she remained quiet. Abi swallowed again, feeling like the world's biggest idiot. She tore her gaze away, adding, "If you don't want to. I'd be just as happy to cuddle if you'd prefer not to rush. We could go on dates first. Seriously, just being with you tonight is enough for me."

"Is that what you want, Abi?"

Biting her lip, Abi expelled a trembling breath. It was difficult to meet her gaze. "I just know I don't want to screw this up. Again. Last time, I—"

A soft chuckle came from Tess. "You're so sweet. Thoughtful. And so stunning." Strong fingers gripped Abi's jaw, gently guiding her face back to Tess's. A hooded pair of magnetic brown eyes pulled Abi in, her breath catching as the night's intent became clear.

"It was me," Tess continued, her voice low and soft. She traced Abi's hairline first, slowly moving downward to explore the contours of her nose, her cheekbones. Tess's touch was so light, hardly a whisper against Abi's skin, and yet shivers raced through her at the contact.

Abi's eyes drifted closed. Her lips parted, about to ask Tess what she meant, but those same fingers ghosted over her mouth. A contented sigh left her as Tess traced the outline of Abi's top lip first before sliding down to her bottom. She jolted at Tess's voice so close to her ear. "You could never screw this up. I wasn't ready for you before. For the connection I feel when I'm with you ... how *strong* these emotions are."

Tess's tongue traced the shell of Abi's ear at the same time as her index finger dipped into Abi's open mouth. Abi moaned softly, her stomach tightening as arousal pooled between her legs. She opened her eyes, quickly focusing on Tess and hyper aware of the finger exploring her mouth. Flicking her tongue, Abi stroked Tess's finger before closing her lips over and giving it a suck. A guttural sound came somewhere deep within Tess, her eyes turning almost black as she watched Abi.

Abi loved witnessing the hunger taking Tess over, the worries that so often controlled her now disappeared. It was the most beautiful thing Abi had ever seen, and they weren't even naked yet. Her smile for Tess was unrepentant, her teeth scraping the skin on Tess's finger as she pulled back. The shudder passing through Tess was intoxicating. Abi reached for her, sinking her hand into Tess's messy locks and pulling her in for a deep kiss.

There was no more hesitancy in their embrace as their lips came together, fusing with so much passion and desire, Abi was lightheaded from it. Tess nibbled her bottom lip, nipping and then stroking the bite with a soft swipe of her tongue. Abi whimpered, feeling her nipples harden as their kiss deepened. She slid her hands over Tess's smooth shoulders and back as Tess's tongue explored her mouth exactly how her fingers had done earlier. She reached Tess's waist, slipping her fingers under the tank to feel the smooth skin beneath.

I'm the luckiest woman right now.

Abi knew it, but after seeing Tess's need for her, merely touching wasn't enough. Tonight, Abi wanted to get drunk off Tess. She wanted to bury her face between Tess's thighs and drown in her succulent juices until Tess was screaming out her name. With her lips still on Tess's, Abi slowly walked them the few feet to the bed, only stopping when she felt Tess's legs connect with the mattress. Abi broke the kiss, feeding off Tess's glazed eyes. Certain her own eyes sparkled, she flashed Tess a seductive smile. "Arms up, beautiful."

The tank top came off, and then they were kissing again, Abi's hands skimming over the satin skin of Tess's back. She gripped Tess's shoulders, leaving her lips and kissing her way down Tess's throat. "You really are something," she murmured, her hands gliding sensuously over Tess's breasts. She gave them a light squeeze, relishing all of Tess's soft noises, before bending to give one of her pebbled nipples a long, slow lick. A shaky breath left Tess, their gazes colliding as Abi sucked on her breast.

"Abigail."

Tess hissed, her back arching in response to Abi's touch, and her fingers sank into Abi's hair, holding her head in place. She grinned at the deliberate way Tess said her name. "Mmm," she hummed, keeping her eyes locked on Tess as she switched to the other breast.

Tess peered down at her with eyes filled with awe, hunger, and something Abi couldn't recognize. She cupped Abi's cheek in her palm, choking, "I've never felt ... you make me—"

"I know." Abi placed a soft kiss on Tess's nipple before straightening and capturing her lips again. "I feel it too," she admitted between kisses, her voice so incredibly husky, she almost didn't recognize it. Her body quaked as she reached for her own tank top, stripping the material away, and before it even left her fingertips, her mouth was on Tess's again. Abi ravaged her with kisses, their tongues sliding in a sinuous dance as their hands explored one another. She shuddered as Tess's nails scraped lightly along her back. When Tess cupped Abi's breasts, she broke the kiss, uttering low words of appreciation.

"So beautiful. You're stunning, Abi." Tess's cheeks flared hot, but she didn't shy away as she lifted her gaze to hers. Abi smiled, her pulse picking up at the compliment. Instead of replying, she pushed Tess gently down onto the bed and straddled her, burying her face in the crook of Tess's neck.

"I love you," Abi crooned, swiping her tongue out to lick the shell of Tess's ear and smirking when she felt her tremble underneath her. With one hand supporting her weight, Abi used the other to glide over Tess's skin as she continued to place deliberate kisses and nips along her throat and shoulders. Her fingers found Tess's nipple again, rolling the tight bud between her fingers before giving it a light twist. Tess gasped in response, her nails digging into Abi's arms, but she seemed content to let Abi take control for once.

Her lips reached Tess's breasts once more, latching onto the neglected nipple while her fingers played with the other. She loved listening to the sounds of pleasure coming from Tess, loved the glazed expression in her eyes as she gazed down at Abi from where her head rested on the pillows. Abi had been born for this, born for no other reason than to bring Tess to ecstasy.

"Oh, God," Tess whimpered, squirming as Abi's lips popped off her breast. Her nipple was wet from Abi's tongue, tightening even more as the cool air reached it, and the delicious sight had Abi's thighs squeezing together to stave off her own desire. She was dizzy with it, torn between wanting to go slow and wanting to tear her shorts off and sit on Tess's face. She kissed her way down Tess's abdomen, licking around her navel before reaching for her underwear. Abi's fingers shook as she tucked them into the waistband of Tess's boy shorts, pausing to admire the new artwork on Tess's upper thigh. She bent her head, pressing a lingering kiss over the sunflower.

"A–are you sure?" The strain in Tess's voice was palpable, the turned-on yet insecure question lifting Abi's eyes to greet hers. She nodded, knowing Tess likely meant going down on her, since Abi never had before. It had been one of those things she'd kicked herself over the last few years, since Tess had cut the night short their first time together.

"So sure." She smiled, dropping her head to kiss the sensitive skin between Tess's navel and mons. Her fingers found purchase against the panties' hemline, where they hovered in temporary limbo. Her nose grazed the apex of Tess's thighs, and she breathed in Tess's arousal deeply. A slight tremor washed over Abi as just the scent of Tess made her feel tipsy. Before she knew it, she was darting her tongue out to taste her through the material.

"Fuck," Tess cried, her thighs quivering with need. Abi's clit throbbed so much, she worried she'd come just from getting this far. As much as she wanted to rush things, Tess's pleasure came first tonight. Abi wanted to see how far she could wind Tess up before she came undone.

Tugging the material slowly down Tess's legs, she planted open-mouthed kisses on any newly exposed skin. While her lips discovered each dip and freckle, Abi's fingers followed the path from behind. She skimmed over the luscious curves of Tess's backside before raking her nails across the back of her thighs. The boy shorts landed on the floor, and Abi didn't waste time spreading Tess's thighs apart to see the slick arousal coating her lips. "You're so fucking sexy, Tess," she declared, lying between Tess's legs and pulling her hips closer. When her exposed pussy was within eating range, Abi did just that, spreading Tess's lips with her fingers and burying her mouth between the silky folds like a woman starved. She breathed her in, unable to get enough, already addicted to Tess's sweet, musky scent. Tess's throaty curses resounded throughout the room as Abi tasted her, swirling and flicking her tongue over her clit before sucking it into her mouth. Low mewls escaped Tess, her eyes squeezed shut and her hips rising off the mattress like she was trying to ride Abi's face. Her chest and throat were flushed, evidence of how turned-on she was, and she was fisting handfuls of her pillow. The moment was everything Abi had fantasized about, but still, she wasn't close enough.

She pulled away from Tess long enough to lift Tess's leg over her shoulder for better access. Then she parted Tess's folds and dove back in, burying her face in Tess's pussy. She took her time bringing Tess to pleasure. Exploring, teasing, prodding her sensitive sex. Abi flattened her tongue, stroking Tess's slit from the bottom to the top before tormenting her clit once more. Tess's ragged pleas were the sweetest sounds Abi had ever heard.

"*Please* ... Abi, fuck me."

Abi smiled, raking her teeth over Tess's clit and easing two fingers inside her. They both moaned, and a tiny voice in the back of Abi's mind screamed, *finally*! Now that she had Tess, she wouldn't dare let her slip away again.

Tess's fingers tangled in Abi's hair now, clutching at strands and not afraid to guide Abi's face closer. Abi fucked Tess slowly, building the friction, curving her fingers to hit Tess's g-spot. The closer Tess came to release, the more she increased the pace, adding a third finger while still licking and sucking Tess's swollen clit. Seconds later, Tess clamped around Abi's fingers, trapping them as her body spasmed. Tess cried out as she climaxed, her juices drenching Abi's fingers and lips.

Abi continued to pump her fingers, her tongue lapping up Tess's climax as she wrung out the last of her orgasm. Tess visibly shook when Abi finally pulled away, and she gently retracted Tess's leg from her shoulder to set it back down. They were both panting, and as Abi crawled up Tess, she frowned at the lone tear leaking from her lover's closed eye.

"You okay, babe?" Abi asked quietly, easing Tess into her arms. She sprinkled light kisses over her damp forehead and hair, hearing the gulp of Tess's swallow.

She nodded, a wobbly smile forming as she met Abi's worried gaze. "That was ... sheesh, I have no words."

Abi rested her forehead against Tess's, her hand closing loosely over Tess's throat as she chuckled. "Good, I hope, because I'm pretty sure you've ruined me for anyone else." *Fuck, isn't that the truth.*

Tess's laugh was low and raspy, and regardless of the tears still seeping out, she leaned into Abi and captured her lips in a long kiss. As her tongue teased Abi's, occasionally dipping from her mouth to stroke or nibble her lips, Tess traced a path down Abi's body, lighting a fire low in Abi's belly. Her breath hitched the moment Tess bypassed her sleep shorts to push aside her panties. At the first graze of Tess's fingers on her clit, a long moan left Abi. She was drenched and could already feel her climax rising to the surface once more. It wouldn't take Tess much to send her crashing over the edge.

"Oh, fuck, *yes*." Abi ground down on Tess's hand, her back arching as those talented fingers slipped deep inside her. Arousal flushed her cheeks, her wide eyes connected with Tess's smug expression. She kissed Tess, hard this time, reaching for her free hand and guiding it to her breast. "Faster, baby. Yes, that's it," she panted once Tess's fingers picked up the pace. She toyed with her other breast, her hand squeezing the firm mound before rubbing the nipple between her fingers.

Tess kissed Abi's throat, scraping her teeth over Abi's shoulder before replacing her hand with her mouth. All it took was one long lick of Tess's tongue across her nipple before Abi was coming undone, going rigid in Tess's arms seconds before she was screaming out her pleasure in the quiet room.

When Abi woke hours later, the first thing that registered in her sleep haze was the cozy, sensuous naked body pressing into hers. Not bothering to open her eyes, she smiled, snuggling farther into Tess's arms. Soft snores that sounded more like the purrs from a kitten tickled Abi's neck each time Tess exhaled, quickly lulling her back to sleep.

A desperate urge to pee had Abi stirring sometime later. She opened her eyes to find a tattooed arm resting heavily on her bladder and Tess's hand tucked under her side. She lay still for as long as her body allowed, wanting to savor the moment, to savor Tess. They fit together like Abi always knew they would. A jigsaw puzzle finally completed. Their legs were tangled like a pretzel, which was cute, except that Abi was moments away from utter humiliation.

She carefully dislodged her legs first and then lifted Tess's arm off. Once she'd eased out of bed, she tiptoed to the bathroom, eager to do her business and get back to Tess. Abi glanced around the tiny bathroom. Although the space was scarcely sufficient for one person, Tess had figured out a way to make the décor seem quaint rather than cluttered. After she'd washed her hands, Abi rinsed her face and used one of Tess's hairbrushes to clear out the knots.

"Tessa Moore, you sexy lover. You're seriously lacking in the makeup department," she muttered, riffling through the cosmetic bag on the back of the toilet. She gave up after a minute, deciding there was at least an eighty-five percent chance Tess wouldn't notice or care about any of Abi's blemishes.

She gargled with rinse before turning off the light and heading back to bed. Still sound asleep, Tess's blonde hair obscured part of her face as she lay on her stomach with both arms bunched under her pillow. Abi couldn't help but smile at the sight, her eyes softening as she took in Tess. Like clockwork, the pulse in her throat quickened, and her heart got all fluttery. All these years later, and Abi still swooned, except now Tess was beginning to feel the same. Through the night, Tess had given Abi more than just her body. In that subdued, serene way of hers, she'd opened herself up in ways not many people got to witness. Whether or not Tess knew or even understood, she had shown Abi glimpses of her heart and soul.

Abi crawled under the covers, scooting as close to Tess as possible. She pressed a lingering kiss to Tess's bare shoulder, breathing her in. "Good morning."

Tess groaned softly, shifting onto her side. The bedsheets slipped off, flashing a gorgeous pair of breasts, her nakedness making Abi's mouth go dry. Tess cracked an eye open, a sleepy grin appearing as she gazed at Abi. "C'mere," she croaked, snagging an arm out to tug Abi on top of her.

"Eh — morning breath, sorry," Tess mumbled as Abi kissed her. She made a lame attempt to push Abi away, but Abi slid her hand to the back of her neck, tugging her forward once more.

"I love you, morning breath and all." Abi captured Tess's lips again.

"Mhmm, you're so brave." Tess smiled between kisses. She stilled in Abi's arms, darting a glance over her shoulder at the analogue clock on the wall. "Shit! I've gotta open the shop today!"

"You are? It's Saturday, and the bachelorette party is tonight." Abi frowned, checking the clock as well. It was already after eight. She slid off Tess, silently watching her lover scramble out of bed.

"Yes, and I have a few clients booked." Tess leaned over to land another kiss on Abi, whispering against her lips, "Thank you for last night. I'm sorry to have to rush out."

"Not a problem." Abi watched as Tess hurried to the bathroom, the black boy shorts from the night before the lone piece of clothing covering her assets. Abi smiled, nestling back into the covers. She must have dozed off again, because the next thing she knew Taunya's distinctive ringtone was blasting through her phone.

Abi yawned, dragging herself from the bed. It took a minute to locate her cell, which had fallen off the nightstand sometime through the night. By the time she'd retrieved it from under the bed, she was breathless and still half out of it from being jarred awake. "Tauni, you better be calling to say you have a coffee made with my name on it."

Taunya's laugh was rich, working like a magic potion to Abi's fleeting crankiness. "Well yes, but also the gossip mill is off the charts here this morning. Mom and Dad know you slept at Tess's last night, and Dad saw Tess drive off an hour ago." She lowered her voice. "Between me and you, I think one of them is about to crack any minute and come knocking."

"Uh-huh, and you're not dying to know if Tess and I are an item?" Abi snickered, setting the call on speaker so she could get dressed.

"Nope, I had a feeling from the moment you two set eyes on each other again."

"Uh-huh. Who knew you could be so optimistic?"

"Har-har. See you in a minute. Love you!"

"Love you back." Hanging up, an exuberant sigh left Abi as she glanced around Tess's home. She flopped back onto the unmade bed, knowing she would tidy the small space before she headed back to the main house, but for now she just wanted a few more precious minutes by herself to reflect on the night before.

Sex with Tess had been everything she remembered and more. While they were in the early stages of their relationship, Abi knew for certain that Tess had wanted her just as much. Goosebumps broke out on her flesh just thinking of the skillful way Tess had brought her to orgasm, or how she'd held Abi in her arms afterward. Tess was almost too good to be true, and it left Abi to consider her plans for the future. She couldn't take her old job back, not if it sabotaged something more with Tess. All the freshly laid out business incentives in the world wouldn't tempt Abi the way Tess could. She would just have to explain that to Margo.

Chapter Twenty

Abi

"I can't believe we're gonna be late even after you had the day to get ready!" Tess grumbled from her bed. Abi could feel her brown eyes burning holes in the back of her head as she rummaged through the selection of clothes laid out on her open suitcase, now in Tess's bachelor pad. Maybe it was a bit forward on her part, but now that they were unofficially together, Abi had no intention of using Tess's old room any longer.

She was currently down to two of her semiformal dresses after trying on the pantsuit she'd brought and thinking it too business-style for their night out. "How about this one?" She held up the sexy black crew-neck mid-length bodycon dress she'd bought on clearance last fall. While it had a full back, the front of the dress left bits of her torso and cleavage exposed.

"Abigail."

Abi heard the muted exasperation in Tess's gentle chiding tone, like saying her full name was all she dared to do. Abi stood up and grinned, watching Tess's gaze trail up her body as she pulled the dress on. "*Tessa?*"

A controlled breath was expelled past Tess's lips as she fought an inner battle for patience. Abi loved getting a rise from her, knowing that her brattiness had a way of frustrating and turning Tess on. "It's a gorgeous dress. The other dress you have there might be too … revealing for tonight. Wouldn't want you confused with one of the dancers."

"Dancers? Where exactly are we going?" Tess had been hush-hush about details of Taunya's bachelorette party. In fact, the only thing she'd let the bridal party in on was that it wasn't a black-tie event. That did *not* narrow the night's options down any, and Abi didn't want to dress too casual. Where would they be going that included dancers? Abi bit her lip, a far-fetched idea forming. Scantily clad women on a stage, performing... She swung around to face Tess, agape. "Are we going to a strip club?"

Tess's mouth twitched in response, the only telltale sign Abi was on the right track. She left her place on the bed, coming to stand beside Abi, only to run her hand down Abi's arm. As she laced their fingers together, Abi caught a whiff of her perfume and shivered. Once again, she was thanking her lucky stars for Tess. Abi observed her now, casually dressed in a pair of slim-fitting black chino pants and meadow-green blouse with the first three buttons undone. Tess looked dashing, a light dusting of makeup on her face and her simple gold necklace nestling between the crease in her small breasts. "You okay?"

Nodding, Abi lowered her head to capture Tess's lips in hers. She tasted like mint tea and the chocolate dip donut she'd not so discreetly stuffed in her mouth when she returned from the main house. Abi pulled away, resting her forehead on Tess's. "Never better. Just wondering what I'll do if a gorgeous woman gives you a lap dance tonight."

Tess snorted a laugh, pushing Abi away. "I have no idea what you're talking about. I never said where we were going."

"I think," Abi's smile came slowly, teasingly, and she tapped her index finger against her chin, "that I'm not the jealous type. Honestly, I think I'll enjoy someone giving you a lap dance. Immensely."

Tess's blush was everything.

"I love when I'm right," Sloane stated as the bridal party stood just inside a strip club an hour later. A sole dimple appeared as she gave her twin a smug grin, holding out her hand, palm up, and wiggling her fingers. "You know what to do."

Coy narrowed her gaze at the offending hand, a heavy sigh leaving her as she pulled out her wallet. "What can I say? I didn't think the barber had it in her." They were both immaculately dressed that evening, Coy wearing a black pair of skinny jeans and a vintage off-white, men's button-up dress shirt. A pair of black suspenders and Converse sneakers completed the outfit. Like Coy, Sloane had a ring on almost every finger. She wore a pair of black leather pants and ruby red crop-top, which showed hints of her abs whenever she moved.

I should take up mountain biking. The random thought had Abi grinning, especially knowing for a fact that she never would. Voluntarily sweat and get dirty outside for hours at a time? *As if.*

"At this point, I don't know why you bet against me. You must lose four to every one you win."

Abi watched the display, the nature of their bet slowly dawning on her. She laughed, digging out her own purse and handing Sloane a five-dollar bill as well. "I'll pay up too, because up until we were getting ready, I thought we were going to a hotel."

"Right? I thought at most the barber would have sprung for a casino."

"Ah, my friends, but a casino wasn't on my bucket list," Taunya said, wobbling over to them. Even with her ankle wrapped thick with gauze and a pair of crutches, Abi had never seen her smile so wide. Her brown eyes were gleaming with excitement, and if she wasn't injured, she'd likely be rocking back and forth on her heels. She looked ten times better than she had yesterday, wearing a pair of dress capris and halter top. The stitches on her cheek weren't as noticeable as Abi thought they'd be. Taunya's ankle was bandaged, and on the opposite foot she wore a summer sandal with pretty pink toenail polish. "My sister is the best, and nobody tell me differently."

"Oh, I am in full agreement," Abi replied, just as Tess was walking back from where she had been talking to one of the club staff. Krystal was with her, smoothing out last-minute details for whatever Tess had planned for them that night. To any onlookers, Tess appeared calm and collected tonight, but Abi called her bluff the moment they'd stepped inside the club.

Tess sidled up on her right side, her fingers brushing Abi's hand as she brought them up to her face. She swiped away the perspiration dotting her forehead, announcing, "Everything's a go,"

There was a slight tremor in her voice, but when Abi opened her mouth to quietly ask Tess if she was okay, a gorgeous, half-naked woman approached their party. "Good evening, ladies, my name is Jasmine. If you'll follow me?"

Coy let out a low whistle, openly ogling Jasmine's honey-colored skin and long black hair before coming to rest on the woman's full red lips. There she gave Jasmine one of her heart-stopping smiles, the kind that made both dimples pop and her eyes sparkle. "Baby, I will follow you anywhere."

Abi rolled her eyes, slipping her hand in Tess's and squeezing. As much as she adored Coy, she was supremely glad she'd never become one of those "notches" in her headboard. Leaning close to Tess's ear, she asked, "You okay, babe?"

Abi had been to a strip club once before with her roommates in Toronto, so she felt somewhat prepared for the atmosphere. Tess, on the other hand, looked completely out of her element. Her eye kept twitching in time to the beat of the bass from the speakers, and when she'd gotten her first good look at the exotic dancer performing on the main stage, Abi was worried she'd faint. Even as they made their way upstairs, Tess paid more attention to what her feet were doing than what went on around them.

She nodded, darting an appreciative gaze in Abi's direction. She seemed to hesitate before crooking Abi closer once again. "It's too loud. And busy. Worse than I expected!"

Abi grimaced; she'd had a feeling it was something like that, but besides leaving, there wasn't much that could help Tess tonight. She'd already taken her evening meds, and Abi had helped gather last-minute bachelorette party items while Tess was at work. Instead of replying, she just squeezed Tess's hand again, not letting it go until Jasmine showed them into a private booth area.

"Holy shit, this is epic," Taunya crowed, pushing out ahead of the group. She hobbled to the leather U-shaped sofa sitting against the back wall.

"It's so big up here. And you can see the main stage!" Krystal's excitement was a lot more subdued than the rest of Abi's friends, but she looked in a hurry as she raced Sloane to the railing overlooking the club's main level. Like Abi, Krystal wore a dress, but hers was a lot more modest.

"Have a seat, get comfortable," Jasmine instructed, and Abi didn't miss how her gaze slid more than once in Coy's direction. "Lily or myself will be around to assist with anything tonight. Can I start you off with your bubbly now, or something else?"

"A bottle of Grey Goose for now, please, along with six glasses." As she spoke, Tess's hand found its way to Abi's lower back, as if the physical contact helped ground her. Just being away from the crowd on the lower level did wonders to help Tess visibly relax.

"Sure thing, cutie."

"Cutie?" Coy echoed once the group was alone. She sniffed, slumping down onto the other end of the sofa. "Surely she wasn't talking about the barber."

"Coy, don't be a dick. This whole room is filled with hot chicks, not just you," Sloane tossed back, punching her shoulder as she took a seat beside her sister.

"Yeah, but I'm the only one slaying these sexy suspenders."

Abi chuckled, taking Tess's hand and leading her to the middle of the sofa. Since the moment she'd realized she had won Tess over, there was something Abi had been eager to test out. Her gaze collided with the other woman's right before she gave her a gentle push backward into the sofa.

"Wha—" Tess's voice died off as Abi sank down on her lap, her arms quickly wrapping around Abi's waist as if they'd been there for years. Abi caught Taunya's knowing smile.

"You guys are perfect together."

Taunya's compliment had Abi breaking into a silly grin. She rested her head against Tess's shoulder, her lips grazing the warm skin along her neck as she whispered, "You hear that, babe? We're perfect." Tess swallowed, her throat bobbing up and down under Abi's lips.

"So what's the plan tonight?" McCoy interjected, sitting close enough now that Abi could see the black eyeliner darkening her green eyes. Her attention was directed to the main stage below. The redhead now gliding up and down the pole was covered in tattoos, and other than what must be seven-inch heels, she was completely nude. Bills littered the stage in front of her. "Are we just drinking and enjoying the dancers killing it on that pole? Because I'm totally okay with that."

"Tess has a few games up her sleeve," Abi supplied, reluctantly sliding off Tess's lap.

"Yeah, I planned out a truth-or-dare game before our entertainment later on," Tess supplied, looking around Abi to see her sister, and, Abi noted, purposely avoiding Coy with the answer. Abi raised an eyebrow. Maybe she was annoyed with Coy for her earlier comment.

"Sounds fun," Krystal and Sloane threw in, and Abi could have kissed them. Tess had been worrying since she'd left work that her plan for tonight would crash and burn. She'd already been beating herself up over forgetting the typical "straight woman" bachelorette party incentives. Abi was happy she'd forgotten, because the last thing she wanted to do was sip out of a penis straw. *Bleh.*

Jasmine returned with their bottle and glasses, giving the group a tantalizing view of her tattooed upper thigh as she bent over to place them on the table. "Has anyone told you in the last ten minutes how gorgeous you are?"

Abi whipped around to see McCoy now perched on the edge of her seat, her fingers loosely holding their servers. *You've got to be kidding me,* she thought with another eye roll. Coy had a one-track mind tonight.

Never mind Coy's dashing effect; Jasmine's seductive smile could melt the panties off someone's grandma, and Abi wasn't at all surprised when she wasn't the only one to groan. "In this club? Baby, I hear that every two minutes. You know, so far your charms are just average. You'll have to do better than that, darling." With that, she slipped from Coy's clutches, winked, and left their booth section.

"Fuck sakes, I'm in love." McCoy smacked a palm over her chest before slowly sliding to the floor.

"Annnnd you owe me another five bucks," Sloane declared, reaching over and giving her twin a swat to the back of the head.

"Ow!"

"Already! That's gotta be a record. You really, *really* shouldn't bet on yourself, Coy."

McCoy was rubbing her head, but she was all smiles as she pulled herself onto the sofa again. "I legit can't help myself. I might be addicted."

Taunya laughed. "Whose idea was that? Playgirl can't go to the grocery store without hooking up with someone."

"Too true. I'm my own worst enemy sometimes."

They got into the Grey Goose, divvying up the bottle into six glasses on the rocks. Their attention was split between the main stage and Tess's game, but Taunya looked happy, and that was what mattered. Jasmine came by again to check on things, paying extra attention to the twins before disappearing again. The server was either exceptional at her job, or the idea of sleeping with the twins was part of her kink. Whichever it was, McCoy was lapping it up, showering her with compliments and a tip.

"Okay, Tauni. Truth or dare?" Krystal asked, giving the two Ziploc bags in her hands a light shake. She held them out to the bride-to-be.

"Truth!" Taunya crowed, digging into one of the bags and pulling out a small piece of paper. "'Have you ever had a threesome?'" she read aloud and rolled her eyes at Tess, who threw up her hands in defense.

"Hey, I didn't know who would get that question." She chuckled.

"I actually know this," Abi admitted, sipping her drink and watching the performance going on downstairs.

"So do I!" Krystal gleefully added. "Great story, as I recall."

"The short answer is yes, once." Taunya snickered at Tess's slackened jaw. So much for Taunya telling her everything, Abi mused. "About a year into my relationship with Derek. We took a girl home from the bar. That's when I figured out dick was more my thing."

"What the hell!" McCoy exclaimed, but she didn't seem overly upset. "You promised *me* that fuck!"

"Not with my boyfriend I didn't!" Taunya roared with laughter, leaning back in her seat so far, Abi had to grab her before she fell off the sofa. "Can you imagine? You would have crushed Derek's ego."

"No way. If anything, I would've taught him a thing or two."

"You're an asshole," Sloane informed her twin, nudging her out of the way to refill her glass with ice and vodka.

"Next question!"

"Tauni, you pick who goes next," Abi reminded her. The truths had been enlightening so far. The dares were limited to their location but still hilarious. Sloane had already convinced an older gentleman to let her put lipstick on him.

"Tessa, you go. Truth or dare?"

Tess shrugged, reaching into the dare bag. Her cheeks were flushed from the alcohol. She studied the paper, her blush intensifying under the lowlights of the club. "'Text your parents and tell them you got arrested.'"

At this, Abi laughed. "Ooh, can I do it?" she asked, snatching Tess's phone from the coffee table. She punched in the code, quickly bringing up Audrey's contact info and shooting off the text.

"If anyone out of this group got arrested, it would be Taunya or McCoy," Krystal vowed, clinking her tumbler against Sloane's.

"Pretty much."

Audrey's reply came, and Abi burst out laughing as she read the message. "She said, 'You're funny, Tessa. Hope you're having fun at the party.'"

Tess snorted, ignoring everyone's giggles. "Good to know I can't count on her if the day comes."

"You're too sweet to be arrested," Abi replied, giving her a quick kiss.

"McCoy, your turn."

McCoy set her drink on the table, wiggling her fingers before dipping one hand into the truth bag. She arched an eyebrow, a slow smile crossing her features. "'Have you ever made a sex tape?'" Her eyes left the paper, grinning wider when she noticed Jasmine now in their booth. "I think I should get a second chance, since everyone knows the answer to that." Without waiting, she retrieved another question and immediately groaned. "Hell, Tess, did you come up with these? 'Have you slept with anyone in this room?' Seriously, Barber?"

Tess shrugged, glancing around at them all. "What? It's a fair question."

"Is it, though?" McCoy tilted her head, briefly studying Tess before she smirked. "The answer's no, but I'm hoping to change that by the end of the night." Her sly grin was aimed at Jasmine.

"Excuse me, ladies. I hear there's a beautiful bride-to-be in this booth?" A man's deep baritone cut through Coy and Jasmine's sexy glances, and they looked up to see a muscular guy behind Jasmine. He was exactly Taunya's type, wearing some kind of sexy black chest strap top and a matching pair of *very* short shorts. His smile was meant to have the same effect as Jasmine's, and Abi could tell it worked because Taunya squeezed her arm.

"That's me. That's so me tonight." Taunya beamed, and as the man danced closer, she looked happier than Abi had seen her the entire time she'd been home.

"I booked two, one for the rest of us," Tess whispered in Abi's ear.

As soon as the words were out, a woman sidled up beside Jasmine wearing a similar chest strap to the guy but sporting a G-string. She was the same one who had danced on stage earlier, and her ginger hair flounced about as she swayed into their booth. She'd been stunning on stage but was absolutely breathtaking up close. Abi's gaze followed the mysterious woman, wondering what she would do.

"Jaz, you wanna have some fun with these girls while Brady takes care of the bride-to-be?" she asked their server, who wasn't in matching outfits but looked every bit as capable of acting out a woman's fantasy.

"Thought you'd never ask, Lily." Jasmine was pouring shots for everyone. She handed them out before tossing hers back.

"Fuck," McCoy groaned loudly, watching in awe as Jasmine shimmied out of her thong and headed straight for her.

Abi figured Lily would dance with Brady, so when the dancer stopped in front of Tess, she wasn't sure who was more shocked.

Chapter Twenty-One

Tess

"Oh um ... h-hey." Tess sucked in a sharp breath, her hands bracing either side of her on the sofa as Lily straddled her.

"Hey back. First time here?" Lily smiled, and the lights above Tess captured the golden flecks in her hazel eyes. Yes, that's what Tess focused on. She wasn't looking anywhere else, especially not —

"Jesus. Yes, first time," Tess breathed, relaxing back more on the sofa when Lily rubbed her breasts into her face. This was by far the most erotic thing she'd ever done. Her skin was flushed all over, arousal pooled between her legs, and Abi was skimming her hand over her bare back. "You?"

"Is this my first time? No, not quite." Lily laughed softly, arching her back and letting her wild mane shimmer down as she rocked her hips against Tess's pelvis. Tess swallowed hard, her gaze dropping to watch the movement. Lily's strength and confidence in working such a beautiful body was so mesmerizing, Tess doubted she'd be able to pull away if she tried. She was merely a passenger, a voyager on the most exciting ride of her life.

Well, that's embarrassing.

"I've gotta admit…" Abi's sensual voice in her ear sent shivers down Tess's spine, and for a fraction of a second she was worried she'd spoken out loud. But Abi nipped the shell of her ear, her hand slipping into the waistband of Tess's chinos to squeeze her ass. "I am so hot for you right now."

"Y–yeah?" There was no disguising the tremble in Tess's voice. She felt parched and gratefully accepted the glass of Grey's Abi handed to her. Taking a long swig, she sighed as the wetness hit the back of her dry throat. She licked her lips, and that was when she noticed Lily reaching for the clasp on the only garment shielding her nipples from view. "W–wait!" Grabbing the dancer's wrist, Tess stopped her progression. Her eyes were wide, unable to believe what almost happened. Forcing out a laugh, Tess was all too aware of the deep blush now staining her cheeks. "Please don't take that off."

"You are too cute." Lily's laugh was barely audible, but she did as Tess requested. "How long have you two been together?" she asked, easily transferring to Abi's lap but turning around in the process. Tess let out a relieved sigh, relaxing as she watched the gorgeous dancer shake her ass in Abi's face.

"Oh … like, less than a week." Technically speaking, it was more like twenty-four hours, but it seemed wrong to have to explain their complicated situation to a stranger.

Abi caught Tess's gaze, and she grinned, turning her attention back to Lily. Her palm struck the dancer's bare ass cheek gently, and Tess's shocked gasp was louder than Lily's. *"Abigail."*

Abi only giggled, her arm snaking out to wrap around Tess's neck. She hauled her closer, her lips eagerly searching for Tess's. "Are you wet right now?" she asked, her eyes still trained on Tess as she leaned back against the sofa.

Tess floundered for a response, fidgeting restlessly in her seat. Her heart seemed to be perpetually stuck in her throat tonight, and her gaze landed on Lily as she reclined fully onto Abi. Her ass was grinding against Abi's front as she moved, her back sliding sensuously up and down against Abi's torso. Lily saw Tess staring — gawking, if she was being honest — and reached for her hand, saying, "You two look amazing together."

"Thank you." Tess cleared her throat, pulling her hand from hers and glancing around at the rest of the bridal party. Krystal and Taunya were wrapped up in Brady's attention as he danced naked for them. To her left, Tess saw a fully naked Jasmine entertaining the twins.

The bubbly that came with the custom bachelorette package was finally opened and shared around. Lily was the first to leave, still clothed and with a wad of twenty-dollar bills, blowing Abi and Tess a kiss before floating away from their booth. "That was crazy."

"*You're* crazy. I can't believe you told her to keep her bits covered!"

Tess's brow furrowed, tentatively feeling out if Abi was serious or not. She was drunk but not falling-over or pass-out drunk. Even so, she needed to tread lightly because Abi was at least tipsy. Vicki used to get angry and accusing when she drank. It was hard for Tess to know what Abi was like with so many people around. Tess reached for her, sliding her hand over Abi's shapely thighs before stopping at her waist. "I only wanna see your bits, babe. Sorry if I ruined it for you."

Abi rolled her lips inward, the faintest smile tugging her lips, and she yanked Tess closer. Tess ended up straddling her, her hands falling on the sofa on either side of Abi's head. The mix of bubbly and vodka was strong on Abi's breath as she whispered, "I fucking love you." Then her mouth was on Tess's, the tangle of tongues and teeth drowning any impulsive chance she had to reciprocate the words. The kiss was messy and desperate, and as Abi sank her nails in Tess's hair, it felt like it was vital to her sanity.

"I love you both," Taunya grumbled behind Tess. She gave her a shove. "But can you maybe not screw each other in front of me?"

Tess slowly inched away from Abi, skimming her fingers across the other woman's cheek as she addressed her sister. "Your dance done already? I didn't even see Brady leave."

"Yeah. I was so close to hiring him for another half hour, but he said he was booked elsewhere." Krystal threw herself down beside Tess, and for a few minutes they watched McCoy and Sloane finish up with Jasmine. The moment she left, the twins were fighting over who she liked more. The last bottle was opened and poured, and Tess found herself curled into Abi as she sipped her drink.

"Tonight was epic," McCoy commented, raising her glass to Tess's for a toast. "You did good, Barber."

Tess snorted. "Thanks?"

"Just think Tauni, after tonight Derek will be the only guy you ever see naked." Sloane looked in deep thought as she spoke, or maybe it was the alcohol affecting Tess's vision. She squinted, watching her sister's reaction.

Taunya merely smiled. Then she laughed, clinking her glass against Sloane's. "I know, and I can't wait."

After a week of functioning on limited sleep, Tess was operating solely on fumes, caffeine, and a miraculous amount of second winds. And now sex, if the past two nights were any indication. A lazy smile curled her lips as she scrolled through her phone, careful not to wake Abi. Sloane had already tagged her in a handful of pictures of the last few days, and she found herself going back to the one where she and Abi were kissing at Twin Falls. It was a great image, perfectly cropped and filtered so that even the plainness of Tess's features appeared captivating. Through Sloane's lens, Abi and Tess looked hot together.

Fatigue and faint traces of a hangover lingered from the night before, but waking up to the tender woman currently tucked into her side made everything worth it this past week. She lowered her head to kiss Abi's hair, sighing in utter contentment. She was no longer terrified of the constant fluttering in her chest and stomach. Falling for Abi was inevitable, and truthfully, it'd be the best damn thing ever to happen to her. The thought of Abi returning so soon to Toronto caused momentary bouts of anxiety and insecurity whenever it crossed her mind, and so she tried not to think about it. She had this sinking feeling that Abi would get home only to realize her feelings for Tess weren't at all as profound as she'd first thought. Being dismissed again for something or someone else was probably Tess's worst fear.

Tess and Abi were perfect together, their bodies and hearts connecting like long-lost lovers. It sounded corny, but it was almost like Abi was made for Tess. All her past failures with Vicki and Chantelle dissolved whenever Abi looked at her. For the first time in Tess's life, she felt complete. And after last night, she decided she'd start a bucket list of her own. She hadn't known getting a lap dance from a stranger would be one of the top five on said list, but now that it was, she had a burning desire to experience more of life. If things with Abi flourished, Tess had a feeling her girlfriend would be right there with her, ticking off boxes and helping her fully live. Tess had been cooped up in her own box for too long, living vicariously through others.

An incoming message displayed at the top of her screen, and she inwardly groaned when she noticed Vicki's name. What did she want — to inadvertently ruin Tess's good mood? The woman was insufferable; never had Tess thought Vicki of all people would try to win her back. She clicked on the message and immediately wished she hadn't. There was a link to Sloane's post in Vicki's message, along with an accusation so outlandish, anger burned its way up Tess's throat.

Vicki – 9:26AM

> And you blamed me for cheating. Everything is so clear now! You're a fucking hypocrite, Tess. May you and your side-piece get splashed by the biggest puddle and then shit on by a family of seagulls!

Tess didn't know whether to laugh or cry at Vicki's diabolical statement. How hadn't she noticed before how unhinged her ex was? Honestly, she'd say at this point that Taunya had been doing her a favor when she broke up with Vicki on her behalf.

A family of seagulls, V, really? Not even a flock? Tess snorted, but another message came through. This one had unshed tears rushing to the surface.

Vicki – 9:28AM

> She'll never love you. You gave up the only person who had the patience to look past

all those disgusting faults. Remember that,
Tess. P.S, I hope she likes leftovers.

What a horrible, horrible *woman!*

Tess tossed her phone to the side, wishing like hell she could reverse time to five minutes ago. The weight of Vicki's insults sank Tess's jolly mood like a lead balloon, and she batted runaway tears off her cheek with the back of her free hand. What if...

Stop, don't think it. Quit being your own worst enemy, she thought darkly.

Abi nuzzled Tess's breast, awake now, and strands of her hair tickled Tess's ribs in the process. Placing a soft kiss over the same spot, Abi shifted to rest her cheek against Tess's chest, a long yawn escaping. Their eyes met. "Morning."

"Hey, good morning." Tess forced a smile, wanting desperately to go back to being on cloud nine and just soak in how lovely Abi was first thing in the morning. She was obsessed with the roughness in Abi's voice when she first woke; it was unbelievably sexy and unintentionally erotic. It reminded Tess of the numerous times the night before when Abi had screamed her name in the throes of pleasure.

Early-morning light slipping through the crack between her curtains cast a glow over Abi's sun-kissed skin. With her hair tangled and mussed in a delicious, *well-fucked-look* mess, she was the hottest woman Tess had ever seen. And Abi wanted *her*. It was hard to fathom and harder to ignore Vicki's parting message. Why would someone like Abi want her?

"What are you thinking about?"

Tess's smile faltered, her gaze slipping past Abi to stare at her guitar resting on the wall. "You mean my face hasn't given it away?"

She slid her hand over Abi's arm, relishing the slight tremor emitting from her lover.

"You have tells I can read, mostly in your body language. What your hands are doing, that sort of thing," Abi admitted, capturing Tess's hand in hers. She kissed Tess's knuckles, examining them closely before lacing their fingers together.

Tess assumed as much. She'd always felt like such an open book when she was around Abi. How else could Abi disarm the irrational side of Tess so easily? "I was just thinking of how lucky I am that you're here with me," she whispered, tangling her free hand in Abi's locks.

It was a lie, and they both knew it. Tess's breath caught with the intensity in Abi's eyes, temporarily riveted to the bed and blinded by the sheer beauty of those blue eyes. Abi never hid herself from anyone, especially not Tess, so why waste time doubting herself again? Ever since she'd known her, Abi had worn her heart on her sleeve for the world to see. The old expression about eyes being the window into the soul described Abi perfectly, and yet for years Tess had ignored what they'd been telling her.

"Ditto, babe. Every moment so far with you has been perfect, but what are you really thinking about?"

Tess hesitated, knowing she was overthinking but unable to stop it. "The future."

Tess watched as her reply registered in Abi's gaze, and she gripped Tess closer as a result. "I was waiting to say something because I wasn't quite sure yet," Abi began, placing a soft kiss on Tess's chest. Tess stroked her hair as she continued, "But I think I wanna stay."

"Stay? Stay here?" Tess clarified, ignoring the obvious astonishment in her voice.

Abi nodded, nuzzling her face against Tess's breast before turning to look at her. Tess's heart clenched with the way Abi smiled. "That's what I was thinking, yes. I'd have to go back to pack and everything, but I could be living in Vancouver again in a month or two."

"Seriously? That would be..." Tess shook her head. "But why?"

Abi giggled, tickling Tess in the ribs. "A lot of reasons, not just you. Although getting you naked multiple times a week is the best incentive so far."

They both laughed, and the excited thought of Abi moving home pushed Tess's current doubt away, at least for now. Silence filled the room again, but rather than discomfort, serenity settled over them. Tess toyed absently with Abi's hair, her fingers gently probing her scalp before running through a tendril. Abi was tracing her index finger languorously over Tess's clavicle. Tess watched intently as the other woman wandered, the noticeably shorter nail on that finger teasing Tess's nipples, first one, and then the other. The sensation as it trekked a careful map down Tess's sternum had goosebumps breaking out over her body. Her touch was so light, it was ticklish.

Tess flinched, an uncharacteristic giggle slipping from her lips. "Abi."

Abi bit her lip, trying and failing to hide a pleased grin. She knew exactly what she was doing, the imp. "Tell me something I don't already know about you."

Abi tickling her made it hard to think. They'd had sex only a few hours ago, but already Tess was once again aroused. Her heart pounded, wild from the stimulation, but she took a deep breath anyway and tried to concentrate. She let it out slowly, her lips still twitching. "I think peanut butter tastes great with almost any dish."

"Something I *don't* know," Abi repeated, tweaking Tess's nipple.

"Ow!" Tess poked Abi in the ribs, then tickled down her spine, guffawing as Abi squirmed away. "Well, did you know I went through a phase in my twenties where I ate breakfast sandwiches every day for two months? I'd melt cheese on two fried egg whites, and instead of using mayo on the English muffin, I'd coat it in peanut butter. Then I'd sprinkle cinnamon over top before adding the egg. It was..." difficult to describe. Grinning at Abi's revulsion, she brought her fingers to her lips and kissed them. "Chef's kiss, I swear."

"If you say so, weirdo."

"Hey! Are you saying you've never eaten anything before that didn't seem to go together?"

Abi smirked. "Yes. Pineapple on pizza."

"Now you're just being a brat."

"I know, but you love it."

Tess couldn't take her eyes off Abi's mouth, wanting to kiss her again. She licked her lips, and her pulse quickened even more when Abi noticed. "I do," she admitted.

Abi moved to close the distance, her firm breasts eliciting a silent gasp from Tess as they brushed against her own chest. Abi cupped Tess's face in her palms, brushing sleepy, unhurried kisses over her cheeks and chin. Reminders of Taunya's bachelorette party lingered on her breath, but Tess didn't mind as she sank deeper into her pillow. Her eyes drifted closed at the simple intimacy. "God, I don't deserve you." The hushed admittance tumbled out, and Tess gritted her teeth, wishing she could call the words back.

"Absolutely you do." The hot, wet, glide of Abi's tongue over Tess's lip had her groaning in pleasure, the fleeting moment of insecurity vanishing as quickly as it had come. Spreading her legs out more, Tess wasn't at all surprised when Abi fit herself between them seconds later.

Tess opened her eyes in time to see Abi dipping lower to take a nipple in her mouth. She jolted off the bed, always taken by surprise at how her body reacted to Abi's touch. Her hands went to Abi's back, digging the nails lightly into her unblemished skin. "You're insatiable."

Abi's laugh was muffled behind a mouthful of Tess's breast, but her mischievous gaze met Tess's briefly. She suckled and swirled her tongue around Tess's nipple, kneading the small mound in her hands until Tess was squirming underneath her. When Abi popped off to move onto Tess's other breast, she said, "I want you to take me for a ride on your bike today. Will you?" She licked the already taut nipple. "We can have our date."

Tess's breath hitched in her throat as her pussy clenched in need. God, she'd never tire of the skillful ways Abi brought her to climax. "I can't think right now," she gasped, dots dancing before her eyes as Abi began thrusting her pelvis against Tess's. The friction had arousal trickling from her legs, the muscles in her abdomen tightening as her body got ready for yet another release. Tess's hands landed on Abi's shapely ass, palming her cheeks. She gave them a firm squeeze before sliding lower, catching Abi's soaking folds on her fingertips. Withdrawing, Tess brought them to her mouth, a soft moan escaping as she licked her fingers clean of Abi's arousal. The scent and taste of Abi was liberating and intoxicating in a way Tess had never experienced. Distracted from her task, Abi's blue gaze darkened as she fixated on Tess.

"Fuck, that's hot," she grunted, gripping Tess's wrists to pin her arms above her head. The action made Tess's breasts pull together and heat shoot to her core. There was a wicked gleam in Abi's eye as she crushed Tess's lips with a kiss, and with each stroke of Abi's tongue, the worry from earlier quickly became inconsequential.

Chapter Twenty-Two

Abi

ABI SCREAMED AS A gush of water sprayed into her face that afternoon, a direct result of a cannon-ball into the pool. She sputtered, wiping her face and glaring as Derek's best man resurfaced moments later. "What the hell, Matt?"

"Watch where the hell you're jumping!" Taunya added, splashing him back. "You could've hit us."

"Sorry! I thought I was further away." Matt cast a sheepish glance Abi's way before taking off after Puck, Derek's other groomsman.

The bridal party was smaller today since the official prewedding activities were over — at least until the rehearsal dinner. Krystal had a family thing, and last Abi heard, Sloane and McCoy were still sleeping off their all-night bender with Jasmine — and, surprisingly, Lily. Tess had even disappeared at some point after their late-morning frolic between the sheets.

"Lucky for him, I'm in a forgiving mood," Abi joked, catching the Nerf football that her bestie had just thrown. Glancing past Taunya, she spotted Mr. Moore on the back deck, placing steaks on the grill. Audrey sipped wine on a lawn chair, but there was no sign of Tess. Abi's shoulders drooped a little, which was pathetic. She'd never considered herself the clingy type, but she'd also never truly wanted any of her previous partners. Only Tess.

Always Tess.

"I always knew you had U-Haul potential," Taunya teased, splashing Abi. "'Can't breathe without them' frame of mind."

"There should be a rule made where heterosexual people can't stereotype their lesbian friends. Do you even know the definition of a U-Haul lesbian?" Abi tried to sound upset, but she really wasn't selling it. She *was* severely attached to Tess, to the point where she refused to consider any other outcome than one where they lived happily ever after. She'd been waiting years for Tess. She deserved everything life could offer, every piece of Tess she could give to Abi.

Taunya's knowing smirk said she also didn't believe her. She caught the ball Abi chucked back. "Don't think I didn't notice you moved all your clothes into Tess's place yesterday. Prime example, babe."

"It's more convenient."

"Sure it is." Taunya's voice dripped in sarcasm, but she was laughing. "It's convenient to share the lone dresser in my sister's bach pad."

Abi didn't comment, but she didn't have to. They both knew Tess's living situation would need to change if she and Abi ever moved in together. It simply wasn't large enough. *Not an if, a when,* she reminded herself, the corners of her mouth twitching. *When* she and Tess had a home, *together*. God, she loved the sound of that.

"There she is."

Abi followed Taunya's line of sight, and sure enough, Tess was joining Bobby and Audrey on the deck. She was carrying a glass of wine in one hand and tucking her cell phone into her denim shorts with the other. Abi's gaze roamed over the other woman, appreciating those smooth legs and loose, matching blue t-shirt.

"We still playing, or...?"

The Nerf ball hit her in the head, snapping Abi out of her stupor. "Sorry." Abi shifted her focus to Taunya once more, just in time to catch the rolling of her eyes. A giggle bubbled out of her as she picked up the football again. Their game of catch resumed, eventually turning into teams as Derek, Puck, and Matt joined in. Abi couldn't concentrate, her stomach a steady case of butterflies knowing Tess was watching them. When the ball finally launched accidently across the yard, their game was cut short. Abi wasn't complaining. The moment Taunya was distracted by the boys, she waded over to the pool's ledge. The conversation between Tess and Audrey came to a halt once they noticed Abi. She smiled. "Hey."

"Hey back. Having fun?" Tess's voice had a higher pitch to it as she focused on Abi. She wasn't wearing her sunglasses, and Abi's grin widened when she saw Tess's intense gaze travel slowly from her hair to her torso and back up. For a heated moment, she lingered on Abi's breasts before their eyes met. Tess squirmed in her seat, looking very much like she'd been caught with her hand in a cookie jar. Abi smirked, thoroughly enjoying the sense of sexual prowess Tess evoked.

"Can I have a sip of that?" Pointing to the wine glass in Tess's hand, Abi batted her lashes.

"You two, I swear." Audrey shook her head, laughter racking her shoulders as she got to her feet. Her eyes were hidden behind a pair of large sunglasses, but somehow Abi knew their edges were crinkling with happiness. "I'm glad this is happening, by the way."

"Mom, please," Tess muttered, a blush breaking out over her throat and cheeks. She averted her gaze.

"What? I'm just saying, as an outsider looking in, it's about time." Audrey grinned, raising her wine glass to them both before heading inside.

Abi rolled her lips inward, silently gauging Tess's reaction to her mother's input on their relationship. "I'm sorry about her. She can be ... intense," Tess murmured after a moment, her eyes flickering to Abi's once again.

"Don't worry about it. I've known your parents forever, remember?" Smiling, Abi held out her hand. "What do you say to that sip, babe?"

Tess arched one sexy eyebrow before slowly sitting up, her smooth legs straddling the lounge chair and her cell phone resting in the middle. "Want me to get you a drink from the cooler?"

"Just a sip of yours will do. Please?" Pouting seemed to do the trick, and her mouth went dry as Tess stood up. Her gaze dropped to Tess's bare feet as she closed the short distance between them. They were a part of the anatomy she'd never bothered to appreciate before, save for how they felt against her while sleeping. But if feet could look sexy, Tess's fit the bill.

I am so fucking strange.

Tess squatted in front of her, her wry grin a staggering kryptonite to the throbbing between Abi's thighs. She was breathless as she reached for the wine Tess was offering. "Thank you." Winking, she lifted the glass to her lips and downed the rest of the wine.

"Hey!" Tess's mouth fell open, struck dumb when Abi smacked her lips in delight. She was silent as she set the glass on the deck away from Tess. "That was *way* more than a sip."

Smirking, Abi stood on her tiptoes and beckoned Tess closer with her finger. "There's something I need to confess."

"Oh, yeah? Like how you drank all my wine and aren't the least bit remorseful?" Tess deadpanned. She leaned closer, though, getting Abi right where she wanted her.

"I'm sorry, but ... I just can't help myself!" Abi snatched fistfuls of Tess's baggy shirt and gave her a yank, a wide smile appearing when Tess shrieked seconds before she hit the water.

"Babe, you didn't!" Taunya's roar of laughter from somewhere behind her was contagious, and when Tess resurfaced, the only one not cackling like a fool was her.

"You!" Water droplets rained off the hair hanging in Tess's face as she pointed at Abi. She shoved strands out of her eyes with one hand, standing up in the pool in absolute shock as she gaped at her. "You ... brat!" she sputtered.

Abi's mouth fell open. "You did not just call me a brat?"

"Oh, I so did, Abi. I call it like I see it." But Tess's eyes were twinkling as she waded toward her. Before Abi knew it, she was getting the splash of a lifetime.

"Tess!" Abi giggled, splashing her as well. "Take it back!"

"You're the one who pulled me in, clothes and all." Tess was giggling too, and they sprayed one another until Abi got close enough to grab Tess's wrists. She was breathing hard, addicted to Tess's smile, addicted to her light-hearted side. There was no one but Tess in that moment, those lush brown eyes glinting up at Abi and their chests rapidly rising and falling as they regarded each other. Tess's drenched t-shirt clung to her body, accentuating mouth-watering curves and hardened nipples. Abi groaned inwardly. Her fingers tingled, itching to touch Tess. Her body *burned* for Tess.

"Get a room!"

Watching the Fraser River zoom past as she clung to Tess on the back of the Ducati was an absolute epic rush. The wind whipped into the open collar of her jacket, chilling and stinging the exposed skin beneath, but Abi didn't mind one bit. It was no wonder Tess loved riding so much! The adrenaline pumping fear was different from her phobia of heights. Abi wasn't sure if it was because they were low to the ground or that she simply felt safe clinging to Tess, but it was freeing in a way she'd never experienced before.

They were making their way north with no real destination in mind. The weather was cooperating, and the view of the mountains around them was spectacular. As they sped down the road, the decision to move back to her hometown was as clear to Abi as the blue, cloudless evening sky. How had she managed to grin and bear it under Margo's thumb for so long? The woman was a bully who relished degrading her staff just so she could feel better about herself. Abi had her business degree and two years' worth of marketing experience. Starting over would be a cinch, and who knew? With her interpersonal skills, building her own marketing company wasn't such a far-fetched idea.

Tess veered the bike onto an exit ramp, her gloved hand leaving the handlebar to brush Abi's arms situated around her waist. Abi held her tighter, loving the fact that even though they couldn't exactly talk while on the bike she still felt close to Tess.

The Ducati slowed down, and moments later Tess steered the bike into the parking lot of a convenience store, parking at the gas pump. Abi climbed off first, eager to stretch her arms and legs. She'd never complain to Tess, but man, she was using muscles she didn't know she had sitting slumped on the back of the motorcycle. She flipped open her visor, watching with internal glee as Tess unmounted. Those legs may have been on the shorter side, but the strength hidden beneath those tight jeans had naughty thoughts running through Abi's mind. She fanned herself, not caring one iota how it looked to the guy pumping gas across from them.

Tess took off her helmet, ruffling her slightly matted down hair before arching a brow at her. "You doing okay? Oh, you can take that off." She gestured to Abi's helmet as she set her own down on the bike.

"Y–yeah." Abi was aware she was perving, but checking Tess out as she began to pump gas was suddenly the most important thing she should be doing. Biker Tess exuded a level of confidence that non-biker Tess could only *dream* of. It was as if she turned into a different person! Not a better one, because Abi was head over heels for bashful Tess, but she had to admit sexy biker Tess was *hella* fine. "Riding with you is as fun as I'd hoped it would be."

She saw Tess bite her lip, pulling the nozzle out of the bike's tank and returning it to the holder. She flashed those brown eyes on Abi, an adorable blush dusting the tops of her cheeks. "You meant that? And here I thought I'd have to sell it."

"Your Ducati? Oh no, nuh-uh." Abi shook her head, fisting the front of Tess's leather jacket and reeling her in for a kiss. "Why would you even consider that? You love this bike."

Tess's gaze wouldn't meet hers, but she cleared her throat and muttered, "Vicki hated it. Chantelle too; basically, anyone who has ever dated me."

Abi pursed her lips, annoyance over Tess's stupid exes dampening her stellar mood. "Well, it's a good thing your taste in girlfriends has improved."

"Girlfriend?" Tess echoed, eyes widening.

Abi panicked. "Too soon?"

A horn honked behind them before Tess could reply, and she glanced at the waiting car before meeting Abi's gaze once more. She grimaced. "Sorry, I guess I'll just pull up front. Want to meet me inside?"

"Of course."

Abi was smiling as she made her way across the other set of gas pumps and into the store. Tess found her in the junk food aisle not long after, chuckling at the handful of goodies in her arms. "I can't decide," Abi pouted, holding up the candy bars for her to see. "Snickers or Aero?"

"Oof, that *is* a dilemma. Tess's soft voice was teasing, but Abi loved every minute of it. She loved how every moment they spent together broke Tess out of her shell a little more. Her hands closed over Abi's, and she raised up on her tiptoes to give her a kiss. "Why not get both?" she murmured against Abi's lips. "You can split them with ... your girlfriend."

Abi's eyes flew to Tess's, catching their twinkle, and a gush of relief had her grinning like a fool. "Mmm, good idea. Don't suppose you know where I could find one of those?"

Tess sniggered, poking Abi lightly in the ribs, and she almost dropped the snacks before Tess caught her up in her arms again. She held her close to her chest, and Abi couldn't help but breathe in the subtle perfume Tess had dabbed along her throat earlier. *Delicious.* "Are you always this sure of yourself?"

Abi shrugged, saying simply, "Not always, but when it comes to you I've learned to be ever hopeful. C'mon, let's go home." She flashed a grin. "I'm suddenly eager to see you under me."

Tess let out an adorable squeak, her face and throat flushing with her telltale blush as Abi led her through the store. She insisted on paying for the gas and snacks, knowing it was the least she could do considering everything Tess had put into the past week. Regardless, she knew she would have to make her savings stretch a lot longer, especially if she was serious about moving home. As they left the store, her lack of a job niggled at her. Was it even possible to move back so soon, or would she need to find another job first and save some more?

Tess came to an abrupt stop, the sudden death grip of her hand in Abi's snapping her to attention. Her gaze followed Tess's to the very pregnant woman climbing out of the passenger seat of a car parked directly beside the Ducati. When her face came into view, Abi narrowed her eyes, "Is that...?"

"Yes," Tess choked. Abi glanced down at her, immediately noting Tess's rapidly paling features. She looked like she could vomit at any moment, and Abi's heart went out to her. She'd wager seeing the fiancée who'd cheated on her — and who was now pregnant — was the last thing Tess had expected tonight. And seeing Chantelle's blissed-out face as she rounded the car was a surefire way to kill their happy mood.

Another woman, holding the hand of a little boy, met Chantelle in front of the car, and together they walked toward Abi and Tess. It was obvious they were a family by the way Chantelle held the woman's other hand, and she found her own stomach clenching with fury.

Reel yourself in, Abs. You can't hit a bitch if she's pregnant.

"Tess, hey," Chantelle acknowledged, slowing down as they reached them. She looked the same as Abi remembered all those years ago, except now she had that pregnancy glow people often talked about. It caused her rich black locks to practically glisten under the evening sun and the roundness in her cheeks to pinken. She was annoyingly pretty, but in the way all dangerous things were. Chantelle had, after all, managed to slink her way into Tess's life for years, earning her trust and her love before stabbing her in the back.

"Chantelle," Tess said flatly.

The woman attached to her smiled politely at Tess and Abi before turning to her partner. "I'm gonna run in ahead of you, okay? George needs a diaper change."

"Okay, I'll be right in."

Once it was the three of them standing there, a satisfied smirk had Chantelle's plump upper lip twitching. Her smile grew as she noticed Abi's glare. "Little Abi? Taunya's friend, right?"

"Baby, let's just go." Abi tugged on Tess's hand, ignoring Chantelle's knowing grin. Tess stood ramrod-straight, staring at Chantelle's pregnant belly.

"Wow, isn't it crazy how life turns out?" Chantelle asked, letting out a soft chuckle. She pointed in Abi's direction. "And I guess your Tess obsession finally paid off, huh? Good, I'm happy for you."

"Likewise," Abi snapped, pulling harder on Tess this time. She flipped Chantelle off with her free hand as they walked away, shouting over her shoulder, "Try not to cheat on this one, yeah?"

Chantelle's resounding laughter clapped around them like the startling boom of a storm's first thunder, and Abi didn't miss the way the sound made Tess jump. "Are you okay? God, I'm so sorry, Tess!" she exclaimed as soon as they were out of earshot.

"Of course." Tess shrugged, but her hands shook as she passed Abi her helmet. She started the bike's engine, her gaze anywhere but on the woman climbing on behind. "Let's go home."

Chapter Twenty-Three

Tess

The past had a twisted way of sneaking up on a person. And emotional wounds were the *worst*. Bones and flesh could mend and scab, heal over in time, but the same could not be said about the heart.

Just when she thought she could be happy, that she *deserved* to be happy, all the pain and humiliation of years ago resurfaced to agitate old scars. Seeing a pregnant Chantelle the day before brought up everything Tess had so adamantly pushed beneath the surface. She'd played it off the best she could, taking Abi home and being as present as possible the rest of the evening, but inside, where no one could see, she'd suffered.

It was difficult not to think of what life would have been like had she not stumbled in on Chantelle and her lover. Would Chantelle have stopped cheating? Would Tess have remained blissfully ignorant? They had been planning their wedding, of all things! What kind of person did such a thing to someone? Went behind their fiancée's back and fucked another woman in their shared bed?

Someone who was settling until something better came along. The joke is always on you, Tess.

The clippers currently clasped between her fingers left her client's hair as she reached for the rubber band on her wrist. She pulled it back and released, tensing as the band's snap stung her bare skin. She cleared her parched throat. "D–do anything exciting over the weekend?" she managed, darting a quick glance down to where the flesh around her wrist was angry and red. Her trusty rubber band had seen a lot of action that morning as Tess tried — and failed — to conquer her anxiety. She looked a mess, her concentration was zilch, and it was incredibly hard to ground herself when clients kept walking into the shop. She'd already broken down in the bathroom before opening, and honestly, she didn't think she had an ounce of self-respect left. Here she was, four years later and still struggling to unpack all her Chantelle baggage.

Yeah, well, it was supposed to be our baby growing inside her.

Hell, they'd picked out names for their future children, had a real estate agent on speed dial for the potential forever home they were looking for. What was it about Tess that made Chantelle stray? More importantly, how would she manage to keep Abi from doing the same?

Impossible. She'll leave, just depends on if she'll cheat on me or not first.

Snap!

"—went out on the lake with my wife and kids Saturday," Alan replied, watching her quizzically in the mirror. He was one of her regulars, but their conversations never pushed past the typical pleasantries one said while getting their hair cut. With any luck, he wouldn't ask about her rubber band compulsions, since Tess was not inclined to indulge anyone today.

Vicki's right, Abi doesn't love me like she thinks she does.

Tess shook her head, silently willing the toxic thoughts to pass. In all the time she had known Abi, she never knew her to be anything other than authentic. Then again, Chantelle had pulled the wool over her eyes for quite some time before Tess woke up.

Snap!

She was desperate to finish so she could close the shop early. Her hand gave a slight tremble as she moved the clippers to trim around Alan's ears. "It was a nice day for it," she offered, no longer recognizing her own voice.

"What does the rubber band do?"

Dammit.

Tess flashed Alan a tight smile in the mirror, making sure to briefly meet his gaze before tearing her eyes away again. "It's therapeutic," she explained, going back to the task at hand. "How is work these days?" she asked to change the subject. They continued to make light conversation, and when the job was finished, Alan pressed two twenties into her palm.

"I don't want the change back. Go buy yourself lunch next door. I hear it's quite good there," he said, his eyes kind as he patted her gently on the back before heading to the door. He lifted his arm on a wave and called over his shoulder, "I'll see you in six weeks, Tess. Take care!"

"Yeah, you too... Thank you, Alan."

Tess watched him leave, still rooted to the spot with the cash in hand. It wasn't the first time someone had given her a large tip, but it was the first time done out of pity. It was the only reason to make sense, because there was no way she'd done a stellar job on his hair in her current shape.

Tess blew out a breath, rolling her shoulders as she walked to her shop's entrance and locked the door. Her chest was tight, and as often as she tried, she couldn't get her breathing or thoughts under control today. She found herself swallowing again, even though there was nothing more *to* swallow. Her mouth was as dry as the Sahara desert. With clammy hands, she shoved the cash into her jeans pocket before flipping the open sign over and closing the blinds. She leaned against the door for a moment, absently snapping the rubber band. She took a breath, and another, suddenly feeling too tight in her own skin. She snapped and breathed, in and out, until her wrist was raw and her head light. Slowly, she slid to the floor, her dire reality churning her already upset stomach.

I'll never be good enough for Abi, and eventually ... she'll see it. And then she'll break me, just like Chantelle. Just like Vicki keeps trying to do.

She repositioned the acoustic guitar draped across her lap as she sat with her legs crossed on her bed. Sometimes all there was *to* do was work out all the crap bottled up inside her by strumming her guitar. Some days, the soothing melody and eye-opening lyrics she scribbled down were the only thing to make sense. She could only hope it worked for her today.

Was it cowardly of her to avoid Abi and everyone else rather than talk about how she felt? Probably, but she was no good for anyone like this, stuck in her head like she was, having one pity party after another at no one's fault but her own. *She* was the problem. Tess was too naïve, too trusting, too sensitive, too *everything*. She couldn't face Abi like this. How could she?

"Get out of my head," Tess muttered, plucking chords on her guitar and enjoying the calming way it resonated inside her. Closing her eyes, she allowed all the shit she'd been bottling up since the day before to pour out of her and into the music flowing from her fingers. Before she knew it, the unfiltered and pain-filled lyrics she'd written down flowed from her lips as she twisted her turmoil into song. Tears pricked her eyelids, but Tess didn't let up on her playing as the wetness soaked her cheeks. She was nowhere near as good as her mom with a guitar, but she liked to think it brought something therapeutic to the table.

"Love can be such a fragile little thing," she sang and winced at the rasp in her voice. Way too many tears produced that harrowing sound effect. Her throat burned, but she kept going, strumming, and singing, and purposely ignoring another incoming call from Abi. Tess wasn't girlfriend material. She wasn't wife material, mother material, and it was wrong of her to think otherwise. Abi would be an idiot to move back to Vancouver to be with Tess.

> *"Love can be such a fragile little thing*
> *Givin' your all to someone, somewhere in time*
> *Yet what happens when they abuse it,*
> *abuse the love you gave them*
> *Oh, I'm a damn fool."*

Tess shrugged, and her clammy fingers momentarily slipped off the strings. Hearing the truth out loud just made her more upset, but she couldn't stop once she was in self-destruct mode. Her pulse thundered in her ears as she started in on the chorus.

"What happens then, what happens then
Trust is meant to build you up, not break you down
Oh, well, it's broken me now
I'm a broken mess now
Gave them my heart and trust like they knew I
would
I admit I was a toy in a wicked game
I should've know better but
It was a game they played all too well.
What happens then, what happens then
Trust is meant to build you up not break you down
Oh, well, it's broken me now
I'm a broken—"

The sudden intoxicating scent of vanilla in her room hit Tess. Her eyes flew open, tears streaming past her lashes, and she froze, taking in the striking woman leaning against Tess's closed door. The air in the small space immediately grew saturated as they stared at one another, shock and confusion blatant on Abi's face.

"Tess?"

Shame had Tess breaking her gaze and folding more into herself on the bed. *Abi shouldn't be here.* How did she get in without Tess noticing? *Why would she even come?* The room felt off to Tess. The lone lamp she'd kept on in the corner of the room shone too bright with all the curtains closed.

"S–shouldn't you be with Tauni?" She asked, croaky and short of breath. Or was it McCoy? Tess gave an agitated shake of her head, unable to remember whatever details Abi had told her the night before. She felt off, too hot and too cold at the same time, suffocating. The room was suffocating her.

"What's going on, Tess? You've been avoiding my calls and texts all day. Did you come home early?" Abi sounded close now, too close, quickly becoming an accomplice to Tess's suffering. When Abi's soft hand landed on her thigh Tess flinched. She heard Abi's sharp intake of breath, and she inwardly winced.

Fuck, this isn't what I wanted.

"Okay," Abi began again, and Tess felt the moment she retracted her fingers. Her voice was soft as she continued, "That ... the song I heard when I came in. Who was it about?"

Tess swallowed, despising how her bottom lip trembled as she uttered the words, "You know. You *know*." She saw Abi nod out of the corner of her eye, but still Tess couldn't look at her. She let go of the guitar to press a hand against her chest.

"Chantelle, right? And maybe Vicki?" Abi's voice sounded further away than it should have been.

Slowly, Tess nodded once, but the movement just made her dizzier.

"Do you still love her? Chantelle? Is that it?"

"N–no!" Tess stammered, louder than she intended. Her bleary eyes finally collided with Abi's, and she pulled the guitar off her lap to slip from the bed. "But y–you wouldn't understand!"

"Try me."

Tess took a few steps before stopping, her legs dragging across the floor like heavy steel pipes. She shuddered, aware of her shallow breaths. She kept sucking in air, but the hollowness in her lungs felt unquenchable. She squinted back at Abi, and even in her state she despised the concerned expression on her lover's face. "I–I'm not w–who you want, Abi..." Tess paused, drawing in another desperate breath, another need unfulfilled. She staggered, catching herself against the bathroom door before her knees buckled.

CHAPTER TWENTY-FOUR

Abi

ABI STOOD WATCHING TESS stumble toward the bathroom, no doubt to escape. It hurt, to say the least, but Abi tried not to overthink things. Whatever was happening with Tess, she wasn't in the right frame of mind for any rash decisions.

"I'm not w–who you want, Abi…"

"Whoa, Tess!" Abi cried, lunging for Tess just as her knees buckled. One arm wrapped around the smaller woman's waist, and a hand went to Tess's shoulder, holding her in place. Tess clung to her, allowing Abi to lower her gently to the floor. Her breathing felt heavy and irregular against Abi's throat, and with the perspiration dotting Tess's forehead as well as her glazed-over brown eyes, Abi could only assume her girlfriend was having an anxiety attack.

"L–L–Leave me," Tess wheezed, her body rigid in Abi's arms. Her usual warm gaze had morphed into a hard stare at Abi in suspicion, their disconnect tearing at Abi's heartstrings. She gave a hard swallow, mentally racing through her options as she brushed strands of damp blonde hair from Tess's forehead. She couldn't call Taunya, since she'd disappeared with Derek for the day. Audrey and Bobby were at work as well... Abi pursed her lips, wishing she'd taken time to refresh her knowledge of anxiety attacks.

The door to Tess's Annex opened, and Abi turned in time to see McCoy popping her head through. In all the chaos, Abi forgot she'd left her friend waiting in her Jeep. They'd returned early from shopping when all her messages to Tess had gone unanswered. Had Abi known seeing Chantelle would set Tess off this much, she'd have insisted they have the day together.

McCoy's stare dropped to where she and Tess sat slumped on the floor. "Hey. Anything I can do?" she murmured, coming farther into the room. She sounded concerned, but her presence only agitated Tess more.

Tears made their way down Tess's cheeks as she glared up at Coy.

"What are the chances of the barber having a jar of VapoRub kicking around?" Coy muttered, glancing around the room before looking at Abi. "I saw on TikTok that inhaling it breaks you out of an attack."

"Get out," Tess gasped, and fear and something that looked akin to betrayal shone in her eyes as she swiveled back and forth between Coy and Abi. But why would she feel betrayed? "B–both of you."

Abi stood long enough to snatch Tess's cell phone off the bed. She punched in Tess's passcode, handing it to Coy. "Get a hold of her friend Stacey, see if she can come over."

"On it." Coy nodded, casting Tess another glance before leaving again.

"Y–you love her," Tess accused, batting Abi's hand away when she crouched in front of her once more. Tess's whole body shook now. "McCoy."

"Tess, sweetheart, I love *you*. Let me help, *please*. Isn't there ... shouldn't we be doing a grounding technique or something?"

She'd read that somewhere, hadn't she? Back when Taunya had first confided in her about Tess's condition, she'd spent an entire day googling everything she could about general anxiety. But that was *years* ago.

Think Abi, think...

"G–go, Abi."

Abi huffed at Tess's breathless growl, and instead of listening, she pressed a finger against Tess's lips to shush her. "If you want me to leave, then help me help you, okay?" She slid her hand down to place over Tess's heart. Their gazes locked, and Abi noted the escalating fear in Tess's. Her heart was racing under Abi's palm. "Concentrate. Um, how about we pick a topic?" With Tess's reluctant nod, Abi continued, keeping her voice feather-soft. "Name three of your favorite songs you play with your mom."

She watched Tess's throat bob up and down as she struggled for air. Her eyes shut momentarily, but she stammered, "'F–Fast Car' b–by Tracy C–Chapman."

"That's a great one," Abi crooned, rubbing Tess's arm soothingly and patiently waiting for more.

Tess sucked in a deep breath, the air leaving her lungs as shaky as her next words, "'H–have You Ever S–Seen The Rain.'" Another unsteady breath in, and then Tess opened her eyes to look back at Abi as she exhaled. A faint smile appeared. "By CCR. And ... 'Big Yellow Taxi' by ..."

"Joni Mitchell," Abi supplied when Tess trailed off. She'd heard that song played several times over the years at the Moore house.

"Yeah."

"Good. Let's do another category. What are your three favorite haircuts to do?" Abi wasn't sure why that question popped out, but the distractions were *working*. Tess was noticeably relaxing in Abi's embrace.

"The umm ... the pompadour, the quiff, and the..." Tess hesitated, blinking up at Abi, who watched her swallow. She looked away, whispering, "I–I love doing an undercut and fringe together."

"I don't know what a fringe is," Abi whispered back, reaching for strands of Tess's hair currently hiding her from Abi's view. She gently tucked some behind Tess's ear. "But I love that you do."

"Bangs."

"Oh. Okay."

Tess was mostly calm now, but Abi could tell fatigue was settling in where the tension had been. Her shoulders drooped, and then she surprised Abi by mumbling, "Can ... can you move your things back to the house?"

"*What?*" Surely, she'd misheard. Abi's lips parted, "Tess—"

"You don't want me, Abi. You won't be happy." Their gazes met, and the devastation in Tess's broke Abi's heart. "I won't forget the time we spent together, but ... it'll be better if–if we don't drag this out."

Later, Abi found herself parked beside McCoy at O'Rourke's, occupying the far corner of the bar counter. They each held a pint of Molson draught, Coy's already half empty. Abi nursed hers, never one to drown her sorrows in booze. Truthfully, had it been anyone else but Coy with her, she'd likely be scraping the bottom of a Half-Baked Ben & Jerry's by now. Abi was under the impression ice cream and chocolate solved everything, or at least buried it until all she could feel for a time was the sugar overdose and a welcome endorphin boost.

Witnessing Tess's attack had rattled Abi. For the last hour, she'd done little else but replay those moments, returning over and over to when she'd walked in on the other woman. Tess could have been playing any old betrayal song, but she'd taken the time to compose one. That level of dedication was astonishing. How hadn't Abi realized beforehand that something was wrong? Tess had been quiet since they'd run into Chantelle at the Quick-Stop, but nothing like the utter mess who had — by all accounts — broken up with her.

Sniffling into her glass, Abi made a face as the lukewarm ale rushed over her tongue as she took a drink. She swallowed before shaking her head sadly. "I'm such an idiot, Coy."

"Stop, you're not," McCoy chided, leaning into Abi on the barstool to give her shoulder a nudge. "Lovesick, maybe, but you're no idiot."

"I *am,* though. I went from telling myself I had moved on from Tess to immediately getting sucked in the moment I saw her again. It's not normal, and... well, a part of me feels like she'll never feel the same."

"Hey, no, no, don't do that," McCoy told her softly, her ringed thumb catching one of Abi's tears. Shadows of concern reflected in her green gaze, and Abi sat wordlessly as Coy took her beer from her and set it down on the counter. Then she wrapped Abi up into her solid arms. "Please don't cry."

"Did I come on too strong, Coy? Is that why she's already giving up?"

Abi had always been so headstrong whenever she set her mind to something. In the world of business, it was a trait that had served her well, but maybe the same couldn't be said in relationships.

"Abs, you know that's not true. Tess doesn't seem very sure of herself. I honestly don't think her reasons have much to do with you." McCoy inched away, the pads of her thumbs wiping away more tears. One corner of her mouth tilted upward. "Give her time and some credit, yeah? You can't expect her to jump into a relationship with you and not have fears. From what you've told me, her exes were toxic. Makes sense the barber would have trust issues."

There was truth in Coy's words, but the rejection stung more than Abi thought it could. She'd had it in her mind for so long that if she and Tess ever did get together, they'd sync like two halves of a whole that were meant to be. It hurt that she wasn't successful in reassuring Tess.

"I don't have time," she admitted, her voice thick with emotion. She fluttered her damp lashes, peering into her half-empty glass of beer. Rolling her lips inward, she picked the lager up once more. Taking a drink, she added, "Not really. I um ... I quit my job just before I left. It would be so easy to move back, Coy, to start over again in Van but..."

"Not so much without Tess."

"Yeah."

"Damn," Coy said, drumming her fingers on the countertop. She reached for her own beer, draining the glass before signaling Sloane for another. "Why'd you quit?"

Abi huffed, "Boss tried to make me cancel my vacation."

"Ah. I can't imagine someone doing that."

"Not everyone has a cool boss like you." Abi's lips twitched, and Coy cracked a grin.

"I'll make sure to tell Pops you think he's cool."

"The coolest."

Frankie approached them from behind the bar, pushing another beer into Coy's hands and darting a scrutinizing gaze between them. "Coy," she acknowledged, her voice low and steely. The pub owner was fashionably dressed tonight in another suit, this one a black pinstripe one-piece with a wide belt. It was both classy and sexy, with the chest loosely fastened with drawstrings. Frankie was gorgeous and — not that Abi would admit to anyone — a little terrifying.

The way most predatory animals are.

In her peripheral vision, Abi saw Coy sit up straighter in her seat. "Miss — Frankie, hi."

Despite the gravity of her evening, Abi started to snicker at Coy's slip-up, but the urge quickly died in her throat as the older woman's cold eyes settled on her. Abi audibly gulped as Frankie's lip curled up in what could easily be perceived as a snarl. "Coy's friend. Everything okay here?"

Abi began to nod, but Coy rushed to say, "Frankie, you remember Abi? She was here with the rest of the bridal party the other night."

"I see." Frankie studied her, noting the redness around Abi's eyes. She tsked. "Was Coy the one to make you cry?"

"What? Frankie, I would never—"

Frankie held a hand up, halting the rest of Coy's protest. Her fingers were free of rings, but her nails were long and beautifully manicured.

Beautiful and deadly.

The random thought popped into Abi's head, and she made a mental note to ask Coy later what Frankie's story was. She blinked, aware Frankie was still staring at her. *She's waiting for a response.* "Coy was cheering me up. She's a good friend," Abi corrected, wondering what Frankie would do if Coy *had* made her cry. She glanced at her friend, smiling a little.

"She is," Frankie agreed, finally focusing on her lover once more. She leaned across the bar counter, fisting the collar of Coy's shirt and pulling her forward for a heated kiss. Abi's eyes widened a little, and she turned her attention to where Sloane was busy with patrons several feet away. Frankie's power play had Abi remembering Taunya's words the night of their bonfire. Jealous and possessive. How did someone like Frankie navigate an "open" relationship, as Sloane had put it?

"If you plan to drive home, let this be your last beer, McCoy," she heard the older woman say, and when Abi glanced over again, Frankie was back to standing a respectable distance away.

Coy's cheeks had a slight flush after that kiss, and her lips were swollen, but she grinned, clearly appreciating Frankie's dominance. "Yes, Mistress."

Fascinated, Abi stared as Frankie's brown eyes flared for a second, and then her lips twitched in amusement, "Brat," she muttered before walking away.

Coy propped her elbow on the counter, and Abi followed suit, both of them sighing as they watched Frankie leave. Although Abi had just met her the other night, it was obvious Frankie cared a great deal for Coy. It made Abi long for Tess something awful.

Fresh tears stung her eyes, and she lifted her phone out of her purse. She hung her head, her heart squeezing at the lack of messages.

"Still nothing?" Coy asked, and seconds later she was rubbing slow circles on Abi's back.

"No," Abi sniffled, unlocking her phone and quickly typing a new message for Stacey. She and Coy had left as soon as Tess's friend arrived.

Abi – 7:53PM

How is she?

Stacey – 7:54PM

Sleeping atm. Taunya came and went, now we're just cuddling. Check back in the a.m.?

"Tauni checked in on her; that's good, right?" Coy murmured close to her ear. She was hovering over Abi's shoulder, reading the text.

"I'm surprised she hasn't messaged me yet," Abi admitted, gnawing her lower lip. She met Coy's eyes, "What if —"

"Quit overthinking, Abs. No one is in the wrong here, okay?" Abi's cell buzzed again, and Coy glanced down at it in her hand. She chuckled. "See?"

Stacey – 7:57PM

Taunya's phone is dead and she had to meet Derek's parents. Tess regrets what she said to you, so check in tomorrow. I'll stay awhile longer, but I think she'll come around.

Abi read Stacey's newest text, sighing in relief. There was still hope.

Chapter Twenty-Five

Tess

Tess had never felt more mentally or physically drained. The last time she'd experienced an anxiety attack that bad, she'd just left the apartment after walking in on Chantelle and her mystery lover. Tess had made it out to the parking lot before the crushing weight on her chest became too much. In that moment of utter desperation and humiliation, there was no Abi to save Tess from herself. She'd lost minutes, which had felt more like hours, alone and huddled between two parked cars. The hyperventilation during her attacks were always scary, but at least this time Abi had been there to soothe her, her silken voice wrapping around her mind and body in the world's biggest bear hug.

After long bouts of crying in Stacey's arms, and again in Taunya's, during which she also filled her sister in on everything that was happening, Tess had come to a few conclusions of her own: she wasn't sure when it had started, but at some point over the years, she had stopped truly loving herself. Whether it was pre-, mid-, or post-Chantelle wasn't clear, but the fact remained. For so long, Tess had focused too much of her time trying to please everyone else, all without stopping to care for herself. Instead of confiding in her sister her reservations over planning the bridal party week, Tess had silently taken on the daunting task. It was like she no longer believed in voicing her own opinions, from maid of honor duties to harder life decisions such as romantic relationships. Was that what Chantelle had seen in her? Instead of talking to her about it, she'd woken up one day and decided she needed a woman with more backbone? Tess wasn't built for pissing off or confronting loved ones. Even when she'd caught Chantelle in bed with another woman, Tess hadn't gotten angry. She'd internalized every feeling until she could break down privately from the betrayal. She was a peacekeeper, not a woman to speak her mind with no consequence. When she'd finally gathered up the courage to end things, she'd packed all her bags and left a note. *Like a coward.*

"I can hear you thinking."

Tess blinked. Taunya's melodic tone flooded her overloaded senses and worked wonders to relax her mind. She sighed, relaxing into the comfort of her sister's arms. Times were changing; usually it was Tess catering to her little sister, not the other way around.

"Sorry."

"Wanna talk about it?"

"Mhmn, honestly, I'm a little talked out. Can we just lie here a bit longer?" she whispered, aware of Taunya's gentle fingers playing with her hair as they lay in Tess's bed.

The Heat, starring Sandra Bullock — one of Tess's on-screen crushes — played in the background, but she couldn't even concentrate. Monday was now Tuesday, and early morning she guessed by the first rays of light shining in through the slits of her curtains. Despite the upcoming wedding, Tess had followed her sister's lead through the night and eaten through her feelings with chocolate, two bottles of homemade red wine, and a stale box of Ritz crackers they'd found in the back of Tess's cupboard.

"Of course, although don't take offense if I nod off." Taunya let out a yawn, her arms tightening around her sister. Moments later, her chin was resting against the top of Tess's head, and she murmured, "I need to hear how —" another yawn "—you plan to get Abi back."

Tess couldn't remember the last time she'd been held like this, and it came as a surprise to her that it wasn't their mother doing the holding. As close as the sisters were at times, Taunya wasn't usually one Tess would think of turning to. She was so often hot-headed and self-absorbed, so the change filled a longing Tess hadn't realized she'd been harboring. One corner of her mouth curled up in a sad smile. "I can't be what Abi wants. She thinks she knows who I am, but how, when even I'm not sure?"

Taunya was quiet, so Tess continued to whisper, "Do you know why I stayed with Vicki? I wasn't happy, but the thought of failing at yet another relationship made me more miserable. I don't want to fail Abi, Tauni." Silence answered her, and she craned her face up to see that Taunya's eyes were closed and her breathing had evened out.

"That was fast," Tess muttered, dropping her gaze again. After spending so many hours with Stacey, or Taunya, or both, she was reluctant to be alone in her thoughts once more. It was then that they raced away from her, conjuring the worst tales imaginable until they became an obsession. It was there Tess berated herself, and those same illusions had her believing every negative thought her creative brain could fabricate. How could she begin to believe in herself and start looking at life like a glass half-full? She didn't want to live half-empty anymore.

Careful not to disturb Taunya, Tess slipped from the mattress and headed for the bathroom. She was stiff from lying so long in bed, and she felt yucky overall, but couldn't bring herself to shower. She flushed the toilet, not daring to look at herself in the mirror as she washed her hands. If she felt like hell, she no doubt looked it, and honestly, she couldn't bring herself to look at the woman who'd made Abi cry.

Tess left the bathroom, a forlorn sigh escaping her as she glanced around her small living space. Abi's perfume still lingered in the air, proof that even for the shortest time, Tess had been unbelievably happy. It was the lack of clothes and footwear that made her chest squeeze with newfound agony. Without pieces of Abi littered across the floor and by the door, the small home had never felt so unbearably lonely.

I'm sorry, Abi. I'm so very sorry, Tess thought, fighting back fresh tears. She wished whole-heartedly that she hadn't sent her lover away.

Once Taunya left, Tess allowed herself the rest of Tuesday to wallow in self-pity and in and out of a fitful sleep but reluctantly opened the shop the following day. Now it was Thursday, and while her emotional hangover had mostly dissipated, a hard awareness had sunk deeply into Tess's heart and hadn't let go. Abi had yet to call or text her. Even though Tess *knew* Stacey had warned Abi to give her space, a part of Tess hoped Abi wouldn't listen. Tess had feared as much, and yet hadn't it been exactly what she requested? She'd been the one to send Abi away; she'd watched in silence with Stacey as Abi packed her belongings and left, knowing very well she was breaking the other woman's heart. Tess hadn't believed it possible then, and now she wondered if she'd been correct all along in her assumptions. Abi not reaching out was proof that a relationship with Tess wasn't what she wanted. It was true what they said: the truth hurt, a *lot*.

"Doing anything fun this summer?" Tess asked the kid currently occupying the swivel chair in her barbershop. Before they'd begun, the boy — Donovan was his name — pointed to a picture on his phone, showing Tess a trendy hairstyle she was well familiar with. She'd lost count in the past year of how many clients requested a line-up and skin fade combination.

"I went to camp already with my best friend Ben, and Mom says soon she's taking us to Playland!" Donovan's gleaming blue eyes shone with the kind of fervent excitement only a child could still possess. Hell, it almost made Tess happy, and she wasn't even going.

"I believe my words were maybe, Don," his mother gently corrected from where she sat by the window. She was smiling, though, and Tess found their happiness contagious. They were new, walk-in customers, and Tess always felt a certain degree of pressure to impress with her skill so they'd return. Today, most of her underlying pressure was more of a personal nature.

"That would be fun if you did get to go. I went a few times when I was younger," Tess told him, sounding gruff even to her own ears. Picking up her small neck duster, she cleaned away bits of debris from his hairline before doing a final check. The line-up and skin fade were an edgy, distinctive, all-around fun design for Tess to do. Getting the sharp lines even along the hairline and temples typically gave her a sense of pride, and when she topped the line-up off with the slick skin fade with her clippers along the back, her customers left looking like a million bucks. Today, pride was far from what she was feeling, and she just hoped it didn't show in her work. Client complaints would be the last thing she'd need with Abi so much on her mind. She swapped out the clipper guards and started on the fade.

When she finished and the mother had paid, Tess asked if she could take a picture of Donovan's cut to post on her Instagram. The woman agreed, and after Tess snapped a few photos, they left, with Tess's assurance that she'd tag them in the picture. It wasn't until they'd disappeared that it dawned on Tess she never got the mother's name.

"Just my luck," she said under her breath, her shoulders sagging a little as she reached for the broom. Emotion clogged her throat as she swept up the kid's hair, tears blurring her vision until they were splashing onto the dustpan. She paused in her task to snap back her rubber band, hissing as it met the raw skin on her wrist. In Monday's upset, cracking her rubber band repeatedly had caused deep welts to form. They had since scabbed over.

Tess swept the hair onto the dustpan but clumsily unloaded it in the garbage, and a good portion ended up back on the floor. More tears gathered and fell, and she swiped her shirtsleeve over her damp eyes. It was almost shocking how much she missed Abi. It had only been three nights, about as long as they'd been sleeping together, but hell if she didn't miss every single little thing about the other woman. Her voice, her hair, that smile, those eyes, and the way they seemed to light up when they saw Tess...

Tess's heart squeezed, like someone had reached inside her body and wrapped a huge hand around the muscle. She sank into her office chair, snatching the cell phone off the desk in desperation. She had to know: why hadn't Abi reached out? Tess's fingers trembled as she pulled up their previous text thread, her thumbs belting out a rapid message before she reconsidered.

Tess – 5:08PM

> I'm sorry, Abi. Please don't be mad at me. I couldn't bear it.

Tess sucked her teeth, hesitating, before deleting the last part. Her thumb hovered over the send button, unsure if she should try at all. After Tess had all but thrown her out, Abi had every right to be pissed.

The bell above her shop's door jingled as someone entered, startling Tess, and she dropped her phone onto the desk with the message left unsent. McCoy stood there, still dressed in her work clothes. She had stripped her navy-blue grease-stained overalls off her torso to bunch up around her waist, where it was tied in the front, like people often did with a hoodie. Her work boots were scuffed and marred by engine oil, but the forest-green dropped-armhole tank top she wore appeared relatively clean. "You working late, or just forget to turn the sign off?"

Tess sat up straighter, checking her watch and silently praying her face didn't show signs of crying. Sure enough, it was ten after five, and she muttered a curse, vaguely wondering where the afternoon had gone.

"The latter," she admitted, studying McCoy warily. The younger woman seemed out of place in Tess's shop, her hands shoved into her overall pockets and grime streaked on various parts of her handsome face. By the off-color of Coy's septum ring, there was a high chance grease had made it up her nose as well. "What brings you by, Coy?" she finally asked, having to force the question out past her clamped lips. She didn't *want* to know the whys; in fact, the arrogant mechanic was the *last* person Tess wanted to see today.

"A haircut, actually, if you're up for it." Coy shrugged. "If not, maybe just a beer. I'm thinking we could both use one. You still keep a few in the back fridge, right?"

Tess narrowed her gaze in suspicion, studying her some more, trying to find an ulterior motive. Bringing the topic of Abi into conversation was the obvious choice, but if that was her angle, then McCoy was content to detour for a time. Presently, all Tess could see was an open friendliness, far more sympathetic to Tess than she'd ever been. It should have been raising flags, but it wasn't. She sighed. "Lock the door and close the blinds, then."

As McCoy did as she asked, Tess got her station ready for one last customer before heading to the back of her shop and her mini fridge. Although they'd always been more acquaintances than friends, it wasn't McCoy's first time showing up after hours for a cut and beer. Tess liked to keep a few cold ones on hand for long days but so far hadn't applied for a liquor license. She wasn't sure she would, either, knowing it could potentially impact her younger clientele. And she loved when kids like Donovan came into her shop.

"I turned the sign off, too," McCoy mentioned, plopping down in the seat Donovan had recently vacated. Fatigue and weariness cast shadows in her green eyes, and all Tess wanted was to ask about Abi. She'd learned from Taunya that Abi had taken up Coy's offer of a spare bed when Tess kicked her out. The idea of Abi in such close quarters to a womanizer like Coy caused more than her chest to burn, and Coy's small smile caught Tess off guard.

"Thanks," she said, accepting the beer.

"Long day?"

Coy shrugged again, cracking the tab on her Molson and taking a long swig. Tess waited, curious about this side to Coy that Abi knew intimately. They were close, closer than Abi and Taunya in some ways. McCoy wiped her lips with her arm and let out a long sigh. "Just the usual bullshit that comes with working in a male-dominated field. Another self-righteous, bigoted asshole throwing a tantrum after finding out a woman had replaced his exhaust and rear rotors. 'Cause you know, us women are too stupid and can't possibly tell the difference between a filter, lug, or socket wrench."

"Ugh, that's gotta be so annoying," Tess sympathized with a grimace. She sipped her own beer, setting it off to the side and gently turning McCoy in the chair so she faced the mirror. "You want the usual?"

"Please. With any luck, my face will be buried between a set of great thighs by the end of the night. I wanna make sure she can feel the fresh under-cut while I'm eating her out." McCoy chuckled as Tess's face drained of color in the mirror. She winked, adding, "Not Abi, Barber, promise. I'm squeezing in a guy's night at the club with my buddy Naz."

"B–but," Tess stammered, swallowing the lump in her throat, "why would you bail on Abi?"

Coy raised the beer to her mouth, taking another long swig before saying, "Abs borrowed Sloane's car yesterday to go visit her parents. Won't be back until sometime tomorrow."

"Oh." Tess's hushed response wasn't lost on the mechanic, and she quirked her eyebrow in the mirror.

"That's why I'm here dirty. Didn't have time to wash up before giving my sister a ride to work."

"Oh." Tess frowned, wishing she could think of something more to say. Concern for Abi was on the tip of her tongue, but she reeled it in, not wanting to get upset all over again. She fastened the cape around McCoy's neck, unable to meet Coy's perceptive gaze.

"You would know that if you had reached out to her, Tess."

"I ... I know that," Tess rasped, emotion thick on her tongue. She began jerkily unraveling McCoy's small braid. She'd sported a disconnected undercut for as long as Tess had known her, the only changes being the way she chose to style the top day-to-day. Her straight chestnut hair was usually plaited down her scalp or thrown into the topknot, with her shaved bottom boldly on display. It was an easy style for Tess to tidy up every couple of weeks.

"So why haven't you? Do you know how hard it's been for Abi to give you space?" McCoy shook her head, resulting in a firm grip from Tess to hold it straight. "Pushing her away out of fear will only hurt you both."

"She's..." Tess trailed off and reached for her sheers before trying again. "She's giving me space?" Was that all it was? Had Tess been worried over nothing?

McCoy's dry chuckle had Tess blushing. It was no surprise when the rugged woman replied, "Tess, my awkward new friend, you know shit-all about women. I had to confiscate Abi's phone for a while yesterday morning just to keep her from calling you. I ex-plained — and more than once, I might add — that whatever you're going through has nothing to do with her, and she needs patience."

"You ... did?"

"Why sound so surprised?"

Shrugging, Tess blushed even more, and she kept her eyes trained on Coy's haircut. "I thought maybe... Er, never mind."

"That I was trying to steal Abi from you?" With Tess's subtle nod, Coy laughed, moving so much in the chair that Tess had to pause and hold her still again. Her green eyes were bright and rife with humor as she gazed at Tess in the mirror. "Dude, I've been trying for *years* to get Abi underneath me. She isn't into friends with benefits, and besides, even if I wanted to, I couldn't hold a candle to what you mean to her. Tess, no offense, but fucking open your eyes, yeah? Abi isn't *like* anyone you've dated in the past, and frankly, it's insulting for you to think otherwise. That girl has loved you forever, and if you don't wanna be with her, now or ever, you at least owe her an explanation."

Chapter Twenty-Six

Abi

Friday's dinner rehearsal arrived gradually for Abi, the hours trickling by as sluggishly as the last drops inside a bottle of pure maple syrup. Even with constant distractions to take her mind off Tess, it hadn't been enough to speed the week along. Maybe it was because none of the distractions had *worked*, so Tess was still ingrained in every piece of her mind, body, and soul.

Abi gnawed on her bottom lip, the stem of a half glass of Pinot Grigio dangling between her fingers as she hid inside the Moores' bathroom. She was perched on the closed lid of the toilet with her cell in her other hand and Margo's number, already dialing. She wouldn't normally have bothered the woman outside of work hours, especially when it was late in Margo's time zone, but it had taken this long to come to a decision. Life was hard in general, but love, she was figuring out, was damn near impossible.

"Abi, I'm glad you called," Margo gushed. Her voice was entirely too pleasant, and Abi suspected she had gotten into a bit of her own wine that evening. It always worked wonders in loosening up the older woman.

The thought brought on a sad smile. "Hi, Margo."

Silence, then, "Is everything okay? You sound, I don't know … like you need a hug?"

Abi barked a laugh, acknowledging the truth in the words. She'd been held more times than she could count over the last four days, but not by the one person she longed for. The crack in her armor grew, threatening to take her over, which was what had led Abi to dial Margo in the first place. "I'll be okay, though I'm grateful for your concern."

"Of course, Abi. I know things between us got complicated recently, but I'll always care for you." The statement was made in a much more demure tone, which surprised Abi. Curt and brazen were practically Margo's middle names as of late. She'd be lying if she said she hadn't missed the old Margo, the one who stayed up all night talking and brought breakfast in bed. Abi's throat burned, her chest constricting with Margo's concern. *Why couldn't love be a choice?*

"I um, thank you," she said thickly, blinking back tears. She took a gulp of her wine, "I–I just wanted to confirm things with my old job. I'll take it, if … if it's still mine to have."

"Of course it is." There was no hiding Margo's elation, and Abi hesitated. Would she be able to keep things professional between them?

She cleared her throat. "*With* the stipulations I laid out last week? Can you agree to that, Margo, or are we deluding ourselves here? I care about you too, but I have no interest in anything more than a business relationship."

"I understand. While I don't necessarily like it, I promise, Abi, things will be better this time if you come back to work for me."

"Okay, then. I guess I'll see you bright and early Monday," Abi whispered, standing up as a few tears slipped past her lashes.

"Sounds good, Abi. Enjoy your weekend."

"You too, Margo." Abi ended the call, setting the phone down on the vanity before peering out the large bathroom window. Close friends and family of the bridal party mingled in the backyard, some setting up for the evening meal and others in deep conversation. Even Abi's parents had come to celebrate Taunya and Derek, and, she supposed, to have a long-overdue visit with the bride's parents. Everyone seemed to be having a grand time, well, everyone but Abi. It wasn't possible to be any happier for the bride-to-be, truly, but it was time for Abi to leave. Her trip home hadn't turned out at all like she'd planned, and once again she'd be leaving Vancouver with her tail tucked between her legs.

Fuck, it hurts, maybe even more than the first time.

Abi squared her shoulders, taking a deep breath as she scanned the crowd outside for Tess. Like the newfound coward she was, Abi had been trying like hell to avoid her that evening, and it was just as well; it wasn't like they had anything further to say to each other. For the first two days after Tess ended things, Abi had remained optimistic. She'd taken McCoy's advice to heart, thinking that if she gave Tess time, things between them would work out. *Yeah, right, as if loving Tess could be so easy.* Frankly, Abi was over the constant rejection. She was mortified at how quickly she'd wrapped herself up in Tess, and, by proxy, Tess's problems. She was usually more dignified, but just as she had all those years ago, as soon as Tess had shown her any attention, she'd become an obsessive teenager all over again.

Abi polished off her wine, absently rubbing the deeply centered ache in her chest. Her heartache was stubborn and profound, but the pain didn't stop there. Unrequited love was like living with slivers of glass in your stomach or acid burning your skin from a corroded battery. The discomfort ate at Abi, day and night, never fully exiting her body. And unlike four years ago, she now had a crater-sized hole where her heart lay. She didn't think she could hurt any more than when she'd left Tess's bed the first time, but she was wrong. Loving Tess, *truly* loving her, only to be rejected in the end—

The toilet lid was flipped up, and Abi had just enough time to drop to her knees before she emptied her stomach contents. She heaved again, tears trekking down her cheeks as she got sick. "God," she choked out, reaching up to flush the toilet. She was shaky as she climbed to her feet to wash her hands and rinse out her mouth in the sink. "Two more days. You can do this," she vowed, staring back at her pale reflection in the mirror. She took a deep breath, retrieving the small makeup kit from the vanity before letting out the gust of air from her lungs.

Fixing her smeared eyeliner and adding a bit of blush to her cheeks to disguise her horrid state, Abi picked up her empty wine glass and left the bathroom.

"Where did you disappear to?" Taunya asked, catching Abi by the elbow the moment she stepped outside. Her friend looked stunning tonight in a casual mauve sundress and sandals. The stitches on her face were barely discernible, and there was a fresh bandage wrapped securely around her ankle, but Abi knew it was just a precaution before the wedding. Taunya planned to remove it for the big event.

"Just the bathroom. Sit with me?" Abi asked, taking Taunya's hand and guiding her toward the long rectangular foldout table. Others were already seated, but Tess was still nowhere to be seen.

Had she skipped out already? She couldn't be sure, but the maid of honor leaving the dinner rehearsal early seemed like bad form to Abi.

"Abs," Coy greeted her, reaching out to pinch her lightly on the arm. The friends sat down, Coy on one side of Abi and Taunya on the other.

Taunya leaned in to whisper, "Were you crying? Wanna talk about it?"

Abi grimaced, giving the other woman a slight shake of her head. No, she didn't want to *talk* about it. That was what got her into this whole mess. If she'd never opened up to Taunya the day she landed, she probably never would have pursued Tess on this trip. The only positive thing to come from everything was getting Tess away from Vicki.

"Hey, baby," Taunya said, offering her lips to Derek as he took his place beside her. He looked like he'd won the lottery, eyes lit up and eager for the weekend. He was so smitten with Taunya, it was almost unbelievable love like that existed.

The rehearsal got underway with Taunya's parents welcoming everyone to their home. Tess snuck in a few minutes after, quietly taking the vacant seat beside her mother. She caught Abi's eye, surprising her with a shy smile. Forcing a smile of her own, it lasted all of two Mississippis before she tore her gaze away. There was a microscopic possibility that Abi's toxic trait of "loving too damn hard" would fade with time, but in *this* moment it hurt to look at Tess. It felt like a physical blow, and she sucked in a breath, her hand faltering when she reached for her water glass.

"Shit," she hissed when it tipped over, liquid gushing over the tablecloth. Her cheeks were on fire as Coy jumped to her rescue, batting up the sopping mess with cloth napkins.

"No worries, Abs," she murmured, rubbing Abi's back as she worked. She closed the remaining distance between them, her lips grazing Abi's hairline. "You're doing great."

Abi closed her eyes. If only she believed that.

She didn't dare look at Tess again during dinner, and it wasn't until the speeches were halfway done that she understood how ridiculous she was being. Taunya needed her to be present, in *all* ways, not merely a body but with a mind elsewhere. She needed to bench her personal baggage, pronto. Except that was easier said than done, and she almost choked on her grilled steak when Tess clinked her glass to garner everyone's attention.

"I'll, um, I–I'll keep this brief," she began, and Abi had no choice but to look at the woman she loved. If she could give Tess nothing else, she hoped at least to provide courage somehow to speak in front of others. Their gazes collided across the table, and the obvious bundle of nerves on Tess's face melted to one of relief. This time her smile was tremulous, and she stared directly at Abi for several seconds before she blinked, taking in the rest at the table. "Sorry, I um, lost my train of thought."

Light chuckles and murmurs erupted around the table, but Abi held her breath as Tess plowed on, "I can't believe I'm supposed to do this speech twice," she expressed, her voice an octave higher than usual. More laughter ensued, causing Tess to let out a stressed giggle of her own.

"We love you, Tess!" Taunya rang out, thumping the table and making the beverages slosh around in their respective glasses.

"Love you too," Tess returned, an adorable blush breaking out over her throat and cheeks. Abi itched to say the same, but she couldn't, *wouldn't*. Seconds later, Coy's hand was in her palm — almost like she'd read her mind — and Abi gave it a grateful squeeze.

"It's easy to say to your family that you love them. If you're blessed with a good one, it's easy to feel loved and to trust in it." Tess's words wobbled a bit as she glanced at the dozen faces around her. Abi's heart squeezed as those magnetic brown eyes landed on her. Tess frowned, her gaze distant. "What's not simple is going out in the world and … and *giving* yourself to someone new. That's hard, for some people more than others. You risk everything to fall in love, trusting that they'll come through for you and you won't regret having tried."

Tess blurred in front of her, and when Coy's finger swiped an errant tear off her cheek, Abi knew why. She let them come, saying the hell with it, knowing very well Tess was trying to tell her something important. Leave it to the gentlewoman to disguise a deep conversation into a maid of honor speech.

"Derek, you gave that to my sister, and I…" Tess paused to clear her throat. She reached for her glass of water and took a sip, her fingers swiping away her own tears. She smiled at her future brother-in-law, her eyes gleaming with dampness and affection, "I can't thank you enough. I've had the honor of watching you both mature these last six years. You've grown as individuals and as a couple, and time and time again you've proven how much Tauni means to you. That is the basic definition of love, and honestly, I can't wait to officially call you brother."

Applause broke out around the table, and Abi tearfully watched as Derek got up and walked all the way around the table to give Tess a hug. It was such a meaningful display of familial love, something Abi might never be a part of. She felt a sob building in her chest, and she willed the sucker down, taking a deep, calming breath and another drink of wine.

Her Sunday evening flight couldn't come soon enough.

Chapter Twenty-Seven

Tess

TESS COULDN'T FIND ABI anywhere.

She'd already looked inside the house and again in the backyard, but she was starting to think Abi didn't want to be found. Or she'd left the dinner rehearsal early. *Or both*, Tess considered, craning her neck to scan the corner of the yard over Krystal's shoulder. There was a high chance Abi had left the dinner to get away from Tess, especially after her failed attempt at an apology via the maid of honor speech.

Taunya left her place between the twins and approached Tess with a smirk, raising her wine glass to clink her sister's. "That was quite the speech, sis, but you've always had a way with words."

"Thank you." Tess's lips twitched, and she glanced around the yard again, her attention not fully on Taunya. "And I meant every one of them."

"Lose something?"

Tess frowned, lifting her glass to her lips and muttering, "Maybe." Sipping her father's homemade sweet wine, the butterflies in her stomach plummeted as her anxiety revved.

"She's not exactly a 'something' when she has a set of glorious legs and a heartbeat," McCoy tutted, because of *course* Tess couldn't have a private conversation with her sister.

Tess's face pinched, aware of Sloane and Krystal looking at her as well now. *Thanks a lot, McCoy.* "Do you know where she is?" she asked in a tight voice.

Coy replied with a casual shrug of her thick shoulders. *How irritating.* "Hey now, I'm not the one who lost her."

A frustrated growl escaped Tess, surprising her sister's friends. Sloane guffawed, gesturing in Tess's direction with a flip of her hand, the silver rings on each finger reminding Tess of a rock star. "Dude, Abi wasn't feeling well, so I gave her the keys to my car. She was headed back to the apartment."

"Damnit, how long ago was that?" Tess rocked back on her heels, deep in thought. There were a couple ways to get to Richmond. She could take her bike and try to catch up to Abi.

"Fifteen minutes, maybe?"

"Okay," Tess said slowly with a faint grin. She handed off her wine to Taunya, a nervous laugh escaping. "Okay! I'm going after her."

"Hell yes you are!" Krystal exclaimed, giving Tess a light shove.

"It's about time. I've been shipping you two from the beginning," Sloane added, high-fiving her twin.

"Go get our girl, Tessa!" her sister added, then wrinkled her nose. "Not like my *girl*, girl, like my friend—"

"I got it, sis." Tess laughed, planting a quick kiss on Taunya's cheek before taking off. "Wish me luck!" she called over her shoulder.

"You don't need it!" Coy's voice rang out.

Cheers and hollers shot up around Tess as she hurried away from the dinner party. Instead of going through the house, she made her way around the front to where she'd last parked her bike. The driveway and grass were cluttered with vehicles from their guests, and Tess slowed to a stop as she calculated the small spaces between them.

"Just my luck," she grumbled as she realized she'd have to walk her bike out of the driveway if she planned to go after Abi. That would be a lot of pushing and possibly unrealistic. McCoy could do it.

Tess perked up at the thought. "Coy could totally do it!" Wow, the mechanic was quickly moving out of Tess's annoying category and into her helpful one. Her heart knocked against her chest from the sheer adrenaline of what she was attempting to do. It'd taken her too long over the last few days to decide what was right for her, and it wasn't until McCoy's visit to her shop that the truth and depth of Abi's feelings sank in. Tess had wasted so much time comparing herself with Coy, deciding that the mechanic was more suited to a woman as incredible as Abi, that she hadn't stopped to consider — to *believe* what Abi had been telling her all along. Tess still had a long way to go in that department, but she knew she couldn't live with herself if Abi left Vancouver without them trying to fix things.

Spinning around to head back to the rehearsal party, Tess spotted an older-style red T-top Trans-Am two car lengths away. It was in mint condition, the roof panels off, and as she noticed Abi's caramel locks bobbing to the low music playing, she figured Sloane's car up-keep was thanks to her twin. A huge sigh escaped Tess, her shoulders slumping with relief at having caught Abi. For a moment she just studied the other woman, gauging what mood she was in but also not wanting to startle Abi over the music playing in the car. Tess was unfamiliar with whatever pop song Abi was singing along to, but it didn't look like she was crying, so she took it as a good sign.

Squaring her shoulders and drawing in an encouraging breath, Tess ambled into Abi's line of sight, catching her eye through the windshield. Her hand went up in an awkward wave, a gust of relief escaping when Abi reached over to shut the music off. For a moment, they just stared at each other, Tess taking the chance to soak up Abi's features. It felt like weeks since she'd been able to look at Abi fully, not days, and her heart grappled to understand. "H–hi," she stammered, rubbing her sweaty palms over her dress pants. "Sloane ... she, um, said you weren't feeling well. Are you leaving?"

A wary look crossed Abi's face as her gaze dropped to where Tess still absentmindedly rubbed her hands. Their eyes locked again. Abi lifted her hand to point behind Tess. "Sara's jammed in here tighter than a sardine can."

"Sara?" Tess said, her brow crinkling in confusion. She glanced behind her at all the vehicles blocking Abi's path, and the problem became clear.

Abi patted the steering wheel of the Trans-Am, a faint smile appearing. Her lovely blue eyes sparked with humor. "Sloane's car is Sara, Coy's Jeep is Tegan." When Tess just gave her a muddled look, Abi tsked. "Please tell me you've heard of Tegan and Sara, the twin indie pop duo."

"Sure I have, I just didn't know people actually named their cars." Laughter bubbled from Tess's chest. "Especially not after celebrities."

"Getting to know Coy, does that surprise you?" Abi shook her head, her kissable lips still curled up at the corners. She tilted her head to the passenger side of the Trans-Am. "Join me?"

Tess sighed, the butterflies in her stomach easing. "I thought you'd never ask." She slipped in beside Abi, shutting the heavy door behind her.

"How have you been?"

Abi's question caught Tess off-guard. Here she was, still putting Tess's feelings above her own, even though it was Tess who had pushed Abi away. Tess didn't deserve her in the slightest, but maybe, depending on where they ended up tonight, she could spend the rest of her life proving herself to Abi.

"I'm so sorry, Abi," Tess blurted, her brows knitting. She clasped Abi's hand, interlocking their fingers and giving them a gentle squeeze. She swallowed hard, but her gaze didn't leave Abi's. "I'm sorry for ever pushing you away. Seeing Chantelle messed me all up, and I let my insecurities take over. I should have trusted you."

"It's okay, Tess, I get it." Abi ducked her head, staring down at their hands instead of at Tess. Her thumb began stroking the back of Tess's hand, and she added quietly, "It isn't like we were together long enough for you to get there emotionally with me."

"Maybe so, but ... but I want to," Tess whispered back, reaching up to tuck a loose strand of hair behind Abi's ear. She was slow to pull her fingers away, tracing the line of Abi's jaw as she went. Her pulse jumped in her throat, and she croaked, "What do you say? Can we ... can we give this another shot?"

Abi's tearful gaze reluctantly met hers in the dim light. Tess watched as her bottom lip trembled. "I took the job. I start back Monday morning."

"Oh." Tess blinked, slowly pulling away from her. The familiar burn of tears in her own eyes was coming full-force. "Oh."

"Yeah."

"But I had thought..." Tess trailed off, her throat working overtime as she got her emotions in check. Her shoulders sagged, and she ducked her face away from Abi's so she couldn't see the tear that slipped out. Clearing her throat, her voice was gravelly as she finished lamely, "I thought you would move back. It's what you said."

"I was, but after..." In her peripheral view, Tess saw as Abi shook her head. "I decided leaving Toronto right now wasn't the best thing for me. Also, I owe you an apology, Tess." When Tess looked at Abi, her vision swimming with tears, Abi leaned in and placed a kiss on her cheek. She rested her forehead against Tess's, whispering, "I'm sorry for coming on so strong. You're not ready for this, and we basically U-Hauled from the get-go. I've always been too much."

"What?" Tess abruptly pulled away and scrutinized the woman before her. "You are *not* too much, Abi. In fact, through my eyes you're practically perfect. All I've ever wanted in a relationship was someone who loved me for me and wasn't afraid to show it. *I* am the one who's sorry, because like an idiot, in the last four years, I let every excuse there was act as a barrier between us."

Abi sniffled. "I'd always assumed you regretted that night."

"I regretted a lot of things, but never how it felt to be with you. Abi, I..." Tess shook her head, closing the gap again and giving Abi a teary kiss. "I don't want this to end. I don't... I don't want you to go. Please stay?" She wasn't above begging, if that's what it took.

"I love you, Tess, but this week has given me nothing but time to think." Abi lifted Tess's hand to her lips and placed a sweet kiss on her palm before resting it against her cheek. Their eyes met once more, and the obvious adoration in Abi's glacier blues no longer frightened Tess as much. "When I move back here, I want to make sure you're ready for everything I have to give. I'll need you to be certain of your feelings for me and want to take the next step toward our future. So ... so if you want to try, let's see how things go long-distance. Can we do that?"

"Yes, anything, just please don't give up on me," Tess murmured, taking Abi's lips in hers again. She kissed the other woman deeply, passionately, her free hand wrapping around Abi's slender neck and drawing her closer still. She let out a groan when Abi pulled away. Their gazes held, Tess watching under hooded eyes as Abi used her thumb to wipe her kiss from her lips. "What?" She leaned forward for another kiss, but Abi stopped her pursuit.

"I know it's hard to gauge how quickly it takes to heal, but I want you to tell me where you're at emotionally, and often. Communication is everything if this is going to work."

"I promise I will," Tess avowed, bringing Abi's hand to her chest, right over her heart. "Abi, I don't *want* to be like this, questioning your every intention. I want what I've always wanted, and I think ... well, I hope that it can be with you."

Abi's eyes lit up; her smile was hopeful. Tugging Tess to her once more, she whispered, "Excellent answer, sweetie."

CHAPTER TWENTY-EIGHT

Abi

TAUNYA WAS EYEING HER reflection in the tall, standalone mirror when Abi walked in two days later.

"Wow, Tauni, you are *gorgeous*," she gushed, marveling over her friend's exquisite wedding dress. It was an off-white, almost cream-colored strapless dress with the beaded corset bodice hugging Taunya's slight torso so well, it looked like the silken material was made for her alone. The bottom half of the dress flared out into a long, ball-gown style. Taunya's mid-length coal black hair had been curled and pinned up, and baby's breath flowers adorned the loosely fastened bun in the back.

Tears sprang to Abi's eyes. "I can't believe how beautiful you look!"

"Save all your fawning for my sister," Taunya joked, reaching for Abi's hand as she came closer into the room. She gave it an affectionate squeeze before pulling Abi into a hug. "Where is Tess, anyway?"

"Careful, don't smudge our makeup. It's a good thing it's waterproof." Abi laughed, taking a tissue from her clutch to dab gently around her eyes. "Tess was handing your mom off to an usher last time I saw her."

"Awesome, that's great." A gust of air left Taunya, and together they turned back to face the mirror. Abi wrapped her arms around Taunya's waist from behind and leaned her chin on the other woman's shoulder.

Their eyes met. "Nervous?"

Taunya smiled and shook her head. "Not even a little. I can't thank you enough for being here, Abi. I love you, bestie."

"Love you back." Abi tightened her arms around Taunya before releasing her altogether. For the first time since she'd arrived home, everything in her life felt exactly as it should.

"Oof, I know that smile." Taunya gave her a knowing chuckle. "Soon it'll be your wedding we're all getting ready for. And a future FYI, I call dibs as your MOH. I'll throw you the best bachelorette party."

"Not on your life, Tauni. I've got strippers on speed dial. What have you got?" McCoy exclaimed, and they turned to see the rest of the bridal party coming into the church's dressing room. This was the first time Abi had seen everyone in their respectable wedding attire, and she had to admit, although she thought the gray material with pink flowers would be a terrible choice for a wedding, every single one of them looked dashing.

"How did you manage to find a tux that matched the bridesmaids' dresses?" she asked, checking out the skinny style gray dress pants Coy had on. Overtop her white dress shirt was a gray tux jacket with pink flowers scattered over the material. The design was eccentric, to say the least, but Coy somehow made it look passable.

"Derek's mother handled all that. I'm surprised she's not here now, making sure I'm ready to go." Taunya rolled her eyes good-naturedly.

"Hey you." Abi grinned, allowing her eyes to roam over Tess. It was hard to describe, but Tess in a dress was oddly perfect. Whether she wore something masculine or more feminine, Tess could pull off anything.

"Hey back." The way Tess's eyes lit up as they kissed was the kind of reaction Abi had longed for, for years. Looking back at this trip's turn of events, it was sometimes hard to believe they were giving their relationship a chance. Abi had never considered long-distance in the past, but when it came to Tess, some things were a no-brainer.

"It doesn't matter how many times I see you in this dress, Tauni, it never gets old." Sloane let out an appreciative whistle. "You're a complete babe, you know that, right?"

"Sloane's right," Coy added with a Cheshire Cat grin. She arched an eyebrow. "If Derek doesn't pull you into the nearest corner after the ceremony to have his way with you, then the man is without hope, for real."

"I'll make sure he knows that," Taunya said with a smirk. She glanced at her bridal party, clapping excitedly. "We all look a-maz-ing!"

"It's true; excluding my sister, I'd smash any one of you. Wouldn't even have to get me drunk." Coy wagged her eyebrows at Tess. "Even you, Barber."

While the rest of the group laughed, poor Tess just looked confused. "You want to hit me?"

Sloane and Taunya groaned, but Krystal began to correct her. "Coy means that she'd ... oh, never mind."

Abi looped her arm around Tess's waist, still giggling. "I'll explain later."

There was a knock on the door, and Bobby opened it enough to duck his head in. "Ten minutes, Taunya! Hope you're ready, sweetheart."

"Thanks, Dad," Taunya returned before taking a deep breath. "So, *is* everything ready? The whole day has been a blur."

"I think so. We know who's walking down the aisle with who." Abi pointed to the bouquet resting on the table a few feet away. "Your flowers are there."

"Are you reading your vows, or did you manage to memorize them? They were kind of long," Krystal put in.

Taunya's eyes widened. "My vows! I haven't even looked at them since this morning. Tess, where did you put them? Maybe I can look over it quickly."

Tess froze. "Er..." Slowly, her eyes widened too. She glanced back and forth between Abi and Taunya, seemingly frantic now. "I–I don't have them, I... Let me go check my bag." She sputtered before darting from the room.

"What do you mean? Tess!" Taunya hollered, her cheeks flushed.

Abi placed a comforting hand on her arm. "I'm sure it's in her bag. She was throwing everything in there before we left this morning."

"Do you have it saved in Google Docs or something, just in case?" Sloane asked.

Krystal nodded. "Good thinking. Tauni could just read it off the phone, worst-case."

"Yes, but that's not what I'm worried most about."

Abi was about to ask Taunya to clarify when Tess barged into the room again. She was out of breath and flushed and looking every bit like she'd been caught doing something horrible.

"Taunya, I–I'm so sorry," she exclaimed, rubbing at her naked wrist like the elastic band she'd taken off earlier would just appear as needed. It already looked as if the makeup Abi helped her apply over the welts was coming off.

"Don't tell me you lost the ring, Tess? I'm getting married in ten fucking minutes, and another wedding is booked right after us! We can't hold off for long," Taunya hissed.

Tess bowed her head, staring at her open-toed heels. "I think it's in my backpack in the garage. I–I for some reason I thought I'd be taking my bike here, not riding with Mom."

Taunya cursed again, which only managed to stress Tess out more. Abi had to raise her voice to be heard over their bickering. "Ladies! Let's just go back to the house and get them. We can do that, right?"

"I can do that," McCoy volunteered, glancing at Taunya for confirmation. She was the most cool-headed in the group, so it made sense to Abi, but just as Taunya started to agree, Tess interrupted.

"I'll do it. It's my fault. I'm the maid of honor," she mumbled, sounding close to tears.

"I'll come with you."

Tess shook her head at Abi. "The wedding is starting. Just ... stall as long as possible, Tauni, please? Again, I'm sorry."

Taunya heaved a sigh and nodded. "I know you are. Drive safe and hurry back, okay?"

Abi itched to run after Tess when she left again, knowing the last thing she should do was drive when she was so anxious. If she were being honest, a part of her felt equally responsible for the mix-up. If she hadn't distracted Tess that morning with a quickie right before they'd left, maybe Tess would have remembered her bag with the ring and vows inside.

"Everything will be fine. Something goes wrong in every wedding," Krystal assured them, patting Taunya on the back.

"Can we get you anything? A drink, maybe? I know it's a church and all, but I've got mickeys stored in my overnight bag in the car," Sloane supplied, tapping her chin in thought. "Might even have some of Nana's Imodium pills in my purse, if you're that stressed."

"Eww!" Taunya exclaimed, but Sloane's comment had her eyes dancing with amusement again.

"Or one of us can get word to Derek, if you want," Abi added, not wanting him to think he had a runaway bride on his hands.

"Good idea. Coy?"

"On it," McCoy nodded, spinning on the heels of her dress shoes and taking off.

"What a shit-show." Taunya groaned, heading for the nearest chair. Abi and Krystal helped her to sit, which was no easy task with the style of dress she had on.

"I may or may not have taken part in Tess forgetting her bag," Abi sheepishly admitted. She grinned. "I haven't been able to keep my hands off her since we made up."

"Double eww!" Taunya shuddered, pinning Sloane with a look. "How many?"

"I'll bring them all in." Sloane chuckled. "Be right back."

"Sorry, I just don't want you to be so hard on Tess," Abi said when it was just the three of them.

"I shouldn't have given her the ring in the first place. Any one of you could have held on to it."

"Yeah, but I get the feeling she takes being your MOH quite seriously," Krystal murmured. It was true. Tess had bent over backward in her role the last two weeks, making sure her sister had the best wedding imaginable.

"Everything will be fine, Tauni, promise." Abi repeated Krystal's words from earlier.

The twins returned, and by the time Bobby popped in to say they couldn't hold off the wedding any longer, Taunya was just finishing her second mickey. Thankfully, all the alcohol managed to do was take her much-needed edge off — *not* get her drunk before heading up the aisle toward her fiancé.

There was still no sign of Tess as the music began, but her absence didn't affect the pairings since the groomsmen were outnumbered to begin with. McCoy stepped up to Abi, lacing their fingers together as Krystal and Matt started down the aisle before them. "Ready, beautiful?" she whispered, lifting Abi's hand to brush her lips across her knuckles.

Abi nodded, glancing around them once more for Tess. She forced a smile, trying to shake off her worry. *Worst-case scenario, Derek gets his ring later. Relax.* "I'm ready, handsome."

Coy guided her to the front of the church, and Abi made the effort to smile at many of the guests that had filled the pews. Having a church wedding wouldn't ever be Abi's first choice, or second, but whatever made Taunya and Derek happy worked for her.

Abi took her position beside Krystal and Coy, smiling warmly at Derek before shifting her gaze to the back of the church. Sloane came down the aisle after, walking arm-in-arm with Puck, and then it was Taunya's turn. The moment she appeared with her father, there was a collective gasp from the guests, followed by several excited murmurs. Abi held her breath as Taunya began the walk, her heart in her throat at all the happiness radiating from the room. She felt bad for Tess, wishing now she'd thought to convince Taunya to grab the ring later. She shouldn't have had to miss this moment for her sister, and Tess would no doubt dwell on her guilt for a long time to come.

Bobby kissed Taunya's cheek before "handing" her off to the groom. "Taunya, you're breathtaking," Derek tearfully whispered, but he was loud enough for Abi and probably the rest of the bridesmaids to hear. From behind her, Coy grunted in agreement.

"If everyone can please be seated, we'll begin," the pastor announced.

"The barber's cutting it close," Coy muttered close to Abi's ear so only she could make out the apprehension in her friend's voice. Abi reached for Coy's hand, giving it a reassuring squeeze.

The pastor started by introducing the couple, and when it came time for their vows, Abi could have kissed Derek when he opted to go first.

"Taunya, I knew I loved you from the second I held your hair back while you got sick in the bushes at Puck's party." Derek grinned when laughter rang out in the room. He held one of Taunya's hands in one of his and his written vows in the other. Clearing his throat, he continued, "You didn't know it, but I'd been following you around that night. Well, not in a stalkerish way or anything," he corrected when more giggles erupted.

"*Dude*," Sloane mumbled, and although Abi didn't turn to look, she imagined her friend's exaggerated eye roll.

Derek barked a laugh as well. He was nervous, but it didn't deter him. "I was drawn to you from the moment I heard your laugh. I tried to be in the same room as you, hoping I could get a chance to steal you away from your friends."

Matt coughed. "*Stalker*."

"Anyway, when I finally got that chance, the scenario was less than ideal, but as for me, I was already a goner." Derek cupped Taunya's cheek. His entire aura filled with adoration as he stared deep into her eyes. "I love everything about you, Tauni, even when you're bossy or hog the remote, or when we're fighting over stupid stuff. You're my best friend, and I love our life together. I can't imagine doing life with anyone else, and I can't *wait* to grow old with you. I vow to—"

The unmistakable creaking of the large doors opening interrupted Derek's heartfelt vows. Abi pivoted in place, craning her head to catch a frazzled Tess entering the church. Her mouth gaped as she took in the sight of her lover hurrying down the aisle, wearing her leather jacket over her now rumpled dress and riding boots in place of the heels she'd had on earlier.

"Sorry I'm late," Tess muttered, a lovely blush staining her cheeks. She seemed completely unaware of her state of dress, and it had Abi smirking.

"Erm ... Tess?" she questioned, ignoring the stifled laughter around them.

"Here you go, Tauni. Sorry," Tess whispered, handing her sister the flash cards with her vows.

The utter shock on Taunya's face as she watched Tess shrug out of her jacket and pass it off to Audrey was the breaking point for Abi. Hysterical laughter bubbled out, and she clamped her hand over her mouth, sure she was about to get chastised, but when Taunya began laughing as well, it seemed as if the entire guest list broke out in a fit of convulsions.

"You're the best, I swear," Taunya teetered, wiping her eyes and pulling Tess in for a hug.

"No, I'm not, I forgot your stuff at home," Tess replied, her voice muffled against Taunya. As Taunya squeezed the life out of her, Tess caught Abi's gaze.

"Don't care. I'm so glad you're here," Taunya gushed, planting a kiss on Tess's cheek. "Now let's get me married, sis."

"Sounds good to me," Tess agreed, her crooked smile making Abi go weak in the knees.

As Taunya got back into position and the room calmed down, Abi looped her arm around Tess's neck and kissed her soundly on the lips. Tess blushed yet again, peering up at Abi under hooded eyes. "What's that for?"

Abi grinned. "For all the reasons I've given already, and for a thousand more yet to come."

Epilogue

T~ESS PULLED OPEN THE~ bi-fold closet doors in Abi's downtown Toronto apartment. Most of the clothes had been packed by Abi the night before, and the handful still on the hangers were pushed to the far right. It gave Tess a bird's eye view of her assigned task, and she squinted at the two shelves resting on the floor full of footwear.

"So, you *weren't* exaggerating," she muttered, sparing another glance at the stack of sturdy banana boxes waiting just outside the door. Selecting the top box, Tess carried it inside the closet with her and squatted down. She began with the flat dress shoes and sneakers, just in case the pointy tip of a stiletto bottom poked through the bottom of the box. "This is ... beyond all reason. Who needs all these?" she breathed, shaking her head in disbelief. After eight months together, traveling between provinces whenever possible for visits, Tess had thought she'd learned all there was to know about her girlfriend. As it turned out, there were still layers just waiting to be pulled back.

Tess couldn't help but chuckle. "Color-coded too."

"Babe?" Abi called, her voice distant like she was in the hallway. "Don't forget the organizer hanging up with my clothes."

"Organizer?" Tess echoed, a dramatic feeling of dread trickling over her as she dared to look up. "You have got to be kidding!"

Sure enough, nestled between two of Abi's cardigans, was an entire other row of high heels. By the time Tess had unlatched the stilettos from their respective clips and finished packing up the last of it, she'd used all but one box and lost count of how many pairs of footwear would soon be taking over her tiny home. She could see it now, shoes for *days*. They would be building a bedframe with storage sooner than later.

Her phone vibrated in the pocket of her hoodie, and she pulled the device out to see a text.

Stacey – 1:55PM

> How goes it, T? Zeke wants you to know he's still pissed you didn't take him with you. LOL.

"What a turd," Tess said with a laugh. Opening the camera app, she snapped a picture of the tower of designated shoeboxes before sending it to Stacey's phone.

Tess – 1:55PM

> You would assume these are filled with dishes, but you'd be wrong. Shoes, Stace. SHOES.

Stacey responded with a row of laughing emoji faces. Deciding to continue the conversation later, Tess tucked her phone away once more and hefted the first box out to the apartment's entrance. She spotted Abi standing on a chair going through the cupboard above the fridge and leaned against the kitchen's archway. Crossing her arms, a silly grin tugged at Tess as she watched Abi, and as usual she wanted to pinch herself. There were moments where she still couldn't believe she'd landed such an incredible woman. Abi fulfilled her in ways Tess hadn't dared to think possible before. She'd known she'd changed after Chantelle, but it hadn't been clear to Tess just how much until she was learning to trust again. She'd acknowledged something else important too: in the months Tess had been with Vicki, she'd never opened up enough to trust the other woman. After falling for Abi, Tess figured she probably never wanted to. Yes, the last eight months had been an almost transcendent experience, bringing Tess out of her shell, and there was one thing she knew for certain: she was the luckiest person alive.

"Need some help?" Tess offered, her gaze lingering on Abi's form-fitting jeans. The denim hugged her thighs and backside in the most delicious ways, and Tess suddenly had an urge to reach over and run her hands up the length of Abi's legs. God, then she could unfasten the button on those same denims and tug the material past...

"You're sweet to ask, but no. I'm just looking for the cutlery set my parents gave me last Christmas, but I can't find it," Abi replied, cutting into Tess's fantasy. Tess cleared her throat, desire unfurling low in her belly. She met Abi's knowing smirk. "Unless you meant to help with something else entirely."

Tess stifled a groan and pushed off the wall. "Don't tease me. I'm still neck-deep in the closet. Marie Kondo would take one look at your shoe fetish and—"

"It is not a fetish," Abi interrupted with an adorable pout.

Tess only laughed, her steps light as she headed back to the bedroom. She called over her shoulder, "Sure, babe, whatever you say."

"Still on board for living together?"

Abi's question had Tess pausing at the door leading into the bedroom. Although at times terrifying, the answer to that hadn't changed in the weeks since they'd first discussed it. The moment Tess had brought up her readiness for the next step in their relationship, Abi announced she would give Tess another week to think about it. On the eighth day, after Tess's confirmation that her decision was still valid, Abi had promptly typed up a resignation letter and emailed it over to Margo.

Butterflies had been taking up residence in Tess's stomach ever since.

She turned to catch Abi staring, waiting for a response, so she gave her a wide, sure smile and nodded. "All the shoes in the world couldn't stop this move, Abi."

Tess's response had Abi's shoulders sagging in relief, and she giggled. "In that case, there are more in the front closet."

Tess stumbled her way into the bedroom, stammering, "M–more? Did you say there was more?"

Abi's laughter was the only reply, to which Tess frantically called out again, "Abi?"

Tess carried the boxes down the two flights of stairs, and after the third trip, during which she was panting and her arms were sore, she wished now they had taken McCoy up on her offer to help. Tess's selfishness for time alone with Abi had been the deciding factor on whether or not Coy came with her on the trip, and regardless of how sore she'd be tomorrow, she regretted nothing.

The door to the bathroom was ajar when Tess returned to the apartment, and she peeked in to see Abi bent over the sink, her face angled close to the mirror as she applied her makeup. Tess checked her watch, noting it was half past two. It was late for Abi to be putting on makeup.

"With your early-morning arrival, I forgot all about getting ready," she explained, meeting Tess's gaze in the mirror.

Shrugging, Tess simply smiled. It seemed to her she did that a lot lately. "I didn't notice. You're beautiful with or without it, Abigail."

"You know all the right things to say to get into my pants, don't you Tessa?" Abi volleyed back, but there was a pleased look on her face as she carefully applied eyeliner. Abi's snug jeans grabbed Tess's attention once again. Her gaze raked over Abi's legs first, admiring her athletic calves beneath the fabric and those thighs that had frequently threatened to crush Tess's head in the last eight months. She would have to add Abi's regular gym sessions to her gratitude list.

"You look hungry, sweetheart."

Their eyes met again in the washroom mirror, Abi's smirk igniting a roaring heat through Tess. Her pussy quivered with one look. Arousal gathered between her legs. She *was* hungry. "Starving, actually. Packing a moving truck is hard work," she rumbled, lessening the gap between them. The newfound self-assurance in her come-on was a bonus when she heard Abi's breath hitch. She slipped past her long enough to set aside the makeup strewn over the counter, placing several items on the back of the toilet instead.

"Tell me — am I the appetizer, main course, or dessert?" Abi batted her freshly done eyelashes, yelping when Tess grabbed her hips and lifted her onto the vanity.

"I'm hoping for all three, like an exquisite Abi buffet," Tess quipped breathlessly. She reached for Abi, pushing the open flannel shirt she'd stolen off Tess from her shoulders. Then she swiftly yanked her t-shirt up.

"A pussy buffet." Abi flashed a devilish grin, moaning when Tess slid her hands under her bra and cupped her breasts. She tweaked the hardening nipples. "Fuck, Tess, I didn't know you had it in you. Taking me in the bathroom. My roommates could come home any minute."

"I might be mostly vanilla, but I'm not a prude." Tess snickered, bending to suckle the tip of Abi's breast in her mouth. "And you and I both know they're working till five or later."

Her lover's wobbly inhales were invigorating, breaking Tess out of her typical shyness. She toyed with Abi's nipple, running her tongue over the taut bud and making it good and wet, relishing the way it further tightened before her eyes. Grinning, she licked across the sensitive flesh before dragging her teeth to where her tongue had been seconds ago.

"Oh!" Abi's gasp turned to a muffled groan as she buried her face in Tess's hair, her fingernails digging into the scalp.

Tess moaned, deserting Abi's breast to capture her mouth hungrily. She traced Abi's bottom lip with her tongue, licking between her parted lips. A sigh left her as Abi obliged the silent demand, and her tongue slipped in the moment Abi deepened the kiss. Abi sucked

Tess's tongue into her mouth, stealing the show, taking control of their kiss and rendering Tess immobile. Her knees trembled, and she collapsed against Abi, her hands going to either side of her hips and praying the countertop held her upright. Abi's hands sank into Tess's blonde locks, her thumbs kneading the pressure points behind her ears. Tess's eyes drifted closed of their own accord, and she knew she needed to regain the upper hand before Abi was topping her on the cramped floor.

She was panting as she ended the kiss, feeling a little dazed as she stared at her girlfriend. She felt as flushed as Abi looked, from the blotchy skin on her neck and throat to her swollen lips. Her shirt and bra were still bunched up over her breasts, her rosy nipples an erotic display for Tess to enjoy. The contours of her abdomen were slight with definition, toned and sexy with a stud navel piercing. Tess was of the opinion that Abi had the piercing done merely to taunt and tease her. She didn't know why, but there was something about a woman's abdomen that had always driven her crazy. Abi was no exception.

Tess reached for the waistband of Abi's denims, watching her tug her bottom lip between her teeth as Tess unfastened the clasp. "Yes. God, yes," Abi hissed as Tess massaged her hand over her wet panties. She wore a lacy orchid purple thong today, and the thin strap of fabric hugging Abi's sexy hips had Tess's own excitement saturating her panties. With the boy shorts she wore, she was hyper-aware of the trickle of arousal drizzling down her thigh.

Abi arched her back, her hips jutting forward to give Tess more access, and, like any decent gentlewoman, Tess took the offering and spread Abi's legs wider. Sliding her panties to the side, Tess plunged two fingers inside Abi's soaking sex, reveling in the way her pussy contracted with the invasion. Abi whimpered, throwing her head back and scarcely missing the bathroom mirror. Tess sucked her teeth at the passion rolling through her, her clit a quivering mess. Tess was hot all over at Abi's disheveled appearance, her nerve endings a fiery inferno readying to combust at the faintest signal.

"Tell me what you want, Abigail."

"Your mouth, your fingers, I—" Abi's words were cut off by another soft moan of pleasure as Tess rubbed her swollen clit with her thumb. Her wild gaze collided with Tess. "I want them all over, baby. Inside me."

Tess loved her confidence, loved it even more when Abi sank her fingers into Tess's hair and guided her head toward her exposed breasts. She had absolutely no qualms making demands, and Tess was only too happy to comply. She drew Abi's puckered nipple between her lips, wetting the sensitive flesh with her tongue before sucking it deep into her mouth. With her free hand, she skimmed her fingers over the hot skin of Abi's abdomen, blindly exploring the dips and soft flesh there while fingers of her other hand slowly slid in and out of her pussy. When she'd explored every inch of exposed skin, Tess came to a stop on Abi's lower belly, right above her mound. There she pressed into her, holding her in place, and kneaded the erogenous path to Abi's sex.

As it turned out, she was an excellent multitasker, because soon enough Abi was trapping Tess's fingers as she cried out in ecstasy. That was fine with Tess, and she wiggled her fingers inside Abi to draw out more pleasure as the orgasm washed through her. She left Abi's breasts to pepper kisses along her throat instead, darting her tongue out to taste the perspiration gathering below her ear. She was so focused on her task that she didn't notice until Abi's hand dipped into her panties that she'd even bypassed the waistband of her own jeans.

"Come here," Abi said, her voice still slightly breathless after her orgasm. Her smile was lazy, satisfied, as she leaned against the bathroom mirror. Tess's breath hitched as Abi's free hand came up to stroke her jaw. "I love you so much," she crooned, her hand at the back of Tess's neck now before tugging her in for another scorching kiss.

Tess's heart sped up, from the passion-filled whisper or the persistent fingers brushing against her thighs, she wasn't sure. She'd heard Abi utter the same sentiments every day — sometimes multiple times a day — since they'd become an item, but *this* moment felt different. As Tess kissed her back, a burst of longing filled her chest, and she abruptly pulled away.

"Abi," she blurted, scanning Abi's flushed cheeks and resplendent blue eyes. She didn't know what she searched for, considering Abi had shown her time and time again that she was in for the long haul. Their eyes met, and in that moment, she knew. A huff of laughter bubbled from her throat, and she clasped Abi's face in both her palms, gushing, "I–I love you too, Abi."

Abi's eyes widened with a sort of blissful surprise that only someone who had been waiting months to hear those words could achieve. The timing was terrible, Tess was well aware, what with Abi's hand still intimately stroking the hemline of her boy shorts, but the moment was perfectly imperfect.

"You finally said it," Abi whispered, a wide smile blossoming before she yanked Tess's face to hers again. Their lips smashed together, Abi's tongue slipping inside and making Tess groan with pleasure. She angled the kiss to deepen her tongue's assault, and the moment Tess widened her stance on the bathroom floor, Abi's hand was in her underwear. Her deft fingers trailed the length of Tess's slit before reaching her swollen clit. She flicked Tess's bundle of nerves with her thumb, the delicious sensations scrambling her brain until she couldn't even remember her name.

Abi paused their lip-lock long enough to murmur against Tess's mouth, "How do *you* want it?"

Well, *that* Tess could answer. "Hard and fast."

THREE YEARS LATER

Her back ached daily. She waddled unceremoniously throughout the office, garnering unwanted attention from just about everyone she passed. And her feet! She hadn't fit into her favorite stilettos in months, at least since the beginning of the second trimester. How was it Taunya had hardly changed shape when she was pregnant, yet Abi managed to transform into a beached whale?

She groaned, straightening in her ergonomic office chair to try to get the kink out of her lower back. Her boss had sworn up and down that the chair was the best on the market, but perhaps the reviews excluded nine-month pregnant women. A light knock pulled Abi from her thoughts, and she looked up to see the woman in question standing just inside the threshold. A few years older than Abi, Courtney Cairns was the future CEO of Cairns Corporation. She exuded enough confidence, danger, and sexuality to rival even Frankie, and that said something. It was as if the three traits worked interchangeably with Ms. Cairns' personality. In the two years Abi had worked as the company's junior marketing consultant, she hadn't recalled ever seeing the other woman relax. She was kind, a fair boss, and didn't appear to want to sleep with her, and that was more than Abi could say about her previous employer.

"I know you wanted to wait until the week before your due date, but I've decided to put you on early leave. Paid, of course. Full benefits in effect. You can work from home if you choose, but I'd rather not have you going into labor nineteen floors up." Her tone was brusque, as it usually was, but Abi paid more attention to the concern shadowing her resplendent blueish green eyes.

Her surprise must have shown because Ms. Cairns added softly, "You should relax before the little one arrives. If they're anything like my daughter was, then long, sleepless nights await you and Tess. I hear it can be gruesome."

Abi's curiosity was piqued, but she didn't question Ms. Cairns' unusual statement. Besides a handful of framed photos in her office of her with multiple people, she kept her personal life very private. Abi eyed her engagement ring, wondering about her significant other. Who were they, and did they have a daughter together? None of the people in the photos gave the impression Ms. Cairns was intimate with any of them. A simple Google search into the company before she'd been hired informed Abi of Ms. Cairns's bisexuality but nothing about anyone important. Abi felt at a bit of a disadvantage, considering the other woman knew all about Tess.

"Thank you. I am sore," Abi admitted, feeling herself blush. She wasn't one to complain of her workload, but it was understandable that she'd have growing pains. Subconsciously, she placed her hand over her stomach, instantly feeling comforted. She and Tess had chosen not to find out the sex of their baby, agreeing early on that they wouldn't start their child's life with traditional expectations. "Tess is getting pretty anxious as we count down the days."

"As she should be. I'm sure you'll be wonderful parents, Abi." Ms. Cairns turned to leave, calling over her shoulder. "You can take off now, but Shelley would like to see you in the conference room before you head home." Abi watched her walk away, her mass of auburn curls bouncing with each poised step. She loved stilettos as much as Abi.

Excited to take off, she gathered her things together, enough to serve for the remainder of the week at least. She sent a text to Tess, letting her know she was heading home early, and smiled at their wedding picture on her desk. Plenty had happened in the three years since Taunya's wedding. They moved into an apartment five blocks away from the Moore residence, and shortly after their one-year anniversary, her sweet, shy Tess had gotten down on one knee and proposed. After seeing how stressed Tess was over her sister's wedding, Abi had decided she was more than okay skipping her fairy-tale wedding. They'd eloped in front of the justice of the peace in front of their close family and friends, and afterward, they'd thrown the largest backyard party of the summer.

Abi shut the lights off to her office, glancing around fondly for a moment before heading toward the conference room. She frowned when she arrived, noting the closed blinds. Faint light escaped through the bottom of the closed door. Knocking twice, she grasped the knob and turned.

"*Surprise!*"

Abi's hand shot to cover her mouth as a scream died on her lips. "What's all this?" she squealed, laughter bubbling from her chest as she took in the packed conference room. Most of her coworkers were there, but that wasn't all.

"Your baby shower," Tess explained, her adorable, crooked grin on full display.

Sentimental tears pricked Abi's eyes, and she threw her arms around Tess. She planted a kiss on her lips. "You're just full of surprises! Thank you, everyone. This is amazing." Abi blubbered, fanning her heated cheeks. She spotted Taunya, Krystal, Sloane, even McCoy, and waved. "Oh my god, I can't believe you're here too!"

"Sit down, mama," her friend Shelley from accounting ordered. She and Tess took an arm each, gently guiding her to a leather waiting-room-style chair.

"Are you sure Ms. Cairns is okay with this?" Abi blurted and immediately felt silly. It wasn't like she worked in a toxic environment.

Tess laughed, pointing to the far end of the room. "Okay with this? Who do you think gave the okay to have our friends here?" Sure enough, a head of curly red hair stuck out above all the rest in the room. Tess kissed the shell of Abi's ear, whispering, "How's baby Briar this afternoon?"

Abi's smile stretched ear to ear at Tess's question. She turned just enough to capture her wife's lips, kissing her passionately, not caring who saw them. "Briar Esprit Moore can't wait to join us, babe."

Thank you for reading For The 1000TH Time! If you'd like to keep in touch with updates and new releases, follow me on social media via my linktr.ee here: https://linktr.ee/jenleamercyauthor

And if you've loved Tess and Abi's story, please consider leaving a review. Even just a line or two can really help indie authors' get their work out in the world.

About the Author

Hiya, nice to meet you!

One thing you should know about me is I'm a huge, socially awkward book nerd who needs to ship characters or I get bored. I'm a lover of all types of sapphic romance and have a weakness for dominating ice queens and slightly unhinged fictional women. Buuut I also have a sweet, romantic side and can swoon over small-town gals, so long as in whatever I'm reading the spice is medium to red-hot!

Interests that don't include reading, writing, or daydreaming about future WIPs include: plenty of coffee, mood-music listening on Spotify, binge-watching episodes of *Yellowstone,* and watching the latest Gal Gadot or Cate Blanchett film.

I live in Eastern Canada with my wife and kids but hold an unfathomable adoration for Vancouver.

Tune into *For The 1000TH Time's* playlist on Spotify!

Coming Soon

For The Record (McCoy's story)
Featuring:
Age Gap
Slow Burn
Ice Queen/Playgirl Dynamic
Opposites Attract
Widow

Interested in Kris and Courtney's story? Check out my gritty contemporary romance series under Angel Jendrick!

Claim Me (Claiming Kristopher #1)
Forgive Me (Claiming Kristopher #2)
Love Me   (Claiming Kristopher #3)
Cage Me   (Claiming Kristopher #4)
Hate Me   (Claiming Kristopher #5)

How about queer YA romance? You can check out my debut YA romance, Secret Me, here

Blurb:

Tage seems to have it all: she hangs out with the school's most popular clique and has a handsome boyfriend. She's also living a lie about her sexuality.

Wren, a nonbinary schoolmate, has been the victim of bullying by Tage's clique, which leaves Tage racked by guilt because she's always been drawn to Wren. When Tage picks up Wren during a snowstorm and they are forced to spend a night together, their true feelings emerge.

With Wren's support, Tage has to decide whether to come out to celebrate herself and her new relationship.

www.ingramcontent.com/pod-product-compliance
Lightning Source LLC
Chambersburg PA
CBHW022111310726
48972CB00007B/1989